THE ROAD HOME

Recent Titles by Charlotte Hardy

* available from Severn House

THE ROAD HOME

Charlotte Hardy

This first world edition published 2009
in Great Britain and in the USA by
SEVERN HOUSE PUBLISHERS LTD of
9–15 High Street, Sutton, Surrey, England, SM1 1DF.
Trade paperback edition published
in Great Britain and the USA 2009 by
SEVERN HOUSE PUBLISHERS LTD

British Library Cataloguing in Publication Data

Hardy, Charlotte
  The road home
  1. Family secrets - Fiction 2. Ireland - Social life and
  customs - 19th century - Fiction 3. Historical fiction
  I. Title
  823.9'14[F]

ISBN-13: 978-0-7278-6756-8   (cased)
ISBN-13: 978-1-84751-126-3   (trade paper)

Except where actual historical events and characters are being
described for the storyline of this novel, all situations in this
publication are fictitious and any resemblance to living persons
is purely coincidental.

All Severn House titles are printed on acid-free paper.

Typeset by Palimpsest Book Production Ltd.,
Grangemouth, Stirlingshire, Scotland.
Printed and bound in Great Britain by
MPG Books Ltd., Bodmin, Cornwall.

Brídis an ancient Irish name, sometimes anglicized as Bridget or Bride. It is pronounced 'Breed'.

One

His earliest memory was of sunshine; he was sitting outside the door on a chair and his feet couldn't touch the ground so he must still have been very small. Uncle Patsy was beside him sitting on the step; he had another chair upside down between his knees and was mending the seat, weaving rushes. These were wet and Uncle Patsy would throw water over them to keep them damp. Matt remembered the way the water ran away into the earth and dried out in the sunshine. He couldn't afterwards think why he should remember that particular afternoon but he thought it must have been because he was happy.

Matt remembered another time when Patsy mended the roof. He put a ladder up against the thatch; it seemed a very long way up, a fearful way, and Patsy carried bundles of straw up on to the roof in armfuls. Matt longed to climb on the roof. He so longed for it but Uncle Patsy wouldn't let him. He begged and begged to climb up the ladder and in the end Uncle Patsy gave in. Matt remembered the enormous gap between the rungs, so wide that he could only just reach his legs from one to the next, but Uncle Patsy was behind him and held him. Then, as they got higher and higher he began to be afraid and at last, when they were right up on the roof, he felt quite dizzy but didn't want to show it. Aunt Nora came out of the house and he called down 'Aunt Nora! Aunt Nora! Look at me up on the roof!' She looked up and was proud to see him up so high but she said he must come down again. He thought it was best to come down again too so Uncle Patsy carried him down under his arm. That night as Uncle Patsy tucked him into bed, he said, 'I climbed on the roof today, didn't I, Uncle Patsy?' and Uncle Patsy said he did.

Another thing he remembered years afterwards was the sound of the crickets in the hearth. He was sitting by the hearth on his stool drinking warm milk in his nightshirt, so it must have been evening. Uncle Patsy was in his rocking chair and Matt would stare into the fire as it glowed. Suddenly one of the turves would fall and there would be a spurt of flame before the fire died down again. He wasn't allowed to touch the fire but he watched Uncle Patsy as he would make a hole in the fire carefully and then place a new turf in the hole and it would slowly begin to burn.

As the piece of turf fell in, Matt would hear the crickets with their quick rasping noise as they leaped back and forth in the ashes. He asked Patsy how they made that noise; Patsy said he didn't know but he thought they must be talking to each other and telling each other the cricket news, because crickets had lives and fortunes just like mortal people and they got married and had babies and died, just like mortals. He said they brought good luck to a house and we must never harm them. If someone was building a new house or moving into one then they would send them a couple of crickets to bring the house luck.

Another time he showed Matt how to mend a pipe with blood. Uncle Patsy liked to smoke his pipe though Aunt Nora only let him smoke it outside because of the smell. He showed Matt the broken pipe – it was a clay pipe and the long stem had snapped – and he laid it down in the hearth for a moment and went out of the door. He came back with a thorn, sat down by Matt again and Matt saw him prick the back of his hand with the thorn and a little drop of red blood appeared. Matt was fascinated to see the blood, so bright, so glistening.

Patsy dipped the broken ends of the pipe in the blood, pressed them together, then laid the pipe on the dresser.

'That'll be better than a new pipe in the morning.'

'Uncle Patsy, where did the blood come from?'

'From inside of course.'

Matt stared into the fire, thinking of the bright red blood.

Years later, he could remember too what must have been the first time he ever went with Uncle Patsy to cut the turf. It was a warm sunny day and the sky was very high as if they were on top of the world and there were little clouds that sailed over, very high up.

Uncle Patsy had his slane, a long narrow spade with another shorter blade on one side rising at right angles. They had cut away a long black wall of peat about four feet high and at the bottom was black water. The whole village was there, and they worked all day, it seemed for ever to Matt. He ran through the thick grass with the other children while Uncle Patsy cut the turf.

At first Matt watched Patsy. He stood above the edge of the peat and then drove his slane downwards and cut off a big piece and tossed it on to the pile behind him. All the men of the village were there stretched along the edge swinging the turves up on to the black piles behind them.

Later, they were sitting and eating their bread and butter all together in the long grass. He remembered all the other men and women, how big they were, and their faces red from the sun. Then Uncle Patsy pointed up into the sky and asked could he hear the skylark up there singing his heart out. Matt stared and stared but he couldn't see the bird though he could hear him clearly. After that he never forgot the skylark and whenever he heard one he would stop and look up until he had spotted it. That day he was vexed that he couldn't see the bird in the sky. He asked Patsy to let him hold his slane but it was too heavy for him.

He remembered another time in winter when they were sitting indoors one afternoon and it was raining hard. Uncle Patsy asked him if he knew the riddle of the Irishman at sea; Matt said he did not so Uncle Patsy arranged twenty stones, one of which was bigger than the others, in a circle on the table.

'Now,' said Patsy, 'that big one is the Irishman and they're all on a ship with nothing to eat. So they'll have to eat each other. Now this one here, next to the Irishman, is the Irishman's wife and she's the cook, and she doesn't want to cook her husband. She was fond of him, you see. I'll do the counting, says she. So she stands all the men round in a circle, like these stones. Now, says she, 'tis eleven days we've not had a bit of food, so I'll count off eleven men and she counts off eleven men from her husband.'

Patsy counted eleven stones round from the big one.

'Keep your eye on that stone. Now, says she, there's seven days in the week, so we'll just count off seven men and we'll eat the seventh man, and then we'll count off another seventh man and eat him, and so on till there are none of us left.'

Patsy started counting, first the eleven, and then from the twelfth stone, seven stones and every seventh stone he took out. When there were less than seven stones in the circle, he went round twice and finally there were only two stones left and he counted backwards and forwards and at last there only remained the big stone.

'And there's the Irishman left,' said Patsy and Matt stared at the stones on the table and marvelled at the Irishman's wife's skill that had saved her husband.

'But his wife wasn't saved, Uncle Patsy.'

'No more she was.' Uncle Patsy stared at the stone and looked seriously into Matt's face. 'The Irishman must have eaten his wife.'

Matt made many expeditions through the fields and woods with Uncle Patsy. In one of his earliest memories they were lying on their faces on the river bank and Patsy was pointing to a trout just below them sheltering in the cool shade of the bank from the heat of the sun. Patsy signalled to him to be still and to say nothing.

The fish was nearly a foot long, a speckled black and grey, its nose to the stream and lazily making little movements and with no apparent effort hovering in the stream while all around water weed swirled in the silent flow.

Patsy rolled up his sleeve and Matt held his breath watching him stretching his arm down – so slowly that Matt could hardly see him move – to where the trout lay steady in the current.

Patsy's hand came at last down beneath the fish but he did not take hold of it. He began gently to stroke it and Matt was amazed to see that the fish did not swim away but stayed where he was and as Matt watched he realized the fish actually enjoyed being stroked.

Then all of a sudden Patsy's hand flashed up through the water and there on the bank in the grass the trout was leaping and throwing itself about. Matt drew back, amazed at the energy of the fish, its flashing colours and slippery wetness as it arched itself and leaped and twisted on the bank.

Patsy snatched hold of it and brought a stone down on its head. It lay on the bank not moving any more. Matt felt a revulsion that he could remember years after at the sudden and brutal way the fish had died.

Uncle Patsy smiled at him. 'That'll do tonight for our supper.'

Matt felt reassured and when he was older often came here fishing with the boys from the village.

★   ★   ★

Patsy taught him the name of every creature living round them and years later Matt, when he went out by night with Patsy snaring rabbits, remembered hearing the scuffling noises that signalled a badger was coming towards them and as they stood still and silent, passed quite close to them in the darkness. When he was older he became quite accustomed to breaking a rabbit's neck but the first time he saw Patsy do it, it made him quite sick for a moment.

Patsy owned an old gun and sometimes on winter afternoons he'd go out and see if he couldn't bring down a grouse or two on the hillside. Nora objected to these trips and said he'd only get caught by Milligan and it would cost him more than it was worth but Patsy in his easy way would take her and kiss her and say he knew how to keep out of Milligan's way. One day, when he was eight, Matt went with him. He was speechless with excitement as they buttoned up their coats before setting off in the bitter cold afternoon.

'If the quality's out shooting,' said Patsy as they set off over the fields, 'the noise of my gun will mingle in with theirs, d'ye understand?'

Matt now knew vaguely who the quality were because he had seen them come through the village several times on horseback in red coats when they were out foxhunting. He had come to understand too that there was a castle where the quality lived and that Patsy and Nora were in some sense under them and had to be respectful to them and come out of the cottage and bow to them when they passed by. Finally, he had learned that Milligan was part of the castle and so when they went out to shoot game they had to keep out of Milligan's way. Matt didn't understand why this should be, but he knew that it was so.

On this occasion they were standing by the edge of the woods looking out across a stretch of hillside covered with dead ferns. It was cold and the air was as sharp as a diamond, the Curlew Mountains away to the west as clear as could be and the sun standing above them, a ball of orange as the sky turned through a sea-green to a delicate violet.

Two pheasant rose with a clatter and Patsy let fly at them. Matt was about to run after them but Patsy held him by the shoulder.

'Better wait a moment in case anyone saw the bird go down,' he whispered.

They waited, their breath standing in the cold air, listening. At last Patsy said, 'I think the coast is clear.'

They set out across the open hillside towards the pheasant a hundred yards away and searched among the dead ferns and gorse for the dead bird. At last Matt found it and stared at its brilliant plumage, the iridescent colours, almost magical, shifting in the light, its eyes open, still glistening. Matt shouted across to Patsy that he had found it but at the same moment they heard a shout and looking up saw a man running from the trees towards them.

'Come on!'

Patsy took Matt's hand and they set off at a run down the hill towards the trees and the river.

'Oh Uncle Patsy, what'll happen now?'

'Keep your breath for running.'

They came into the shelter of the trees and crashed down through the woods until they came out on the river bank. They stopped, listening for a moment. There was silence.

'Sure, I think we've shaken him off.'

The river was frozen and Patsy tested it with his foot.

'I think it'll take us. Come on, it'll be the best of our way.'

They ran across the frozen river but heard it crack as they crossed.

'Oh Uncle Patsy the ice cracked,' gasped Matt who was out of breath.

'So much the better,' said Patsy, 'Milligan will never dare to cross. We'll make our way back round through the village.'

They trekked up through the woods on the other side of the river and it was dark as they came through the village. Matt was weary. As they reached home, Patsy told him to run inside and after Matt had gone in Patsy followed him a few minutes later.

Matt was full of excitement as he told Nora how they had outwitted Milligan and got a pheasant right under his nose. Nora was not impressed and when Patsy came in she gave him a hard look.

'So you've been up to your games with Milligan? Is this a life to teach the boy?'

Matt was exultant because they had got away from Milligan. He hated Milligan because he was Uncle Patsy's enemy and kept returning to the subject that evening over supper.

'We beat Milligan, Aunt Nora! We beat him, didn't we, Uncle Patsy?'

Two

The following morning there was a rap at the door and as Patsy opened it he found Liam, a groom at the castle, with an anxious look on his face.

"'Tis his Lordship wanting a word with ye, Patsy.' He nodded over his shoulder. Patsy went outside and Matt crept out behind him.

The earl, in a red coat and top hat, was on his horse in the *bohreen* with two other men on horseback. It was the first time Matt had ever seen him and he remembered ever afterwards the look of him that cold morning. He seemed very high up on his horse looking down at them. Matt remembered his very red complexion, his bright little eyes in his rather round face, his moustache and side whiskers. He was holding a crop and Matt remembered his black gloves.

'Byrne,' he said looking down at Patsy and Matt, 'you've been poaching my game again. It won't do.'

Matt was filled with fear but Patsy sprang forward towards the earl.

'*Poachin*'? Who says so? If some rogue—'

'I'm not arguing with you, Byrne. I'm tired of your depredations. If I hear about you again from Milligan you can look for another farm.'

Patsy was rubbing his hands together. 'Oh, 'tis the times we live in, your honour. Sure, an't I as innocent as this lad here?'

He took Matt's head in his hands and held him close. Matt, who was terrified for Uncle Patsy, clung to him. The other men with the earl laughed, looking down from their horses, and the earl turned to them, pointing to Patsy with his crop.

'This fellow is notorious. It's a wonder he leaves me a pheasant or snipe to shoot. He fishes my rivers. He organizes cockfights and in his youth he was one of the ribbon-men. He probably keeps an illicit still. Take a good look at him for future reference.'

'*Cockfights? Illicit still?* Your honour, don't I pay me rent on the nail, faithful to the day, and would ye slander me to these gentlemen that never saw me in the world before?'

The earl interrupted him as he and his friend jerked their horses into motion.

'Hark'ee Byrne. If ever I find you before me again in the sessions house, on any cause whatever, it's out of that cabin you will go. Is that clear?'

'Oh yes your reverence and thanks be to your reverence, sure 'tis much obliged I am to your honour.'

The three horsemen turned their horses away and already Patsy was forgotten. One of them turned to Lord Elphin.

'By the way, how's young Harry? Married the Richardson girl, I believe?'

'Yes, he's in Australia. PM asked him to go out as Governor General of New South Wales. We had the devil's own row about it. I need him here, damn it. But he said he couldn't stay in Britain, had to get away. And he'd only just returned from India.'

They were out of earshot.

Patsy released Matt's head which he had been clutching tight to him and they went indoors. Matt was full of fear and confusion.

As they came into the house Patsy brought his fist down hard on the table. Matt looked up into his face and for the first time in his life he saw Patsy angry. In that moment Matt hated the earl. Instinctively he understood that Patsy had been humiliated on that cold morning, standing at the doorway rubbing his hands together and nodding little bobbing nods to the man on the horse as he spoke.

Matt was too afraid to say anything while Patsy was angry but later while they were eating their porridge he asked Patsy,

'Uncle Patsy, what are ribbon-men?'

'What?' Patsy had been miles away.

'He said you used to a ribbon-man.'

Patsy broke into a laugh, reaching across and running his hand through the boy's hair. 'Ah Matt, them was times to be sure. And Matt, take no notice of his Lordship. Sure, an't we on the best of terms? Me and the earl – I've known him for years and you mustn't worry about it at all.'

Matt understood that Patsy was trying to reassure him but he remembered how Patsy had been in the *bohreen* and knew Patsy was not telling him the truth.

'But what are ribbon-men?'

'Matt, them was the days, when I was not much older than yourself. Out we'd go of a winter's night, a bright clear night, all the likely lads of the parish. We'd meet at the crossroads beyond, and we'd parade just like the militia, and we'd have ribbons in our hats – that's why we were called ribbon-men – and our orders. Of course we didn't use our real names. I remember the officer was called Lieutenant Starlight; that's what we called him to protect him from the informers.'

Nora interrupted Patsy's narrative.

'Why are you telling the boy all this and filling his head with nonsense of long ago? You'd be better telling him useful things to prepare him for the world. You'd be better to be thinking of sending him to school.'

'And we will, Nora my darling. All in good time.'

'Tell me some more about the ribbon-men, Uncle Patsy.'

Nora snorted and started clearing the table.

'Oh 'twas the grandest thing, to be there all together. Marching to the sound of the pipes and knowing you was of a stalwart band of men, ready for anything, fearless men, bold lads—'

'But Uncle Patsy, what did you do?'

'Matt, we were going to show 'em we were Irishmen and proud of the old country, and the English landlords, and the Peelers and the militia weren't going to treat us as if we were outcasts in our own land. This is our land not the landlord's or the government's in London and we should have the right to rule it ourselves—'

'I won't have you filling the boy's head with such talk!' Nora shouted across the room. 'Landlords, government – it's all idle nonsense and comes of men having too much time and too little sense! If you have nothing better to do, there's that clamp of turnips wants putting a face on if the cows are to eat today.'

Patsy was silenced and looked across at Matt.

'Work to do.' He put on his coat, Matt copied him and they went out of the cottage into the yard behind it where a long earth barrow stood. Patsy took a spade and began to dig into the side of the mound. The earth was hard with the frost and he could dig out lumps only with difficulty until he had made a hole and they began to dig out the turnips. Matt helped Patsy carry them to the byre.

'Uncle Patsy when you were in the ribbon-men, what did you do?'

The cows stood about them, the warmth of their bodies making the air warm in the byre, their breath sounding in the little space. Patsy rested his arm on a cow's back and looked down at Matt.

'Well now, supposing some one of us couldn't afford to pay his rent and the landlord was threatening to throw him out of his farm – throw him out, and his wife and children, into the road to starve. We couldn't stand by and see such a thing, could we? So we'd march up to the castle, we'd face him down and seeing us all there in the night, the landlord would have the fright of his life! Oh yes, he'd soon change his tune! Sometimes, mind, he'd maybe think to brave it out, maybe send for the militia to drive us off. So out would come the soldiers and there'd be a fight of it, us brave lads against the soldiers but nine times out of ten, we'd have the best of it. Their stomachs weren't in it, see? And we, after knowing the lay of the land, we'd make fools of 'em.'

Matt was full of glee. 'What else did you do?'

'Well, there's the elections,' continued Patsy. 'If we knew of anyone was thinking to vote the wrong way, why, around we'd go and just maybe persuade 'em different.'

'What do you mean, voting the wrong way?'

'Well votin' for the landlord's candidate instead of an Irishman.'

'Isn't the landlord's candidate Irish?'

'The majority of 'em's English, Matt, sitting here in the middle of old Ireland in their Big Houses lordin' it over us and then, when the election comes round, thinkin' we'll vote 'em into Parliament like a flock of lambs.'

'What did you do?'

'Well, if we heard of anyone inclined to vote for the landlord's candidate we'd maybe go round to their house in the night and knock on the door and very kindly request them to do us the honour of votin' for the Irish candidate.'

'And did they?'

'Oh they did, most of 'em. Of course, sometimes there'd be a little difficulty—'

'A little difficulty?'

'There'd maybe be someone who'd have to be persuaded.'

Matt was filled with apprehension. Patsy looked into his face with a keen expression. 'We'd have to teach 'em a lesson, for the sake of old Ireland, you understand.'

The boy did not dare ask what sort of a lesson Patsy had in mind.

From this time forth they never discussed politics inside the house, but as they went about their tasks in the yard or in the fields and as they roamed the woods and along by the river Patsy would answer Matt's questions.

'Uncle Patsy, why are the English here in Ireland?'

Uncle Patsy was silent for a while. They were walking through the woods after some snares they had set for rabbits. It was an afternoon in early spring and Matt was nine at this time.

'Well, it's difficult to say for sure. Ye see, Matt, the English have always been here in Ireland, lordin' it over us. But because they've always been here, doesn't mean they have to go on bein' here, does it?'

'No.'

'Ye see, sometimes the Irish people rise up against them to make old Ireland free. There was Robert Emmet. Ye've heard of him?'

'No.'

'Now Robert Emmet was a bold young gentleman who lived many years ago and he was ready to fight the English to drive 'em out.'

'What happened?'

'A dirty informer betrayed him to the English and he was taken and all his brave lads fled, betrayed ye see. He had a lovely sweetheart, Miss Sarah, who loved him dearly. He was brought to trial in Dublin and condemned to a shameful death. A sad day for Ireland, Matt.'

Patsy stopped and looked down into Matt's face.

'What happened to Miss Sarah?'

'After he was executed the poor girl died of a broken heart.'

'I don't understand.'

'She loved Robert Emmet so dearly that after he was executed she just lost the will to live. Because he loved Ireland more than his own life, ye see Matt, he laid down his life for his country and because of his great courage and self-sacrifice, she loved him so much she just didn't want to go on living after he was dead.'

Matt was silent, trying to digest this. He could not understand how anyone could not want to live. It was a mystery to him that anyone could die for love.

'And why was he betrayed?'

Patsy sighed. 'In this world, Matt, while you have men that will die for their country, there's others so base they would betray them for money.'

'So Robert Emmet died for nothing?'

'No Matt!' Patsy turned to him. 'Not for nothing! Not while there's you and me to honour his name.'

Matt was thrilled when Patsy included him.

'We'll honour his name till one day Ireland shall be free, Matt.'

Another name which Patsy taught Matt was that of Daniel O'Connell, the 'Great Dan' as Patsy called him.

'I heard him, Matt,' he said one day when they clearing out the cowshed, and he was leaning on his shovel. 'When I was a lad like yourself I went to one of his monster meetings. That was a sight. A million people and all as peaceable and law-abidin' as you could wish. No sign of a bottle, never a fist raised in anger. Could you imagine that now?'

'A million people,' breathed Matt in awe. 'However did you hear him?'

'He had the sweetest voice you ever heard. 'Twas as if it was strained through honey. He was a Kerryman was the Great Dan.'

'What did he do, Uncle Patsy?'

'What did he do? Why, wasn't he only the "Liberator" himself – wasn't he the man who gave us back our rights? Didn't he force the Iron Duke to do his bidding?'

'The Iron Duke?'

'The Duke of Wellington, the Prime Minister in the Parliament of London. Do you think he would listen to us poor Irish or trouble himself about us? Oh no. But then along came the Great Dan and organized his monster meetings, a million men, Matt, and 'twas a different story. The Iron Duke himself trembled when he saw the strength of old Ireland. All peaceable, mind, but the Great Dan said to him, here we are a million men as mild as milk, only asking for the same rights as other folks and the Iron Duke took one look at all them men, Matt, and he said to himself, well they're peaceful now right enough, but supposing they was ever to be roused?'

Patsy laughed and Matt laughed with him too, excited at the thought of the strength of a million men.

'Yes, says he to himself, supposing they was to be roused?' said Patsy turning again to his shovelling and Matt beside him. 'And that decided him. He gave us our rights back which they should never have taken in the first place.'

'What rights, Uncle Patsy?'

'What rights? Well, the right to have our own churches for one thing and then the right to vote in elections so we'd have a say in the Parliament in London.'

'Have you ever been in London, Uncle Patsy?'

'I never was in London, Matt.'

'Aunt Nora isn't my mother, is she?'

Patsy was taken aback by this, but managed to laugh. 'Why how could she be your mother, Matt? She's your aunt.'

'Who is my mother, Uncle Patsy?'

Patsy was silent, thinking quickly. He dropped to Matt's height, looking the little boy in the eye. 'Ye see, Matt,' he began, 'your mother was a very beautiful lady—'

'Isn't she alive any more, Uncle Patsy?'

'I'm afraid not.'

'Why did she die, Uncle Patsy?'

This was a question Patsy and Nora had thought over many times.

''Twas the cholera,' he said at last.

'What's that?'

''Tis like – well, ye see, Matt, they was terrible sick, so God had mercy on them and took them up to heaven.'

'Why?'

Patsy floundered. 'Nora could explain that better than me.'

'Was I sick?'

'No Matt, you were saved, thanks be. So your aunt and me took you in.'

'My mam and da were taken and I was saved?'

'That's it.'

'Oh.'

Three

'Uncle Patsy, what does bastard mean?'

Matt stood in the doorway on a bright summer afternoon. His shirt was torn and there was dried blood round his nose. Nora leaped at him.

'What have you been up to? Have you been in a fight?'

'He said I was a bastard.'

'Who did?'

'Michaeleen Brannagh.'

Nora took the boy in hand seated him at the table and was wiping his face with a cloth. Matt seemed none the worse for his fight. Patsy watched from the table.

'I'll make a cup of tea. What happened?'

'We were just coming out of church when our lesson was finished and Michaeleen Brannagh said I stole his chalk and I didn't, Uncle Patsy, I never touched his chalk but he said I did and then he said he'd fight me and I wasn't afraid of him I said I never did take his chalk it was all a lie. Then he hit me, just outside the church when Father Geoghegan had gone. He hit me when I wasn't looking, Aunt Nora, so I hit him back. I beat him to the ground because he said I had his chalk. And then he said I was a bastard and the others laughed. What does bastard mean, Uncle Patsy?'

'Never mind such things, Matt,' said Nora, 'they're all silly children, sure it means nothing at all. Pat, are you going to pour the boy a cup of tea or are you not?'

'I'm all right Aunt Nora, never fear, sure didn't I beat Michaeleen Brannagh?'

'You come home looking like a scarecrow, with your shirt torn, and who's to mend it, I'd like to know. Don't go getting into fights again.'

She smacked him round the head but Matt could tell she wasn't really displeased. Patsy poured him a cup of tea and pushed it across the table.

'There Matt, you're a brave lad, and you did right.'

'But Uncle Patsy, what is a bastard?'

There was a pause while Patsy looked at Nora. 'I'll maybe tell you when you're older. Sure, 'tis no matter at all, and you did well today.'

Matt put his cup back on the table and pushed away Nora's hand as she was still fussing about his face.

'Uncle Patsy, I want to know. All the children laughed when he said it. What does it mean?'

Again there was a pause while Patsy looked at Nora. At last she turned to Matt.

'It means a child whose parents are not married, Matt.'

'Weren't my parents married?'

'Yes, they were, Matt, and you're not to listen to such talk.'

'But if my parents were married why did Michaeleen Brannagh call me – that?'

'Pure spite, Matt. Only because you beat him. You're a brave lad.'

Most of the other children had laughed at Matt that afternoon when he fought Michaeleen Brannagh, but not all. Among the girls who looked on at the fight, fascinated and appalled by its violence and energy, Mary Higgins with brown eyes and long hair watched Matt, quivering when he was hit, shuddering at their violence. Mary followed Matt after the fight.

'I never laughed at you, Matt.'

Wiping his nose he looked at her with some surprise. 'Thanks.'

From then on, Matt was always conscious of Mary, picking her out immediately in the group of friends outside the church, waiting for school to begin in the morning, always noticing her and the way she looked at him.

Matt became a more serious child. Both Nora and Patsy noticed it and were distressed yet felt unable to do anything. Matt was growing, he had a reputation for strength and courage and the other children were wary of taunting him. He was known among some of the other villagers as 'that big rough Byrne boy' but Matt was not in fact rough and never offered violence unless he was provoked. Perhaps because of his size the other parents and Father Geoghegan found it convenient to pick on him when they were looking for a culprit and none was to hand.

'Oh, Mrs Byrne, have ye heard?'

Their neighbour Mrs Toole was at the door, a shawl about her shoulders, and clutched across her breast. Her eyes were big as Nora came to the door.

'Have ye heard the news that's in it? The big house above – Castle Leighton that was – is sold!'

Patsy was behind Nora now. 'Sold?'

Mrs Toole nodded vigorously. 'Liam told me – him that was groom to his Lordship – and he said the new owner said none of the staff was to be let go. He said there'd be employment for all and no one was to lose by the change.'

'The new owner?'

Mrs Toole was nodding again and enunciated with a very round mouth, '*An American*! so 'tis said. Liam said the agent told them, only wouldn't say his name or anything about him, only that he was an American with a mint of money and lookin' to settle in Ireland.'

Nora frowned.

'As for his Lordship –' Mrs Toole sniffed – 'never even said goodbye to his servants. No farewells, no ceremony, never a drink – no *tip*! – but there one day and gone the next. And left all the furniture, Liam says. Who would have thought it! The Leightons! Who've held half the county for scores and hundreds of years.'

A week went by, and there was a new rumour in the village.

'The owner of the big house above, Liam said he was there yesterday. Mr Doyle, his name is.'

Nora glanced back at Patsy who was crowding behind her at the door.

'And Liam says he's changed the name of the house,' Mrs Toole went on, 'No more Castle Leighton, says he, but Ballyglin House.'

Still Nora had said nothing.

'An open-handed gentleman too, says Liam. Maybe the old earl never offered him a drink, but the new owner is no sooner in the door than, Call all the servants together, says he to O'Flaherty, and we'll open a bottle. And you may be sure the

servants were happy to drink the health of the new owner. And
is there a Mrs Doyle, sir? says Liam. Ah there is, boys – and ye'll
see her soon enough, says he!'

Mrs Toole was breathless with excitement.

'And soon enough, too, says Liam. Mr Doyle is only waiting
to have the house cleaned and a few things changed round, and
he'll bring his new bride to stay.'

'His new bride?'

'The whole village is talkin' of it, ye may be sure, Mrs Byrne.
On fire to see Mr Doyle's bride!'

It was a month later that word was brought once more to the
cottage that Mr Doyle and his bride were expected that day
and he would be bringing her from the station through the
village on his way to Ballyglin House. The entire village was
gathered on the ragged green between the church and the river
for this event. Nora was not inclined at first to go but Matt
had been caught up in the excitement and Patsy too, so she
had not much choice in the matter. She and Patsy had already
discussed the news.

'That'll be Garrett Doyle that disappeared all those years ago.
After—'

They looked at each other and Nora frowned. 'After the business with Bríd.'

There was a long silence. 'So it seems he went to America.'

'And did well for himself, by all Liam says.'

'Well, good luck to him.' Nora heaved a breath. 'I always liked
him. It was only Bríd couldn't see the worth that was in him.
And look what came of *that*.'

Patsy nodded. 'Sure, Garrett was a man to do well for himself
– wherever he went.'

'And it seems he went to America. Well, well. And now come
back to the village a gentleman. I wonder why?'

The three of them were gathered on the green that afternoon
together with the entire population of the village. The priest
Father Geoghegan, Larry Shaunessy, and the shopkeeper Mr
Carruthers constituted themselves the welcoming committee. The
excitement among the villagers was keen and it was clear there

hadn't been such a piece of news to compare with this in years. There was huge speculation concerning the bride too. Liam was unable to enlighten them.

'He's keepin' it a secret, says he. But 'twill be an American beauty, of that ye may be sure. 'Tis well known the American girls do be the beautifullest on earth.'

'To be sure, 'tis a noted fact, the Americans are famed for the beauty of their girls.'

But at last there was a commotion. A light open buggy, freshly painted and on high springs, behind a well-fed horse was galloping down the road and in a moment was splashing through the ford, scarcely pausing until the driver pulled her up on the green and the crowd gathered round cheering.

'Welcome to Mr Doyle and his bride!' arose from every side, in a welter of cheers.

Doyle stood up and, taking off his hat, held up his hands for silence. He was a tall good-looking man in his early thirties and well dressed in a light-grey suit, a self-confident, self-possessed man, it was evident immediately. The villagers had expected an American millionaire and this was surely he. His bride remained seated, smiling at the crowd. She too fully lived up to expectations. Not only was she strikingly beautiful but she was dressed in the very height of fashion, in the most delicious little straw hat with streamers at the back, and a new pink summer dress. Altogether they made a very impressive couple.

'Friends!' Doyle struggled to be heard. 'Friends! It's grand to see so many here to greet us. So many old friends that I've not seen in years.' The crowd was quietening now. 'Friends, you know I went away to America, and I've done well! I own it, I've been lucky. But friends, I never forgot the old country. All the time I was in America I never forgot Ballyglin and it was always my dream one day to find a wife and bring her back to the village where I was born. And today I've done it!'

More deafening cheers as he gestured to the woman sitting beside him. Nora could see she was straining to keep up a smile.

The welcoming committee struggled forward and Father Geoghegan made a short speech, nothing of which was heard in the cheers which followed Garrett's words. Garrett again held up his hands for silence.

'Now friends, tonight there's to be celebrations. So there'll be a hog roast here on the green and there'll be porter and whiskey for every man – and woman too!'

Soon after he sat again and whipped up the horse as the crowd broke into renewed cheers. Nora turned back up the *bohreen* with Patsy. Matt was somewhere else with the other children.

Nora's face was black. 'She has the impudence of the devil,' she muttered, 'to come back here after she gave her Bible oath never to return.'

'I never was so surprised in my life,' said Patsy. 'Where in heaven's name did he find her? Do ye think she went to America too?'

'What does it matter where they met? The question is, d'ye think anyone recognized her?'

Patsy was silent but after a moment muttered gloomily, 'We did.' He shook his head. 'Well, well, Bríd and looking quite the lady.'

'Lady? She looks like the whore she is. What was Garrett thinking of?'

Patsy sighed and shook his head. 'Well, we know how taken he was with her.'

Nora was silent, thinking hard. 'She's going to want to see Matt. That's what it's about.'

Several days after the arrival of Mr and Mrs Doyle Matt was returning from school when he found a gentleman's carriage standing in the *bohreen* outside the cottage. Its shiny paint, the polished brass and obviously new trappings, all made a sharp contrast with the dusty summer lane, the wild tangle of brambles and briars in their profusion, and the shabby low thatch of the cottage. The coachman, in a neat uniform, was standing by the horse's head and stroking it as it pawed restlessly at the ground. Matt paused for some time to examine this piece of luxury standing so unexpectedly outside his home. As it happened he knew the coachman.

'Liam?'

'Afternoon, Matt.' He nodded at the door. ''Tis Mrs Doyle within there, come to visit.'

As Matt pushed open the door he saw the beautiful lady sitting at the table. Nora was standing, one knuckle on the table looking down at her. As he entered they turned.

'Aunt Nora, there's a carriage—' He stopped, bashful before this vision. The fine lady did not rise but held out a hand, smiling.

'And here's Matt,' was all she said, but he was immediately impressed by her voice, which sounded English but which had a beautiful modulation, a musical quality he picked up instinctively. He was awed into silence, staring at her.

'This is your aunt Bríd come to visit, Matt,' Nora said prosaically.

'My aunt?' He was unable to take his eyes from her face.

She nodded. 'Come and give your aunt a kiss, Matt.'

He approached timidly and she took him by the shoulders and pressed her cheek against his. 'You're quite a big boy now.' She was examining him carefully.

'Is that your carriage in the *bohreen*?' was all he could think of.

'It is.'

'Can I have a ride in it?'

She laughed, and it was the most musical sound he had ever heard. 'Of course you can – if your aunt Nora will permit?'

Now Patsy interrupted. He was seated at the table opposite Bríd. 'Of course your aunt will take you for a ride – but you'll have your tea first.'

Matt sat at the table as Nora proffered him the slices of bread and butter she had prepared. Patsy poured him a cup of tea and there was silence for a moment as he ate until . . .

'I wonder,' the beautiful lady began, 'Matt – I wonder if you like bullseyes?' He looked up quickly at her impish smile. 'Because I just happened to have a bag of them in my pocket – isn't that strange?'

She pulled out a paper twist of sweets.

'What do you say?' Nora frowned down at him.

'Thank you. Thank you – Aunt.' Matt looked between the two women. 'Aunt Nora, you never told me I had another aunt.'

'You see Matt I've been away for many, many years, and I've travelled to so many places, to London, to America—'

'Ye never went to America, Bríd?' exclaimed Patsy leaning forward.

'That's where I met my husband.'

'America?' Matt's eyes glowed. Every boy in the village knew that America was the promised land, and all of them had heard fabulous stories of America's marvels.

'Is it true that they have lifts inside the house so you don't have to walk up stairs?'

She laughed, and ran her hand over his head. It sent a thrill through him. 'Yes, it's true, and many, many other marvels. Some houses don't have fires at all. They have pipes running through the house filled with hot water.'

'Ye never say so, Bríd,' Patsy breathed.

'And trains in the middle of the street to ride through the town?'

'Streetcars? Yes. You don't have to walk anywhere if you don't want to, Matt. You needn't ever walk at all, if you've a mind to it.'

All the time, her voice flowed, enchanting him as he stared up into her face. Bewitched, unable to tear his eyes from hers, he went on, 'And everyone a millionaire, so 'tis said?'

She laughed. 'Not everybody, Matt. But it's easier to become a millionaire, that's for sure.'

He was still staring up at her, over the rim of his tea cup.

'That'd be grand,' he breathed. 'Now can I have my ride, please?'

'If Nora will permit it.'

Nora raised her eyebrows and shrugged. 'So long as you're not too long.'

Liam was waiting and opened the door for them. Matt noticed the fancy scroll work on it and the initials BD worked into a monogram, gold lettering on the deep maroon paintwork.

'What's that, Aunt Bríd?'

'Those are my initials, Matt – Bríd Doyle.'

The carriage itself was out of fairyland, but to have your own name on the door – and there was a little step which Liam now folded down. As Matt climbed in he was aware immediately of the plump velvet cushions where he and his aunt sat closely side by side. Sitting beside her in this dark intimacy, he was intensely conscious now of the crisp freshness of her clothes and the way they rustled as she made herself comfortable. He was aware too of the sweet smell which wafted from her. Everything about her was more beautiful, more bewitching and enchanting than he could find words to express.

Four

That night Matt dreamed of his new aunt. He was still very unclear about their relationship, but he would never forget till the day he died that first ride in her carriage, the closeness of them together in the dark carriage, and the sense of her presence, the fine clothes and the mysterious essence, the fragrance which emanated from her. He daydreamed for days after, constantly reliving that intimate moment, and longing for the day when it might be repeated.

This came the following Sunday when the carriage reappeared in the village, his aunt stepped out assisted by Mr Doyle and they made their way into church greeted by the villagers who made way for them as if they were royalty. Aunt Bríd smiled at Matt as they took their places nearby and he felt a pressure in his chest, a warmth, and smiled a painful smile.

All through the Mass he could not take his eyes from her back, and was nudged once or twice by Nora as he fumbled with his hymn book, forgetful of the place. After Mass as the villagers spilled out on to the green, Mrs Doyle slipped her arm through her husband's and steered him across to Patsy and Nora.

'Garrett, I'd like you to meet my little nephew.' And she introduced them.

'I had a ride in your carriage,' Matt blurted out to Garrett, and turning to Bríd, 'Can I have another ride?' He himself felt the awkwardness of this but was driven to it by a hot embarrassing compulsion.

She laughed, that gay, enchanting laugh which had bewitched him before and which he could never have enough of.

His aunt looked to her husband. 'Shall he ride up with Liam — as far as the cottage?'

'As far as the castle if he likes. Liam can bring him home again afterwards.'

Liam helped Matt up on the bench beside him, and together they rode the three miles to Castle Leighton — or Ballyglin House as everyone had now learned to call it. Matt had seen the house before; several times he and other boys from the village had come exploring this way. They had spied on the gatekeeper, had waited till he wasn't looking, and slipped in through the gate and made their way nervously and excitedly through the park until they had come upon the house and studied it silently and in awe. It spread before them in the sunshine: its tall columns at the front, the row upon row of windows, some open, the curving wings at either side, the glimpses of servants going about their business. Someone soon spied them and they were sent scurrying back the way they came. The house, and the people in it, had about them an aura, as if they were higher beings, not bound by the customary constraints the villagers endured.

'They're Protestants,' was one explanation, a mysterious word somehow redolent of being not quite right.

But this morning instead of hiding in the bushes, Matt was high up on the box with Liam and they swept grandly through the gate where the gatekeeper waited, his hat in hand, nodding as they passed. Liam brought the carriage to the house, Mr Doyle handed his lady down, and Matt followed them up the great stone steps, through tall polished doors into a high hall where a staircase swept up to a balcony above and pictures hung on walls, and statues of naked ladies stood on either side, and then in a blur of wonder into a lofty room with carpets and beautiful sofas, and polished tables and porcelain, and he was placed in a seat by the window. His aunt was pulling off her gloves and coat and passing them to a woman who had appeared from somewhere, and was giving orders. At last she sat in the chair opposite and suddenly reached forward, took his hand and gave it a little squeeze, smiling into his eyes.

He could think of nothing to say, overawed by so much grandeur, and to be alone with his beautiful aunt.

'Liam let me hold the reins, Aunt Bríd,' was all he said in the end. It seemed quite insufficient but fortunately he was rescued soon after by an old gentleman in a swallowtail coat and wearing white gloves who approached holding a silver tray and, bending very graciously, without smiling or saying anything, placed a glass of milk and a plate of biscuits on the low table before him.

'Thank you, O'Flaherty,' said his aunt. The gentleman bowed

again and left still without saying a word. Matt stared at the milk until his aunt said it was all right to drink it, whereupon he took the glass and sipped from it carefully, little sips, and replaced the glass, putting it down and taking it up again, uncertain whether he should drink it all at once or not.

She pushed the plate of biscuits towards him. 'Have one. They're for you.'

He took one and nibbled at it, frightened of dropping any crumbs. She watched him all the time and this made him even more nervous but whenever he looked up she smiled again, and this gave him that warm feeling and he knew she wouldn't scold him if he dropped anything.

Afterwards he tried to remember every moment of the visit, every detail of the room and of his aunt, what clothes she wore and so on, but he could remember nothing of their conversation. Everything was suffused in an air of mystery and glamour, of something quite outside his experience.

He tried to describe it to Aunt Nora and Patsy but although Patsy was ready to hear anything he had to say, Matt quickly noticed Nora was not. She made little 'hmph' noises as she folded the shirts she had been ironing, rattled things about, and went about her various domestic duties, picking things up and putting them down with a quick and noisy efficiency which dampened Matt's eloquence.

Later, outside with Patsy he went on with the description, and Patsy was happy to listen.

'My aunt is very beautiful, isn't she, Uncle Patsy?'

Patsy nodded.

'I never saw such a beautiful lady.'

Patsy nodded again.

'Why has she never come before?'

Patsy drew a long breath. 'She had business of her own, I dare say – being in America,' he said at last, gazing into the middle distance.

'Ah yes. America.'

This made perfect sense: such a gracious lady, so elegant and beautiful could have come only from America. But then – why was she his aunt? Patsy was vague.

'She is of the village,' he explained, 'only she went away when she was very young.' And when Matt pressed him further, Patsy went on, 'she's not exactly your aunt, Matt — more like a relative — my sister's child, only her parents died young. But we call her your aunt Bríd — it's easier that way, d'ye see?'

Matt was content to accept this explanation.

Some few weeks later came a note from the Big House, inviting Matt to visit after Sunday Mass. Again Liam carried him on the box, only this time after his glass of milk, instead of sending him home, his aunt took him out and round behind the house to a paddock where soon after Liam appeared leading two horses, a mare and a little pony.

'Have you ever ridden, Matt?'

He shook his head dumbly, studying the horses.

'And neither have I!' She laughed. 'We can learn together!'

He turned to her in amazement, and she explained. 'Well, Mr Doyle said I had to learn to ride — and I didn't want to do it all on my own — so I thought of you. Would you like that?'

Still unable to speak he nodded vigorously. And soon afterwards Liam had him in the saddle of the little pony — called Maisy — and he was being led in a circle.

'Aren't you going to ride?' he called to Mrs Doyle who was watching.

'Don't worry about me. I can have my lesson later. Hold on tight! Liam — not too fast now!'

Through the summer he went regularly to the Big House on Sunday and practised on Maisy. His aunt had also been practising and soon they were able to ride together. Liam accompanied them, and in time they made their way out of the paddock and up and down the lanes in the neighbourhood. Matt noticed his aunt was now in a splendid riding habit. She looked so elegant and rich that he worried about his own dusty clothes, though he didn't dare mention the fact. The other thing that worried him was that they never rode through the village. When he mentioned this she shrugged and said she preferred it the other way.

As autumn came on the visits grew less frequent. This was due not only to the weather. Mrs Doyle made excuses that it wasn't convenient, and assured him that he could come the following Sunday. There was nothing Matt could do but accept this at face value. He had no idea what other things Mr and Mrs Doyle did though his imagination tried to fill their time – Mr Doyle's business activity and visits to other rich glamorous people.

Then one Sunday the following spring Mr Doyle rode into the village on horseback. The entire village was stunned to see him calmly – or rather, woodenly – take his pew in church for Mass – alone. Afterwards no one dared to enquire after Mrs Doyle. There was always something forbidding about Mr Doyle. He was not a man to cross and it was said he had killed a man once in America. Rumours of Mr Doyle's activities in America had long circulated in the village, of how he had gone there with his pockets empty, how he had started work on the railroad, how he had done well, saved his money – he was not much of a drinker, though always ready to buy you one – and then – here the rumours became vague but the outcome was that Mr Doyle had made his millions – some said in freight, some said in meat packaging, some said in land. But all agreed that he had never forgotten the old country and now he was here again and ready to spend his money in the village. The new windows in the church were testimony to that and there was talk of a bridge in place of the ford – which often used to be impassable in the winter rains.

So when Mr Doyle went to Mass alone, no one liked to ask where Mrs Doyle was. However, it was not long before rumours began to circulate. She had gone to London – on business. And what business might that be, everyone wanted to know? It was unclear. The rumours turned against Mr Doyle. Why couldn't he keep his wife at home? She was a dressy baggage – and they remembered her from before she went away, years ago when she was Bríd Flynn, and very full of herself – and that was never explained either. Mr Doyle couldn't control his own wife it seemed. Some of this Matt heard, and it distressed him greatly. The house and its inhabitants had had an irresistible glamour, something unreal into which he had been privileged to peep. Suddenly things had gone wrong, and Matt felt a cold chill through him, felt it personally as if Mrs Doyle had done it to hurt *him* deliberately.

Patsy could throw no light on the situation. He could only shake his head and stare away across the field. Maybe she had business of her own in London was the most he could think of. It was also rumoured she had brought a fortune of her own to the marriage.

Fortunately Matt was rescued from his confusion and bewilderment a few days later when Liam stopped him in the village after school.

'Matt,' he said, 'Ye've heard that Mrs Doyle had to go away?'

He nodded vigorously.

'She says ye've not to worry, and ye can come and ride Maisy whenever ye like.'

The relief was inexpressible. 'But Liam – why did she have to go away?'

Liam did not know.

'Well – when will she come back?'

Liam didn't know that either.

So throughout that spring and summer Matt walked up to the Big House and took Maisy out through the lanes. His riding ability was secure enough to be able to go on his own though Liam still went with him. They talked about Mrs Doyle. Sometimes as Matt poured out questions about her, he could detect in Liam a certain hesitation – rather like Patsy's – as if he knew more than he was telling. All this merely made her the more fascinating and mysterious.

Then one morning while he was in the stable yard with Maisy, Mr Doyle himself came past. Seeing Matt he paused, was thoughtful, then came across to him. He smiled, glanced at Maisy and ran a hand across her rump. 'How are you getting on?'

'Very well, thank'ee sir,' Matt mumbled.

Mr Doyle looked down hard at him for a long time, studying him, which made Matt nervous, and without thinking he blurted out, 'When is Mrs Doyle coming home?'

The smile disappeared and after a moment Doyle muttered, 'Soon enough, soon enough.'

'But why did she go away?' Matt couldn't help going on.

And to his horror, Mr Doyle seemed troubled, looking away, and then as if not noticing what he was doing, ran his hand over Matt's head. Then as if abstracted, his mind full of thoughts, he turned away without saying a word and Matt watched him walk away across the stable yard and disappear round the side of the house.

This last troubled look was the worst thing of all.

Then as autumn came on again and Matt turned ten, Mrs Doyle reappeared at church. There was no explanation. She simply took her place as if she had never been away. Mr Doyle was completely impassive and there was something about him that prevented anyone asking questions. As they stood on the muddy grass afterwards Matt watched her for a glance and when she finally turned and smiled to him he ran to her and would have thrown himself into her arms but was frightened to; she looked so splendid, so beautiful, and her clothes so smart and new. And the unexplained going away and returning made her even more mysterious than she had been before.

'I came and rode Maisy while you were away,' was all he could say. 'Can I come again?'

She smiled and nodded and he thought for an embarrassed moment she was going to cry. She took his hand, and squeezed it. 'Of course,' she murmured. Then they were gone and Matt watched the carriage roll away up through the village.

During the late summer and autumn work began on the new bridge. Again there were rumours concerning this bridge. It seemed the wrong time of year to start building just as the rains were coming on, and indeed even before Mrs Doyle's unexpected reappearance, the weather had turned and there had been days of winds and rain of constantly increasing severity. The river rose, and work had to be suspended. The wind increased and increased even more, until the news came that the roof had been blown completely off a house in the village. Mr Doyle took charge of the situation, tarpaulins appeared and a temporary roof was secured with ropes. Still the wind and rain increased, and the river continued to swell.

Five

Fair day came in Boyle and Nora and Patsy prepared to walk. The roads by this time were muddy, visibility was low, the sky seemed to hang fifty feet above the ground and there was a continuous drenching rain. None of this deterred Nora. This was fair day, things had to be bought and sold, and there was no intention of abandoning their journey on account of rain. Everyone in the village understood this.

Even so they had difficulty wading across the river which swirled and eddied, rapid, muddy, with leaves and twigs thickly strewn in it. They had umbrellas but even so became gradually wetter and wetter, as the wind blew and buffeted. There was something implacable about Nora this morning, a rigid determination to press on, that neither Patsy nor Matt were inclined to question. So they eventually arrived in Boyle, and made straight for a tavern for a warm drink, and to dry out a little.

The town was crowded with farmers, their wives and daughters, huddled with their heads bowed, the clothes plastered to their backs. Still they bought and sold, hands were slapped, calves and lambs driven away, geese sold. Livestock was traded as if the rain were not there and the air was filled with the lowing of cattle and bleating of lambs taken that morning from their mothers. The square was a mass of churned-up mud and dung and old women huddled in their shawls at street corners with a basket of eggs or cheeses on the ground before them and from somewhere came the pathetic cry of a cockerel.

After a midday dinner, a stew, hot and thick to sustain them for the journey home, Patsy and Matt had emerged and were waiting for Nora when Matt saw Aunt Bríd not far away huddling beneath an umbrella.

'Mr Doyle's at the factor's bargaining for tarpaulins and things to mend the roofs,' she explained. 'Is Nora with you?'

At that moment Nora appeared, hoisting an umbrella.

'Aunt Nora – you're not going to walk home in this?'

'Why not? Not all of us have a carriage to ride in, Bríd.'

'No, of course not – but you'll let Matt ride with us?'

Nora was implacable. 'He'll walk. He's not a milksop. Come Patsy.' She was about to set off but Aunt Bríd hurried after her.

'Aunt Nora! I never said he was!'

Bríd tried to catch her arm but Nora shook her off and turned sharply again. 'Ye'd have us always beholden to your charity, wouldn't ye? Ye'd buy off your guilt and shame, is it?'

She turned away again as Bríd hurried after her. Matt was going to follow but unexpectedly Patsy held him by the shoulder, and whispered, 'Leave them, Matt.'

So Matt and Patsy watched in dismay as Nora and Aunt Bríd had a heated argument beneath dripping umbrellas in the muddy square. Matt couldn't make out what they were saying but was intensely conscious of the horrible tone, the implacable hostility of Nora and the almost pathetic pleading of the other. At last Bríd turned away and disappeared across the square.

Matt watched, mystified and appalled. As they made their way out of the town Matt was afraid to ask why Nora had been so unkind to Aunt Bríd. After all, he had ridden in her carriage many times before and Nora had not objected. Nevertheless, he said nothing. He might be able to question Patsy later, he thought. But he felt cold and frightened at the force of Nora's hatred for Aunt Bríd, troubled and afraid that he might never see her again. How could Nora allow him to go to the Big House after such a scene as this?

They tramped the muddy road to Ballyglin as the afternoon began to close in and the rain continued relentlessly. After a while Matt felt for Patsy's hand. Patsy would be able to explain he hoped. Patsy took his hand without speaking or even looking at him, and the three of them tramped, soaked to the skin beneath umbrellas buffeted by the wind. Only get home, Matt thought, only get home, dry out and go to bed. At that moment he only wanted to sleep, go to sleep and forget the horrible scene he had witnessed.

When they arrived eventually at the river the level had risen even since the morning, and was rushing, swirling, with constant eddies, thick, muddy, with broken twigs and branches carried swiftly down. Their ears were filled with the roaring among the trees as they heaved and swayed above them. They stood for a moment among several other villagers looking at the river in dismay. Patsy turned to Matt.

'You wait here while I test the water.' He set forward into the swift stream. Nora and Matt watched as he struggled to stay upright and was soon in up to his thighs, battling his way across and getting dragged out of his way before he was able to right himself and eventually struggled out on the other side.

'It's all right!' He was about to return for them when Nora called, 'Stay where you are, Matt and I can manage.'

However, as they set forth into the stream which came right up to Matt's chest it was only a moment before Nora, encumbered by her skirts, was dragged off balance and sucked away downstream. Matt clung to her hand as they were swept together but by an extraordinary chance he caught the branch of a willow which happened to overhang the water. In a moment he had lost Nora's hand, and was clinging to the branch. With every ounce of strength he had he pulled himself up further into the tree, strengthening his grip and then turned to where Nora was also clinging to a last thin branch, her head barely above water. Clinging on to the branch, he reached further and further to Nora as the wind buffeted the tree which swayed under his weight. But he was unconscious of the wind or the rain, reaching as far as he could towards Nora. At that moment he was aware of someone behind him, of incoherent voices and of men nearby on the bank shouting and gesticulating. A man was behind him and had already taken him by the waist when with a creak the whole branch lurched forward into the river and Matt found himself in up to his neck but still grasped by a man's arm. In a second it seemed the man had found his footing and was beginning to make his way to the bank, before losing his grip and sweeping several yards downstream again. As the man righted himself for the second time and started to edge his way to the bank, Matt was able at last to turn and see that the man was Mr Doyle himself. He was aware now that there was a crowd of men on the bank shouting and waving at them, and after a moment Mr Doyle had brought him to the bank where men were waiting, half in the river, ready to take him and in a second Mrs Doyle herself had him in her arms.

'Aunt Nora!' he spluttered, before fainting.

When he came to, he found himself sitting in Mr Doyle's gig with a rug over him and Mrs Doyle beside him. It took him a moment to realize where he was and then everything came back.

'Aunt Nora—' he began again, but Mrs Doyle had her arm round him.

'Don't worry. Mr Doyle's taking care of Aunt Nora.'

Suddenly Mr Doyle was before them. He had stripped to his shirt and water flowed off every part of him.

'Is she . . . ?' Mrs Doyle asked quickly.

He nodded. She glanced back at Matt.

'Garrett, I'm taking Patsy and Matt home to dry out. There's nothing we can do for the moment.'

'Don't worry. I'll take care of Nora,' and he was gone again.

The next thing Matt remembered was that they were being led into the Big House, were before a big turf fire, were out of their wet clothes and were in thick dressing gowns with bowls of soup before them. Matt kept asking about Nora but Aunt Bríd always said the same thing. 'Mr Doyle's taking care of her.'

Soon afterwards he was put to bed and was immediately asleep.

When he awoke he couldn't think where he was. The room was dark and he lay, conscious of the strange bed, the thick crispness of the sheets, and the strange nightshirt he was wearing. Then a door opened, and soon afterwards with a clattering of shutters tall windows were revealed and light flooded the room. He instantly sensed that the wind, though still fierce, had abated some of its force and the rain had slackened.

'Are ye awake?' said the lady crossing to him. 'Good – and none the worse for your adventure, I'll be bound. I'll tell the mistress.' She deposited a bundle on to a chair. 'Mr Doyle called at your home last night and brought up your clothes.'

A few minutes later Aunt Bríd came in and hurried to his bedside. She sat on the side of the bed, and leaned over him, examining him carefully.

'Did you sleep well, darling?'

He nodded.

'Would you like to get up? Do you feel strong enough?'

He nodded. 'Sure.' And then, remembering. 'Where's Aunt Nora?'

Mrs Doyle stood up. 'Come down when you're ready and have breakfast. Mr Doyle will explain about Nora.'

Nora was dead.

Strangely, in some remote part of his mind, Matt knew this already. The drama in the river was muddled in his mind with the terrible row at the fair and he had known that henceforth there could not be room in his life for both Nora and Aunt Bríd. One or the other had to go, he realized, so when Mr Doyle took him by the hand, looked him closely in the eyes, and explained gently that they had been unable to save his aunt, Matt was not surprised. In fact he felt inert, unable to express any feeling. It was simply inevitable.

'What'll we do now?' was all he said.

'You're coming to live with us.' Aunt Bríd was sitting beside him.

'And Uncle Patsy too?'

'And Uncle Patsy too.'

So, after seeing Nora buried in the churchyard, Matt bade farewell to the little cottage where he had been brought up, their few possessions were packed up, the even fewer pieces of furniture were distributed about the village and Matt found himself in a room of his own in Ballyglin House. Nearby was Patsy's room, and a strange conversation they had as they inspected these new quarters. Patsy was dressed in fresh clothes which Mr Doyle had supplied and as they talked he would finger the collar of the shirt and shuffle his shoulders inside the strange coat trying to get comfortable. He seemed quite bewildered.

'Mr Doyle's after letting the farm,' he told Matt, 'that was me father's, and his father's too. What am I to do, Matt, with Nora gone? Bríd tells me I don't have to do anythin', but I've worked all me life. I can't be sittin' around all day, can I?'

Aunt Bríd was anxious to placate Patsy. 'You worked all your life, Uncle Patsy, as you say. Now's the time to rest. You deserve it.'

Patsy would go out to the stables and talk to Liam and the

others, and Matt would find him out there smoking his pipe and sitting on a bale of hay.

'Herself would never let me smoke me pipe indoors. Now, here nobody tells me what to do any more. Whatever I want, I just flick me fingers, Matt.' Then he would frown. 'She's very kind, your aunt, but I don't know what I'm doin'. Go indoors, sit out here, 'tis all the same. I don't have to worry about anything, everything supplied. And now Mr Doyle's after lettin' the farm.' He leaned in. 'And for a higher rent, 'tis said.'

Matt was eleven and after long discussions it was decided he must be sent away to school.

'It's for the best, Matt,' his aunt told him. 'Of course I'd rather have you here with me, but Mr Doyle says you must go to the Christian Brothers in Roscommon.'

The school did not accept boarders but lodgings in the town were found, and the following January Matt, dressed in a new and rather stiff tweed suit, went with Bríd to Roscommon and was introduced to a widowed lady with three sons of her own, with one of whom he shared a room, and left his box.

Together they went to the Christian Brothers school which occupied two houses near the centre of the town. Forty boys were educated here by six friars and as they clattered in and out of the rooms for their lessons and ran up and down stairs in their studded boots, the boys got used to the sight of the friars in their chalky cassocks.

The first month was a hard one for Matt. The back pew of Father Geoghegan's church had not prepared him for the wide range of studies into which he was now plunged. Latin, geometry, Irish history, geography, French – it all came as a shock and the transition was a painful one.

Fortunately sharing a house with three other boys helped him to adjust to his new life. He simply didn't have time to feel sorry for himself. Also, feeling set apart from the other village boys as he had been, this transition suited him; he felt he was re-establishing his own dignity and when he came home for the winter holidays and walked into the village in his tweed suit he felt he had been elevated to a superior sphere; already the other boys here seemed rough and ignorant.

They might have resented his new sense of his own identity, as well as the smart clothes he now wore, but they didn't dare show it. Matt had a certain contained quality, a guarded inner feeling, like a coiled spring, and they were wary of teasing him about his new clothes or his speech, which already betrayed the wider world in which he now moved.

Once Matt had adjusted to his new life he embraced it with enthusiasm. He studied hard. 'Make me proud of you,' Bríd had said. 'We'll make a gentleman of you, Matt,' said Mr Doyle.

Some things came easier than others. But far above all, Brother Ronan, who taught them Irish history, had them in thrall. It was partly because from the first what he said chimed in with what Uncle Patsy had taught him about Robert Emmet and Daniel O'Connell; and partly it was due to Brother Ronan's ardent nature and his fiery belief in Ireland's destiny. He made no attempt to hide his contempt for England and his conviction that one day Ireland should be free. His interpretation of Ireland's past was consistent: Erin was the white maid, the *colleen ban*, fairer than the hawthorn blossom in May (he was quoting from an ancient poem) who had been humiliated and insulted, her beauty besmirched by the rough hands of an invader. His meaning was unambiguous and everyone understood it: their manhood had been called into question. Were they humbly to bend the neck beneath a foreign yoke or were they, as men, to rise up and avenge her wrongs? Matt had no difficulty in deciding.

Matt sat at Brother Ronan's feet. Whatever Brother Ronan said sank like a stone into the pool of his consciousness. History needed no memorizing for him. Brother Ronan said it, and henceforth Matt knew it.

One other lesson that was drilled into the boys concerned 'purity'. Their bodies were a temple, they were told, to be kept 'pure' and there was a long list of the perils that awaited the boy who soiled his temple by abuse, including physical weakness, lassitude, imbecility, blindness and the inability to beget children when they were adults. Furthermore, Irish women were the purest on earth, to be treated with reverence and consideration. At confession the priests were eager to learn of any lapses in this department.

★ ★ ★

Over the next three years Matt grew taller than his aunt. Throughout this time he wrote her weekly letters, in which he repeated much of what he had learned, and she replied with news from home. She was to have a baby! And when he came home for the holidays she was indeed great with child, in imminent expectation. The next time he returned, for the long summer vacation, he found her with a baby boy in her arms. Matt was fourteen by now, and although the bond between them was as close as it had ever been, he was inevitably conscious of her need to give the baby her attention.

Then, when he was seventeen, a sister, Rachel, appeared. Matt was grateful that though these children naturally occupied a lot of her time and thoughts, his aunt always had time and to spare for him. During the long vacation they would often sit talking on the lawn beneath the drawing room windows.

Nevertheless the relationship between them had changed. Matt had grown by several inches and, made self-conscious by his extra height, saw that a gap had opened between him and his adoptive family. He now felt a pressure to assert his own opinions. He heard himself being spiky, argumentative, and felt a need to guard his privacy. He himself was conscious of all this, saw sometimes the pained look in his aunt's eyes, yet did not know what to do about it as if he were driven by some hot compulsion which he did not understand.

There was one afternoon in particular when they were together sitting on a rug in the garden. The new baby was asleep nearby beneath an awning and they were nearly asleep too, in the middle of a desultory conversation. Not far away Stephen was playing ride a cock horse, galloping back and forth across the lawn with a horse's head on a stick between his legs and waving a wooden sword. They had both been watching him for some time when she turned unexpectedly to Matt.

'Are you glad to have a brother?' she asked innocently.

Matt was confused. 'A brother?' He could feel himself blushing, but she laughed and reached for his hand.

'I look on you as a son too, Matt. Never forget that.'

Matt replied without thinking. 'But I'm not your son.'

She was checked, and still not letting go of his hand, replied, 'That makes no difference. Not to me.'

'But it does – to me,' Matt muttered thickly, suddenly unable to look her in the eyes and withdrawing his hand. And then, impulsively, 'Aunt – did you ever know my mother?'

There was a pause as Bríd looked away.

'Long, long ago,' she replied dreamily.

'How was she? Was she beautiful?'

'People said she was,' Bríd said in the same tone, still unable to look at him.

'Well – where did she live?'

'I don't know – I only saw her once.'

'Ah.' He was thoughtful. 'And my father – did you know him?'

She nodded, without looking at him. 'Just a little.'

'Well – what was *he* like?' he persisted.

'Your father? He was – a gentleman, but he went away.'

'Went away? Patsy said he died.'

'Well, yes, he did die.'

'Of the cholera,' Matt interjected sharply, watching her.

'Yes . . . yes, I suppose that was it – I wasn't here at the time, but I suppose that was what it was.'

'Where are they buried?'

'Buried?' She looked round quickly.

'Do you know where they are buried?' he repeated.

She seemed completely bewildered. 'Matt, I really don't know.'

'Well, who might know? Would Father Geoghegan know?' He felt hot. 'I mean – someone must know!'

'Matt,' she turned desperately, 'It was a long time ago – soon after you were born. I expect people would have forgotten. Besides – it was before Father Geoghegan came to the village.'

'So – it was in the village? They might be buried in the church-yard?' He looked desperately into her face. 'To think Aunt, to think – to find my mother's grave. My own mother – to see where she lies. To know her grave is safely cared for. To know she is at peace.' There were tears in his eyes and Bríd reached instinctively for his hand again.

'One day we'll know, Matt.'

Six

During this conversation, the master of the house looked down on them from the drawing room window, his hands in his pockets.

Garrett Doyle seethed with an irritated dissatisfaction. He had everything, but as the saying goes, he felt that the things which really mattered, the things he had striven for, somehow still eluded him.

He knew for instance that the conversation between his wife and her son going on beneath him in the garden, was one he had never had, and would never have with her himself. Bríd enjoyed a closeness, a spontaneous intimacy with Matt unknown to Garrett. Of course, Matt was her son, and she had by some miracle been able to recover him after ten years, and Garrett knew by every conversation between them how she dreamed of and for Matt, anticipated his wishes, watched over him, in a way she did not do even for the children she had borne Garrett himself.

He also knew how she longed to clasp Matt to herself and confess that she was his mother, but was prevented from doing so by the thought of all the explanations, and above all by the thought that Matt would have to go through life carrying the stigma of illegitimacy.

He drew a long breath. For the life of him he could not understand why Matt himself had never grasped the truth. The boy had only to stand before a looking glass to see the resemblance to his mother. But Matt was not one to spend much time in front of a looking glass, Garrett had noted with approval.

But there was more than this to Garrett's dissatisfaction. He felt stifled by life in the country. In America, he had stood tall, proud, independent; he had bargained on his own account, made his own money, been a free man. When he made suggestions, had ideas, proposed changes, there were men ready to agree with him, to join with him, to add their own suggestions. Above all there was the space. The sheer size of the country was like a wine and he was made drunk on hope and possibilities and the exhilaration of daring, of risking, of doing new things.

So what sentimental dream had drawn him back to the village of his birth? To do good? To spend his money improving the old place? And what a sad, squalid, poverty-stricken place it had been when he first saw it after all those years. Still, Garrett was not dismayed. He had the money, he could set to work. The first thing he had done was to buy out the old landowner, the Earl of Elphin. This was not difficult. Ever since the famine, which had afflicted the county badly, the earl had been in debt, the land mortgaged. Garrett bought all the mortgages, and sometimes at a heavy discount – 'a shilling in the pound!' he boasted – and the day came when he went to the earl, the mortgages in his hand, and told him to get out. The earl was glad enough to go, a relic of the old rotten rule.

That was how it started. Garrett was now lord of the manor and he had other ideas too. His gift to the church was generous and the priest never tired of thanking him for the new windows. There was the bridge too. 'The finest bridge in the west of Ireland,' they boasted. Ireland was full of boasting, full of windy talk.

And then what? As Garrett began to make acquaintances, to reach out into the country, he ran up against the network of cronies, old pals, family connections, which together made up a blanket which lay across the land and stifled all new thought, all initiative. There was always a reason for not doing things, a reason to talk about it, sure, and to open a bottle of wine and then another, but in the end, nothing was ever resolved, nothing achieved. It was like wading through mud, he would shout at Bríd after a frustrating meeting in Roscommon, everything, it's all sloth, inertia. All talk, but no one ever does anything!

He would move to Dublin, he had decided. There was far more scope there. Besides they would need a town house, for when Matt went to the university.

When he mentioned this to Bríd she was dismayed.

'You wouldn't want to give up this house, would you?'

'Bríd,' he said gently, 'there's no question of closing this house. But we need to have a base in Dublin.'

'Why?'

'Why? Because there's nothing here! I've got to get to Dublin. There are just more openings. I can get things moving. I've been talking to fellows. It's obviously the thing to do.'

'What things?' she enquired nervously.

'Business opportunities, of course. Here, it's impossible; some-body always knows somebody, or is related to somebody else, or owes a favour to someone. Oh they want my money, don't get me wrong. The number of schemes that have been suggested to me! But whenever I look into them, it's to do someone a favour, or rescue someone else from bankruptcy, or to make someone else rich at my expense. They imagine that because I've been out of the country I can't see what they're up to. As if I am some sort of greenhorn!'

He stamped away, harrumphing.

'So – what do you intend?' she asked uncertainly.

'We'll take a house in Dublin and spend part of the time there, part here. I've got to be there!' he repeated violently.

'But couldn't I stay here with the children? I'd prefer them to be brought up here, Garrett. The air's cleaner – and there's the countryside around for them to explore. When Stephen's a little bigger he'll enjoy that. You know how you—'

He had turned and was studying her, stroking his chin thought-fully. 'I shall want you with me,' he said calmly, in a way, she had learned, that meant it was useless to argue.

Garrett's attitude to Matt was ambivalent. There was much in the boy he admired. He was very good-looking – he inherited his looks from his mother – he was tall, he spoke fluently and he always had plenty to say. Mostly about politics. This was one of the things about him which really irritated Garrett because Matt was exactly like Garrett had been at his age. He too had been full of talk about independence, of freedom from British rule, of Ireland taking her place among the nations, a free and inde-pendent republic. Going to America had freed Garrett from such delusions. Politics was all talk, all back-scratching and lining one's own pockets. Nothing really changed. Oh, the flag changed of course, and the national anthem and the head on the stamps, but all the things that mattered went on just the same. Men made money or lost it, they married and had children, land was bought and sold; all these things, the age-old things, went on whatever the nature of the government. This was Garrett's belief. Politics was just a game which men played to their own advantage, and he intended in time to play the game too once he saw his opportunity. This was another reason for moving to Dublin.

But the main reason why Garrett resented Matt was his closeness to Bríd. In Matt this was instinctive and he was not aware of the impact it had on Garrett. He did not see that Garrett was standing in his shadow. But Garrett was bitterly aware of Bríd's infatuation with her son.

Garrett had loved Bríd since she was a little girl. He had never wanted another woman; he had lain at night dreaming of her, planning their life together, and the day after his father died he had gone to ask for her hand. He could offer her the best farm in the village; she would be looked up to as the wife of a prosperous and successful farmer and any other girl in the village would have taken him at his word. Bríd had spurned his offer and run away to London after a whelp of an Englishman. Garrett left the village and went to America.

Then, years later in Chicago Garrett had the shock of his life. Struggling down the street in the teeth of a blizzard, when the temperature was forty below, his hat crammed down over his brows, he glanced up as he passed a theatre and saw the name 'Miss Bridget Flynn', not once, but repeated all down the poster, and on another beside it, and another beside that. And as he made his way through the town that morning he seemed to see the name everywhere. It gave him such a shock because of the coincidence. He did not for a second suspect it might be the same woman, but even so out of sheer curiosity he went that evening to see the play, and as he sat in the audience watching all these historical figures in their doublets and hose and the ladies in their stiff brocaded gowns, as he admired the elaborately painted backcloths, he was studying his programme in the dark. Miss Bridget Flynn was down to play Mary Queen of Scots, which was also the name of the play. Clearly she had the main part. She did not, however, appear in the first scene, which featured Queen Elizabeth of England. Garrett was puzzled, and studied his programme again when the lights came up at the end of the scene. When the curtain rose again, however, it revealed the terrace of a castle, with a park in the background. Several ladies were seated sewing, and for a few seconds nothing was said. Then the one in the middle, dressed in black with red hair, looked up from her needle and sighed, and Garrett actually rocked in his seat as if a mighty wind had buffeted him. It was her. She came down to the foot-lights and began to speak. It was her, it was definitely her. He remembered her voice only too clearly.

Afterwards, he couldn't decide what to do. If he blundered into her dressing room, might he not be rejected as he had been before? Garrett could not bear the thought of a second rejection. Subtlety was called for. What's more he needed to make her sit up and take notice. Garrett had the means to do this. He went early the next morning to a jeweller's, bought one of the most expensive items in the shop, a pair of diamond ear-pendants, parcelled them up and had them delivered to the theatre anony-mously. He also obtained a list of her other engagements and for the next three months followed her, going to see her perform-ances, and sending her other items of jewellery, as the whim took him. He was certain of one thing: she would be on fire to know who her mysterious admirer was, and this gave him a glow of satisfaction. And so it transpired when he finally revealed his identity. It was enough to throw her off balance, enough to give him that opportunity to whisk her into St Patrick's on the morning of her departure and marry her.

That had not been the end of it, alas. Garrett had her hand but he did not have her heart. To his astonishment and dismay he discovered that she had married him only to have the chance of returning to her native village to glimpse her son. She never confessed this until he divined it and eventually forced the truth out of her.

In the end things did seem to come right between them. It was the death of Nora, and Garrett's rescue of Matt which did it. In her relief at his safety, in her gratitude to Garrett, she had flung herself into his arms and his bed. Shortly after, she conceived their first child Stephen, and Rachel followed in due course. It seemed everything was at last right between them.

It was not.

Later he found her in her room changing for dinner. He quickly detected that all was not well with her. Items of clothes were thrown hastily across the bed, she could not decide between one pair of shoes and another, she held up a dress stared at it, and then exclaimed, 'I wonder if I'll ever get back into this,' and threw it down violently, and clutched a hand over her eyes.

Garrett took her by the arm and gently enfolded her in an embrace.

'What is it?' he murmured. He could feel her body shake with a repressed sob before gradually quietening. 'What is it?' he repeated after a moment.

No reply.

'Is it Matt?'

Still no reply.

'It is,' he answered himself. 'What was it about?'

Finally Bríd muttered into Garrett's lapel, 'He asked me about his mother.'

Garrett waited and then, 'And what did you tell him?'

'What could I tell him?' She broke away and sat on the edge of the bed staring out of the window, heaving a deep sigh.

'He'll find out one day,' he said, watching her carefully.

'I know.' She covered her face with her hands. 'Oh God, what will he think? I dread it. How can I ever explain? He will hate me.'

Silence. Garrett stroked his chin for a while watching her. 'You're too hard on yourself,' he said at last. 'And you'll find a way to tell him when the time is right.'

Seven

While this conversation was taking place Matt was tramping down the *bohreen* into the village. It was high summer, and the bushes on either side were thick with luxuriant growth, thick too with wild flowers of every sort, roses and celandine, campion and meadowsweet, crowded with blackberry bushes, while the meadows beyond were high with grass and dotted with buttercups and poppies. The air was filled with evening birdsong; the summer was at its loveliest.

Matt saw none of it. His hands in his pockets, his head down, he strode, conscious only of a black bitterness in his heart, an ache which filled his whole body like a physical wound. He would draw long, long breaths, look up, shake his head and tramp on. There seemed no answer. The world was naturally unjust and that was all there was to it. He, it seemed, he alone had been singled out to be different, singled out to be an orphan, to be deprived of every man's birthright to know his parents. Who am I? he asked aloud to the empty lane. Nobody, came the answer. Nobody at all. They look after me – they took me in, out of their kindness, I'm a relative of sorts, a responsibility they inherited when Nora died. But I don't belong to them. When all is said, her own child, little Stephen will come first. He must. I'm just tolerated.

As he came down through the village, children were playing on the green, and he stopped to watch them for a while. Across the green stood the large grey bulk of the church, dwarfing the little row of cabins opposite. Remembering the conversation with his aunt, Matt crossed and entered the churchyard surrounding it. A path led up to the church door and on either side gravestones stood at various angles, some recent, upright, polished, sometimes with gold lettering, others dulled to grey with bright lichen making patterns on them and leaning at crazy angles, a confusion like old men's teeth, pushing up through the abundant summer grass. Matt made his way through them until he came to Nora's grave and stood for a time, musing on the words. Nora had been born into the world and now she was departed from it, and all there was to show that she had ever been here was this stone. Even this was beginning its long slow journey to obscurity, the polished surface already dulled, the grass intruding on what had once been a neatly kept plot. Everyone is forgotten in the end, he thought, why should I complain?

He thought of Nora. She had loved him, he knew; his earliest memories were of being put to bed by her, and her care for him. Of course she shouted at him – she shouted at Patsy too – but he knew that beneath the gruff exterior she had loved him. He looked about him.

So where was his own mother's grave? He made his way absent-mindedly through the graveyard, reading the names on gravestones, in a sort of desperate hope of suddenly coming across a name he knew.

'Matt?'

He glanced up. Some children were coming out of church after Sunday school and among the chattering little ones stood a tall girl, holding two five- or six-year-olds by each hand. She was wearing a print summer dress and a cotton cap which scarcely controlled the long auburn hair flowing over her shoulders. For a second he stared at her while the two little ones on either side watched him.

'Sure ye know me?'

He made his way over the grassy hummocks to the path.

'Mary?' At last it had come to him.

She laughed. 'Have I changed so much?'

He was confused and blushed. 'No, it's not that—'

'It's been a year or two, all the same. How are ye, Matt?'

He managed to regain control of himself. 'Oh –' he shrugged – 'well enough you know. And yourself?'

'We're all well too.'

'And these—' Matt gestured to the two little ones.

'Ellie and Michael – my littlest brother and sister.'

'And so you're a mother to them.'

'In a manner of speaking. Which way are ye walkin'?'

He shrugged. 'Wherever you like.'

'Come on then, I can't keep these two waitin' for their supper.' She turned to them. 'Ellie and Mikie, this is Matt Byrne, Mr Doyle's nephew.' They made their way out on to the green. 'We don't see so much of ye these days, Matt.'

She caught his glance over the heads of the little ones.

'True – not since I went away to the Brothers.'

'And ye've grown a way, Matt, quite a man now.'

Suddenly Matt felt a devastating hunger for companionship; he had caught a light in her hazel eyes, a light of sympathy, and his soul reached out to her.

'Oh, Mary,' he cried.

She saw the desperate look in his face and stopped. 'Matt? What is it?'

He was studying her closely, unable to put all his confused thoughts into order until, suddenly, everything became clear and he smiled. 'I'm so glad I met you again. I–I was in the graveyard there looking for – you know, I had this stupid idea I might find my mother's grave.'

'Oh, Matt.' She stopped, and there was a pause. Neither knew what to say. 'And is she . . .'

He shrugged hopelessly. 'Nobody knows where she is. I asked my aunt but she knows nothing. I don't even think she's in the village. I don't know what I was thinking of.'

'Did ye never know her, Matt?'

He shook his head. They had reached a door and Mary turned to the little ones, 'Run along in, and tell Ma I'll follow directly.' Without waiting they quickly disappeared indoors.

'I'm so glad I met you, Mary,' he repeated. 'Back there, I was working myself into a stew of self-pity. And then I saw you, and it just, you know, put things back into proportion.'

'I don't think I follow,' she said uncertainly.

'Well, here's you and your little brother and sister and soon you'll go in for your supper – and I'd better be getting back for mine – and you and your family, you're all normal, and that's good and – well, I don't know, it just cheered me up.'

She burst into laughter. 'Well, glad to be of assistance!'

He couldn't help laughing too, and without thinking reached for her hand.

'Maybe I'll see you again?'

She shrugged, looking down at her hand in his. 'Not very difficult Matt; I'm right here in the village every day. I've never even been as far as Athlone.'

'Would you – will you maybe meet me one evening, then?'

'Maybe.' She looked away past him.

'Maybe up by the Fairy Ring?'

'I don't have much spare time, Matt. There are nine of us in the family you know – and I've to help my mam with the wee ones – like ye saw.'

'No, I understand, of course. Forgive me for suggesting it.'

'Still, I dare say I could get away for an hour – if you'd like that.'

'Sure?' She smiled. 'Tomorrow night then,' he hurried on, 'around nine?'

She nodded then turned. 'I'd best be getting in. Goodbye Matt.'

Without saying anything, he watched her disappear into the cottage.

Suddenly the horrible loneliness was lifted from his shoulders, and as he hurried homewards, he felt physically lighter, seemed to bounce up the lane.

As they sat at table that evening dinner was served, as Matt had often remarked, on the earl's china which still bore the Leighton crest. Matt had once asked him why he didn't get new china, why they sat every day staring down at this elaborate design, a falcon displayed, beneath an earl's coronet, and grasping a spear.

'It's *because* it's the Leighton crest.'

When Matt said he didn't understand, Garret explained.

'Every time I eat my dinner, Matt, it gives me great satisfaction to see that crest, to remind me where I am living and who had to get out of my way.'

Matt glanced at Bríd, who had muttered something.

'Did you speak, Bríd?' Garrett asked mildly.

'Yes I did.' She drew a sigh. 'You do it just to make a silly point. As a matter of fact, I would very much like to have my own china.'

'Silly?' He took her up. Garrett was often surprisingly mild in these minor disagreements but he clung tenaciously to his point.

'You think it's silly?' he continued. 'I beg to differ. As your aunt says, Matt, it makes a point. A small point it is true, but a valid one. The Earl of Elphin has gone back to England, good riddance to him, and we sit in his place. And every time I look down at his crest I am reminded of it.'

'Well, I shall insist on new china when we move to Dublin,' she said firmly.

'Move to Dublin?' Matt looked across to Garrett.

He nodded. 'We're going up to Dublin this week to look at houses.'

'When was this decided?'

'Oh –' Garrett was non-committal – 'it's something I've been thinking about for a long time.'

'But why?' Matt was still trying to work out the consequences.

'Business, Matt, business. I've done all I can here. Time to move.'

Bríd laid her hand on Matt's arm. 'We shall keep this house of course. Anyway Patsy's staying here.'

'I've no taste for the city life, Matt,' said Patsy who had been listening in silence to this conversation.

'And we can come down in the summer.'

Later she caught Matt as he was about to go up to his room. 'I didn't want to go. I don't want to at all. I love it here, Matt, and I know you do too. And I don't want you to feel you're losing your home, do you understand? We'll still come down every summer. But your uncle – you know him – restless, never satisfied. We don't need the money, Matt, honestly, but he's never happy unless he's hatching some new plan.' She sighed. 'So it's to Dublin we go.'

'When?'

'He wants to go this week to look at houses. And once we have found something, I suppose we'll go up in the autumn. Besides,' she went on, 'in a year's time you'll be going to the university. You'll need a home, won't you?'

He shrugged. 'I could live in hall.'

'Oh no! I had so looked forward to having you at home while you were a student. Besides, students' rooms are so cold and bare. We'll find somewhere really nice in Dublin. You'll be much more comfortable at home.'

Matt was embarrassed. 'If you say so, aunt,' he said at last and added, 'I'd like that.'

Matt had known the Fairy Ring since a small child. He had ranged across this hill from his earliest childhood even when Patsy held his hand and his little legs could scarcely climb the steep hill. The old cottage was not far distant below them.

This evening he dismounted and walked the *colleen rua* (for such was his horse's name) up to the top where stood a wide ring of standing stones, grey with age and blotched with lichen, a man's height, and one or two leaning in to one another. Mary was not here. He threw the reins round one of the stones and standing with his back to another, always a comfortable place to be, stared away across the village spread out below, the river glinting gold, across the little fields and patches of bog, to the distant Curlew hills, now turning to a dim violet against the setting sun. Staring away towards the sunset, he felt all the time a suppressed excitement. He clasped his hands and closed his eyes.

'Just let her come,' he prayed, 'please, let her come.'

And then, as he opened his eyes again, he noticed two figures appearing over the brow of the hill. He looked away. Who were these? They would see him and Mary if she came now. But then, as he waited, still staring away and hoping they would continue past him, he heard a voice,

'Aren't you going to say hello, Matt?'

Mary was standing before him accompanied by another girl. He looked quickly between them.

'This is my sister Annie.'

Matt felt awkward but Annie was quite excited at this clandestine meeting. 'Do you think I'd let my sister walk out on her own to see a feller?' she said with a penetrating glance.

'Hush!' Mary turned to Matt. 'Annie had to come, Matt, you understand.'

Matt did not understand but said nothing. He could not take his eyes from Mary.

'I had a talk with Father Geoghegan, Matt, about your mother,' she said soon after as they strolled among the stones. Annie was at the other side admiring the view. She reached for his hand. 'I don't think she's there. He said there were several Byrnes, but none that could be your mother. The dates wouldn't fit. So your mother must be from another branch of the family. He said there were Byrnes over in Ardmoyle and Killinch and he offered to write to the priest in those villages, so maybe there'd be a chance of finding her there.'

Matt was overcome with gratitude. He stopped and took her
by both hands.

'You're a true friend!'

'I know how you must feel, Matt; I thought about you after
what you said on Sunday. It was the least I could do. Are you
sure your aunt knows nothing?'

'I've asked her a thousand times. She says it was another branch
of the family and she only saw my mother once long ago. She's
not even sure of her maiden name. And she says my mother died
soon after I was born. Nothing definite. That's what makes it so
difficult; otherwise I could trace her through the registrar of
births, deaths and marriages. If I could only get one definite fact.'
He was so bitter that for a moment he could not speak. 'Can
you believe that I was so unimportant that no one thought to
keep a birth certificate, a death certificate for my mother and
father, a date, an address, nothing at all. Can you imagine how
that makes me feel? I'm nothing, Mary. Quite unconnected, afloat
in the world.' He was overcome and could not go on.

'You're not alone, you have your uncle and aunt.'

'So-called. Even my uncle Patsy who's been a father to me, is
not really my uncle.' He drew a long breath looking up at her
and remembering himself. 'Anyway, enough of that. I'm lucky, I
have more than a lot of men, I live in a big house, I want for
nothing and I'm going to university. It'd be childish to complain.
I'll make my own life, and one day, please God, I'll make my
own family too. And Mary, thanks for your trouble, and for listening
to my woes.'

'University?'

'It's been decided. We're going to Dublin and next year I'm
to be matriculated at the university.'

'So you're leavin' Ballyglin?'

'No! My uncle is keeping the house, and my uncle Patsy is
staying here. We'll come down in the vacations.'

He detected a cooling, a withdrawal in the girl.

'Mary,' he took her hands again, 'I was hoping we could
meet—'

'And what would your uncle and aunt say if they knew you
were keeping company with a girl in the village?' she asked
quietly, interrupting him. 'Mr and Mrs Doyle are very wealthy,

Matt, they go about in the big world. They're bound to have plans for you.'

'Plans?'

'They'll want ye to meet girls of your own class, won't they?'

'My own class? Sure, wasn't I brought up in the village same as yourself?'

'That was then, Matt, this is now.'

'To hell with class! My uncle bought out the Earl of Elphin just to show that class doesn't mean anything any more!'

Mary said nothing, looking away across the countryside, spread below them and beginning to fall into shadow.

'Mary! It doesn't matter!'

She still wouldn't look at him and Matt felt hot with desperation. He took her arm and forced her to look at him.

'I won't let it matter,' he said with a grim determination, and taking her in his arms kissed her hard.

As they separated she looked up and he saw she was as desperate in her way as he.

'I remember once ye fought with Micky Brannagh outside the church, Matt. I never forgot it.' She reached her arms about his neck and they kissed again.

As they separated again he murmured looking down. 'Your sweet slender arms about my neck.'

She laughed softly. 'Slender arms? Them's the arms that lift spuds, Matt, and heave the wet washing out of the tub, and the wee ones into bed when they're bein' naughty.'

'I won't let you go, let my aunt or uncle or anyone else say what they like. I'll come down to see you again, I'll ask your father if I might walk out with you, and one day, God willing, when I'm free, I'll—'

'No. Don't come to our house. I know what my father would say, and I know he'd tell Mr Doyle.'

'What? Why should he?'

'Mr Doyle's our landlord, Matt. Better say nothing. And then one day when you're free, well —' she hesitated — 'we'll see.'

From then on through the rest of the summer, he and Mary met secretly by the Fairy Ring, or sometimes walked by the lake or along the river.

Eight

The train had been slowing gradually and was now making its way through dreary suburbs, through cuttings, that intimated that he would soon arrive at the Amiens Street station. Around him other passengers were beginning to stir, were standing and stretching themselves after the four-hour journey, lifting down valises and briefcases. Matt too lifted down his briefcase and sat it on his knees. A box of books awaited him in the guard's van. He looked out of the window again as the train shifted on to another track with a clattering of points and a lurching to one side. They came under a canopy, slowing, there was a hissing of steam, and the train came to a final stop. The station was busy and already men were leaning out of other windows and calling to porters.

They were everywhere tipping their caps, 'Where to, sir?' and 'If ye'd just follow me, sir.'

On all sides people were jostling and elbowing past: harassed women trying to keep their families together, businessmen in long overcoats and hats pulled down striding purposefully through the crowd. A horse was being led past him, there was a row of milk churns against the wall; everyone else seemed to know where they were going as they hurried past him, and already porters were busily pushing handcarts stacked high with luggage. Matt turned back towards the guard's van, just as a young man in a tweed ulster reaching almost to his ankles with a striped scarf thrown loosely about his neck and hanging half down his back, hurried past followed by a porter pushing his barrow. 'Mind you stick with me!' Matt heard him call over his shoulder in an English accent without slackening his speed. Matt followed him to the guard's van, where other people were searching among suitcases and trunks, boxes and parcels of all sizes and descriptions.

'That one! And that one! And for heaven's sake be careful. Now then look lively, the train was late as it is and I shall catch it.'

Matt watched glumly as this Englishman continued to shower orders over the porter's shoulder. Wasn't that typical? he thought: the Saxon throwing his weight about in age-old style, while the humble Celt jumps to do his bidding. Ireland still had a long way to go.

'You go ahead and find me a cab and I'll bring the rest.' The porter staggered away beneath a pile of trunks, boxes, carrying cases, travelling cases and suitcases while the Englishman clutching several more bags and packages elbowed past Matt. 'Do you mind?' he said in no very friendly voice.

The guard's van was nearly empty and there was no sign of Matt's box. Taking his briefcase, he walked up the platform and stopped a guard.

'I left a box in the guard's van, and it's gone.'

The guard shook his head and went on his way. Matt walked up and down the platform in deeper and deeper perplexity. It must be somewhere. But already a suspicion was forming in his mind. As the porter had been passing him behind his heaped-up cart, there had been something familiar about one of his boxes. Matt ran out to the front of the station but there was no sign of the long ulster.

It seemed hours since he had arrived in Dublin. What a start! No sooner arrived in Dublin than he had lost all his books and the classes started on Monday! And he was late. The family would have started dinner long since. Matt set out to walk to Fitzwilliam Square.

Of all the locations his foster-parents might have chosen, Matt admitted they could not have found a nicer spot. After the mishap at the station, the traffic on the bridge, the crowds in Dame Street and Grafton Street, here was tranquillity, harmony, peace. Matt felt himself relaxing at once as if the trees and shrubs, the bushes and flowers, exhaled a scent to soothe his bruised feelings.

As the maidservant admitted him into the hall he looked into the dining room to his left where the family was grouped at dinner.

'Sorry I'm late,' he muttered briefly.

Bríd started up. 'Darling, where on *earth* have you been?'

Matt drew a sigh. 'The train was late and then I lost all my books.'

'What?'

'Some confounded Englishman walked off with them.' He stood in the doorway, his hands in his pockets looking down at them glumly. 'He had a mountain of luggage and was loudly giving orders to the porter and before I could see what he was doing he'd loaded up my books with all of his stuff and carted them off.'

Bríd could see he was tired and hungry. 'Run up and wash your hands and then come and have some dinner. You look as if you need it. And don't worry about the books. You can get some more.'

'A typical bumptious Englishman,' he went on later in a false English accent as he sat at table and devoured his dinner. 'Eaugh, how de do? Charmed, I'm sure.' Stephen, who was five, laughed, and already the sight of his cheery little face barely visible over the side of the table had taken the sting out of Matt's resentment . . .

During the summer Garrett and Bríd had visited Dublin several times in search of a house and it was Bríd who had chosen the house in Fitzwilliam Square, one in a tall, red-brick Georgian terrace, an 'elegant gentleman's residence', as the agent pointed out to them in the hall, a key in his hand, 'in the most sought-after quarter of the city and eminently suited to anyone intending to cut a figure in Dublin society and to uphold a position such as yourself might wish to, madam. You'll find you have a very select class of neighbours. There's the Earl of Kilgobbin over at number forty-two; Professor Williams at number seventeen—'

'Yes, thank you,' Bríd had interrupted the agent. 'Perhaps you would be so kind as to let us look over the house on our own?' She and Garrett had stumped up carpetless stairs and into echoing rooms, turned back the shutters to look out of the front drawing-room window at the garden in the square, filled with trees and shrubs and neat paths and lawns. 'We'll have a key to the garden, of course.'

The house was taken and she then had an exhausting but exhilarating six weeks painting and furnishing it with chairs and beds brought up from Ballyglin and many more purchased in the city.

Finding and furnishing a house had nothing to do with Garrett though it had been his idea. From the moment he announced it, Bríd seized on the thought that Matt would be able to go on living with the family instead of moving into hall in the university. For a few more years she would have him with her.

During all this time through August and September Matt remained in Ballyglin to prepare for his studies, as he told her. And his room certainly did contain many books. Matt had gradually been evincing a more and more decided taste for politics and the condition of Ireland. It sounded very dry to Bríd. 'Try to enjoy yourself, too, Matt,' she pleaded with him on one occasion. 'It's not all study you know. And I'm sure you'll make many friends.' She hoped he would. Matt had always been a rather lonely boy in the village; perhaps it was out of his loneliness that he filled his head with politics. At that time it was all about Home Rule. Matt read the papers and pronounced his opinions at the dinner table where he sat with Patsy during the quiet days in August and September. Patsy was the one with whom he was closest, the one man to whom Matt could say anything. Patsy listened patiently.

There was another reason, apart from the upheaval in furnishing the house in Fitzwilliam Square and the preparation for his studies, why Matt elected to remain in Ballyglin. In the long summer evenings he wandered about the Fairy Ring hand in hand with Mary Higgins, telling her of his plans. 'I'm going into the law,' he told her. 'It's through the law that everything can be changed.' Mary wasn't sure that anything needed to be changed. 'Everything has to be changed!' Matt insisted. 'Parnell has made a start with the Land Act, and there are people in this very village who have noticed the difference already! But it's only a beginning! The next thing, the really big thing, is Home Rule for Ireland. That would change everything. I want to be part of it.'

Mary listened patiently as Matt poured out his ideas. Belatedly, he would remember her, and reassure her, 'I'll still come down to see you once I'm in Dublin,' he would tell her, as they held hands. 'And one day, maybe I'll be in a position to come to your father and—'

Mary stopped him. 'It's a few years off yet, Matt. Better not to make promises.'

Garrett went with Matt to a bank and opened an account for

him. Matt was astonished when Garrett deposited five hundred pounds in his account.

'A man's got to have money, Matt. Think big. Money elevates a man, lifts him up so he can see farther, breathe deeper. Think of it like a mountain. Your place is at the top, understand? You'll be going out into the world one day; you'll be holding a commanding position, giving orders. I don't want you creeping about, apologizing for yourself. Cut a good figure in society, dress well, hold your head up, and get to know the right people. The university is an excellent place to do that.'

It was one thing for Garrett to open a bank account for him; Matt was embarrassed however when his aunt insisted on taking him to a tailor to have him fitted out with new clothes, the tweed suit he had been wearing on his ill-fated journey up with his books, and others, evening dress, elegant silk shirts, shoes made to measure. 'It's worth it, believe me; they're so much more comfortable. That's something I learned years ago in London.' He took out his new cheque book but she insisted on paying. 'Aunt, I'm not a child,' he said helplessly.

The following Monday he walked down to the university, crowded in with the other new students, and those returning, older men. They were all to be 'men' from now on, or even 'gentlemen' as the porter addressed him as he asked his way to the bursar's office to write his very own cheque for his first term's fees. Matt liked that word 'men'.

There was a visit to his professor's office and a short interview, finishing with a list of books – many of which he had possessed, he told the professor ruefully, until 'a confounded Englishman' walked off with them.

Two days later he arrived for his first lecture, found the lecture hall, his briefcase filled with notepads, pencils and a new and very expensive 'fountain pen' which his aunt had bought him. 'To get you off to a good start, darling.'

The hall, with its steep rows of desks, echoed loudly with chatter, many calls of recognition, laughter, and the noise of boots clattering up and down the steps as the students filed into the rows.

Matt was about to take his place when glancing about him he

saw with a shock the very Englishman who had walked away with his books. For a second he stared across at him; it was definitely the same man. But what a coincidence! He stared. It was the same man, he decided. It was impossible to get to him at that moment, the rows of desks were almost full, and men were settling down and opening folders ready to take notes. A second later the professor walked in, a hush gradually fell and for the next two hours Matt was busy scribbling notes on land tenure and conveyancing.

As the students were once more clattering down and out of the lecture theatre, Matt forced his way through the crowd and as he emerged into the corridor he could see the Englishman just ahead of him. He pushed ahead and tapped him on the shoulder.

'You're the thieving scoundrel who stole my books. You'll hand 'em back if you don't want a thrashing.'

The man, who was a head shorter than Matt, slim, had blond hair, neatly cut, and small regular features, looked him over mildly.

'I take it you're referring to a box I picked up by accident in the train last Thursday? So glad I found you. It's been cluttering up my room. You might have put your name on it then I could have returned it to you.'

'It had a label. Do you take me for an idiot?'

The young man took a moment to reply to this. He glanced coolly over Matt. 'At this moment I'm not sure what I take you for. But I am not a thieving scoundrel. I suggest you moderate your language, old chap.'

'Oh you do, do you, *old chap*?' said Matt with unconcealed contempt.

'By Jove yes I do.' The young man was beginning to get annoyed. 'There's such a thing as manners.'

'Not as far as you're concerned. You deserved it.'

'I did not deserve it. You're confoundedly impertinent.' He took a step backwards, looked Matt over then said carefully, 'I believe I may have to teach you a lesson.'

'That I should like to see.'

'You shall,' said the other coolly. 'Name your day and I'll meet you in the gym.'

'In the gym?'

'Well, I don't want to do you any lasting damage but I'll give you a bloody nose. In the meantime, follow me and you can have your wretched box back.' He turned and walked away.

In silence they emerged into the courtyard and Matt followed the young man who did not once turn round. Across a yard (known as 'Botany Bay') they went towards a grey block, in and upstairs. A key was produced, and Matt followed him into a small, sunny room. The bed was unmade, and strewn with books. A small table was likewise covered with writing materials and a large meerschaum pipe. Clothes hung over the back of a chair and against one wall stood Matt's box.

The man turned and indicated it.

'Label?' he said contemptuously.

Matt examined the box. 'It's been ripped off.'

'Right. I'll meet you in the gym. When?'

'Now,' Matt said firmly. He was beginning to sense that he was in the wrong but was certainly not going to give in to this super-cilious foreigner.

'Right,' said the other again, equally firmly. 'Where is the gym, by the way?'

'You mean you don't know?'

'Why the deuce should I? I only got here last Thursday.'

'Well, there certainly must be one. Come on.'

Somewhat self-consciously, and shoulder to shoulder they crossed the spacious courtyard to the entrance block and called into the porter's lodge. The porter directed them towards the sports' fields, and sure enough they did find a gymnasium. A number of men were limbering up on parallel bars, ropes and climbing frames.

'I say, can any of you fellows lend us a couple of pairs of boxing gloves?' asked the Englishman. Matt was constantly impressed by his cool, confident, manner. Hot, impulsive, angry himself, it was everything he admired and everything he would like to be. He frowned and bided his time as a pair of gloves was pressed into his hands.

'Ready?' The Englishman raised an eyebrow. 'Still want to go through with it?'

'You'll see.' Matt, who had stripped off his jacket and waist-coat, now turned back his sleeves. Another man tied on his gloves.

Some of the other athletes had by this time noticed what was going on and had stopped to watch. One of them appointed himself referee and umpire.

'Now – how many rounds do you fellows want to go?'

'Until he's had enough,' said the Englishman contemptuously. Matt said nothing.

They squared up to each other. Matt had boxed at school and he had been in more than one fight in the village. He was certainly used to defending himself and circled his opponent warily, parrying a few opening jabs and biding his time. The fellow had pluck, Matt gave him that; his skill might be another matter. After a few more of these feints and jabs, Matt had the measure of his man and the next time he opened his guard Matt laid him on the floor.

Matt waited in silence as the referee knelt to see how he was. The young man raised himself on an elbow and shook his head for a moment. He got up and stood for a moment, looking about him with a bewildered expression and trying to get his balance. Shaking his head once more, he faced Matt.

'Good hit, fair and square. Now come on!' and once again he raised his gloves. Matt wasn't so sure. The man still looked uncertain on his feet and Matt did not raise his gloves.

'Honour's satisfied, as far as I'm concerned,' he said. 'And you were in the right of it. I spoke in haste. My apologies.' He held out his gloves for the ref to untie and a moment later offered his hand to his opponent. The young man did look faintly relieved, Matt could see.

'Spoken like a gentleman,' he said. 'And by Jove, the least I can do is to stand you a pint.'

Nine

'I intend, old man,' said Fred as he filled his meerschaum, 'I intend to swim every day, right through the winter, rain or shine, snow or sleet, to harden the body, don't you see. Down at the Forty Foot rock. There's a capital swimming spot.'

'To harden the body,' Matt echoed, his fist on the table and fixed him with a serious look. 'For the struggle. I feel we are like knights of old, Fred, sworn to do service for our lady – the white maiden Erin. We must hold ourselves ready for the struggle,' he repeated and held out his hand.

'The struggle that's coming, when Ireland shall be free.' They shook hands firmly.

'And we'll see who breaks first. By Jove, every day! Christmas Day and all!'

'Essential. To be fit. *Mens sana in corpore sano*. By the way, old man, your glass is empty; allow me to proffer the beaker of friendship.' He rose unsteadily and approached the bar. 'Rosie! Two pints of your sour black nectar, if you please.'

'This is mine.' Matt lurched beside him, his hand in his pocket.

'Absolutely not, dear boy, I insist.' Fred laid his hand on Matt's arm. 'I invited you to partake of a beverage, of a—a foaming potation . . .'

They resumed their seats in the snug. Beneath the table stood Matt's box.

'Is this your first time in Dublin?' Fred struck another match. He had not fully mastered the art of smoking a pipe. 'Dublin. *Baile atha cliatha* – whatever that means,' he added inconsequentially. The pipe was at last puffing satisfactorily.

'The fort of the hurdle ford.'

'Pardon?'

'That's what it means. It's Irish,' Matt repeated.

'And what is a hurdle ford – when it's at home?'

Matt had a childhood memory in his foggy brain of Patsy throwing down sheep hurdles in a stream to make it easier to cross. The words wouldn't come out straight, however. 'It's to . . . cross – to cross easier. Dublin – that's Irish too: *dubh linn* – the dark pool. Didn't they teach you Irish at school?'

''Fraid not old man – the parents sent me to school in England.'

'Sassenach,' said Matt contemptuously.

'Isn't that curious, by the way, that a city should have two names? Don't know of any other city with two names, do you? Wish they'd taught us Irish,' Fred went on wistfully. 'Sight more useful than Latin and Greek, if you ask me.'

Matt leaned forward, suddenly serious in his drunken state. 'It's our native tongue, Fred – which the Saxons tried to destroy – but we'll bring it back to life.' He looked about him, moodily. 'Though my uncle says it's a waste of time.'

'You're absolutely right old man – our native tongue! You can teach me.'

Matt looked up suspiciously from his pint. 'Why should a Saxon want to learn the Irish?'

Fred lurched forward over the table. 'Haven't I been trying to din into your brain, you thickheaded, thin-skinned Hibernian, that I am not an Englishman? Born and bred in the County Sligo, within sight of the roaring Atlantic.' He quoted as if from an estate agent's brochure, 'Ardnashiel House, a most picturesque and commodious gentleman's residence, enjoying modern amenities and extensive views to the sea, and situate in its own demesne of twenty acres. Property of Sir William and Lady Langley and their two rosy-cheeked children.'

Matt had just set down his pint, his fourth. He looked unsteadily across at Fred. 'Rosy-cheeked? I'll take your word for it, too dark in here to see properly. Who's the other child?'

'My big sister Grace, who bullies me; she's a bit of a bluestocking, reads books all day. Fortunately she's in Paris at the moment studying art.'

There was a lull in the conversation during which Matt pulled the watch from his pocket. 'Let me see, the time must be . . .' he stared uncertainly at the dial 'it's either five and twenty to five or else twenty-five past seven, in which case I am very late for dinner. Fred, my friend, dinner calls. And I insist that you join me. I will positively not take no for an answer. It only remains therefore, for us to summon a cab. A cab. Call a cab!' He lurched to his feet. 'Fred, my old friend, if you would be so kind –' he reached beneath the table – 'this box –' he was on his knees – 'give us a hand, old chap, I can't seem . . .'

Carrying the box between them they lurched into the street and heaved it into a cab. 'Fitzwilliam Square. We are awaited!'

As the house door was opened by the housekeeper, Matt entered backwards, holding one end of the box. 'Mrs Connolly, this is Mr Fred Langley, my esteemed colleague and fellow student, whom I have invited to dinner.'

She shook her head gravely. 'Your first day of college and drunk already!'

He glanced into the dining room. It was empty except for a housemaid who was setting the table for dinner. 'Good. We're not late. I'll introduce you to the family.'

Matt led him up into the drawing room where his aunt was sitting by the fire with Stephen and little Rachel. Garrett was out, it appeared.

'Aunt! I've asked my friend to dinner – hope you don't mind?' He lurched unsteadily across the room. 'Come in Fred, don't be shy. Fred –' he turned back to Bríd who had risen – 'Fred has by some miracle restored my books, Aunt, and I am infernally – I mean, eternally – grateful to the dear fellow.'

Fred advanced.

'Allow me to int'duce Mr Fred Langley; Fred this is my aunt Bríd Doyle.' As they shook hands Matt flourished his arm. 'Fred take a seat and don't take any notice of these –' he gestured to Stephen and Rachel – 'small fry.'

What did Fred see as he entered the drawing room? A spacious, pleasant room which seemed to invite him immediately to make himself at home. The colours were rich and strong; plum red for the curtains which were draped on either side of the windows in a theatrical fashion. In fact the whole room and the way it was lit had a theatrical feel about it as if characters were about to appear and act out a scene. Fred had never been in such a room in his life and did not at first take in the rich, intricately woven carpets beneath his feet, the Japanese prints and oil paintings on the walls, the pretty Moroccan table and the comfortable old Spanish leather chairs round it, or the exotic shawl thrown over a chaise longue.

Afterwards as he was walking home he remembered it only in a haze of opulence and comfort.

Rising to meet him was a tall, elegantly dressed woman in a silk gown with the fashionable bustle and cut away to expose her beautiful neck. A mass of dark hair was carelessly put up behind her head, and her face was immediately memorable: strong cheekbones and chin, expressive eyebrows and large dark eyes. There was about her an easy grace and welcoming smile. Even Matt was slightly taken aback by this splendid presence in the room, though he was familiar enough with his aunt when she chose to make an impression.

Bríd could tell immediately they had been drinking. 'Come in Fred,' she said casually, 'take that seat, and tell me how you found the books.'

Matt threw himself into a corner of the sofa where his little sister Rachel immediately plumped herself and curled up against him. Absent-mindedly Matt laid his arm about her neck as Fred recounted the story.

Garrett did not appear for dinner. 'He's out with business colleagues,' Bríd apologized.

Later, as Fred was leaving, Matt said, 'I'll walk a bit of the way with you.' And they set off along the pavement.

'Well, thanks for the dinner old man, different story from my dismal commons in hall, I can tell you. Your aunt certainly knows how to do well for herself. Do you eat like that every day?'

'More or less.' Matt had never thought about it.

They walked on in silence for a couple of minutes.

'You know old man there's something faintly familiar about your aunt. I couldn't help noticing the picture on the wall. And that old poster in the hall: Miss Bridget Flynn – would that have been your aunt by any chance?'

Matt nodded. He had never taken much notice of it, never questioned his aunt about her past, and she for her part, never offered any information.

'I believe I saw her in London when we went over,' Fred went on. 'Years ago – I must have been about twelve, I think. It was a Shakespeare play – *Much Ado About Nothing*. Didn't follow all of it, mind, at that age but I certainly remember her. Difficult to forget. She stole the blessed show. The audience went wild at the end. My sister will be very interested. I'll write and tell her. By Jove, Miss Bridget Flynn eh, who'd have thought it?'

'She was famous?'

'I rather think she was, old chap. Had her name plastered all over the theatre.'

Matt was silent. It was something he knew nothing about. Why had he never asked his aunt about her past? He stopped abruptly. 'I'll leave you here, old man. See you tomorrow, nine o'clock sharp.'

On the way back along the dim pavement, Fred's words were going round and round in his mind. Of course he knew his aunt had been an actress, from little things she let drop from time to time, not to mention the poster framed in the hall. But it had taken Fred this evening to bring home to him what a beautiful woman she was, how stylish and sophisticated. What an easy air she had as she welcomed Fred into her house. Why had he never noticed these things before? And a famous actress. Strange she never talked about it.

The other children were in bed and he found Bríd in the drawing room, sitting by the fire, and writing on her knee. She looked up as he came in.

'What a charming young man. I'm glad you've made friends so quickly.'

Matt shrugged. 'I should pick a fight more often.' He looked up at the large portrait of his aunt hanging on the wall beside him. Full length, full size, it showed her in a costume of the Elizabethan period, painted in subdued hues of silver and grey. As he studied this picture which he had known since his childhood, he said tentatively, 'Aunt, Fred said he knew you.'

She looked up.

'He said he saw you years ago in London in a play.'

She laughed awkwardly. 'Oh that! Water under the bridge.'

'Why did you never tell me about it?'

'There was nothing to tell, darling! It's what a lot of young girls do. Go on the stage for a few years – then get married, and have children. It's called growing up.'

'But really,' Matt insisted, 'he said you were famous.'

'Famous? I don't know about that.'

'He said you had your name all over the theatre.'

'Oh well.' She looked down at the paper on her lap. 'Well briefly, perhaps, just a few months, you know – until they got someone else.' She pretended to go on with what she had been writing and Matt sensed he was going to get no more out of her. 'What are you writing?'

'A menu. Your uncle is having some people in to dinner on Saturday.'

A pause as she went on writing.

'Fred said how much he enjoyed dinner tonight. Do you know where Uncle is tonight?'

She shook her head vaguely. 'Out with business colleagues. He's been busy making contacts ever since we arrived.'

Matt could hardly credit his luck. He had a friend! Fred had accepted him immediately, sincerely enjoyed his company. There was a natural, spontaneous bond between them; they seemed to have endless things to discuss, and talked continuously. Matt looked forward to being with him and they were constantly together, in lecture theatres, in the library, consulting one another on points of law. They also kept their bargain to work on their physical fitness. They played soccer and as agreed went swimming.

The Forty Foot rock is a bathing place down the coast of Dublin Bay, reached easily by a ten-minute train ride, and as the days grew shorter and the weather less friendly, on dark mornings in rain sometimes, they duly took their way to Kingstown. From there they scrambled over the uneven rocks, jumping from outcrop to outcrop, scrambling down to the waterside and at last found a foothold where a few other hardy souls were to be found. Here they stripped. Bathing suits had not yet been invented for men in this secluded spot and by tradition they went in naked. So on a dark and unwelcoming morning when any sensible person would still be huddled in bed, these two, in the name of 'hardening their bodies' in 'preparation for the struggle' looked shivering down at the grey-green bulk of the salt sea breaking regularly against the rock wall where they stood, took a deep breath and plunged in. It was as if a mighty hand clenched Matt's chest and he broke the surface with a gasp as the freezing sea grasped him. It was however a rule that they must stay in for at least ten minutes. 'No point in doing

it, old chap, if we just come scampering out again. Got to harden
the body!' they agreed.

The relief afterwards, however, went a long way to making it
all worth while. After a cup of hot Bovril in a nearby café, they
made the return journey into town, in a haze of contentment.
'By Jove it sets a man up for the day,' was agreed, though they
had a tendency to nod off during the first lecture of the morning
in the unaccustomed warmth of the lecture theatre.

Something else that happened during Matt's first year at the
university was that Garrett invited him to join him at dinners in
town. This meant in hotels where he entertained potential business associates. On their way to one of these dinners, when Matt
addressed him as Uncle Garrett, Garrett said abruptly, 'By the
way, Matt, that's enough of the uncle. It makes me uncomfortable. For one thing I'm not your uncle. Just call me Garrett.'

Garrett also lectured Matt on the usefulness of these meetings.

'You need to get out into the world, Matt, meet people, find
out who can be useful to you, and who your enemies are. Studying
is all right at your age, but it's just a beginning. I never had a
day's schooling myself after the age of twelve. It's the world, the
big world, where a man makes his mark. Where he stands or falls.
Remember that.'

'I need to be qualified,' Matt said with difficulty. 'I must have
a profession. As a lawyer I can help to make a difference. In the
struggle,' he added. 'I'm not interested in making money – for
its own sake. Money's only good if it can be put to use.'

'No one's denying that,' Garrett replied mildly. 'Of course money
has its uses. A man needs to maintain a respectable figure in the
world. Men judge you by how you judge yourself. And one day
you'll marry. You'll need money for that. Wives don't come cheap.
But most of all, money gives you power – it makes you what
you are, tells you that you're alive.'

Matt said nothing more and they rode on in silence until they
had arrived outside the Gresham, one of the most expensive hotels
in Dublin. At the table sat eight men as well as Matt. He remained
in almost total silence as the men chaffed and argued through
the meal. They ate a lot – all the most expensive items on the
menu, he noticed – and they drank heavily too. There was

something gross and materialistic about them; they seized on life the way they seized on their food, greedily, enjoyably. They evidently believed they were entitled to the best of everything.

This was the case in all but one, and as the evening progressed, and as various business projects were discussed, were costed, enthused over or rejected, there was one man who seemed to have less to say than the others, and who from time to time would cast anxious glances towards Garrett. Matt was curious. At the beginning he had apparently joined in the talking and eating and drinking with as much determination as the others. But as the evening wore on, he fell behind. Finally, as the party was breaking up, as they stood about in the lobby of the hotel while overcoats were fetched, Matt noticed this man in urgent conference with Garrett. Garrett was listening carefully, but seemed unwilling to commit himself.

Afterwards on the way home, Matt mentioned this.

'Haynes.' Garrett puffed on a cigar. 'In a bad way. He spread himself too thinly, poor devil, and can't repay his mortgages.'

'So – was he asking for a loan?'

Garrett nodded.

'And – what did you say?'

'I said I'd think about it. He's coming to see me tomorrow, when we've got clearer heads.'

Ten

'By the way, Matt,' Garrett said another time, 'I've been meaning to tell you. All this talk of "the struggle" – it's a lot of hot air. I'll be frank. It'll get you nowhere and it's a distraction from the real world.'

Matt was embarrassed to argue with him but at last between clenched jaws, he began quietly, 'Years ago when I was little and living with Patsy and Nora, God rest her soul, he took me out poaching. Nora said we shouldn't go, but we went anyway. We were spotted by the gamekeeper, and the next morning Lord Elphin, our landlord who was passing through the village, stopped at the cottage and threatened Patsy that he'd throw us out of the farm if he ever tried it again.'

'What did Patsy expect?' Garrett said coolly.

'And then,' Matt went on in this subdued concentrated tone, 'afterwards, when we went back inside the house Patsy slammed his hand down on the table. It was the only time I ever saw him angry. And I swore I would do anything I could, that Patsy and everyone else in the village would never be humiliated like that again.'

Garrett did not reply for a moment. Finally, he turned and clapped Matt on the shoulder. 'Matt, I respect you for your sentiments. You wanted to protect Patsy, and being a little lad, you couldn't. However, we must face the fact that Patsy was breaking the law—'

'The Leightons were an English family, that had no roots in the land and they humiliated him. They should never have been here at all!'

'And if the landlord had been Irish – what then?'

Matt had no answer for this at first.

'You're a lawyer, Matt,' Garrett pressed him. 'What about the rights of property?'

'I believe Irish land should be in the hands of Irishmen.'

'Well then, suppose the Elphins had come over and bought the property legally?'

'They should stay where they are and leave us alone.'

'What about me, Matt? I went to America and made a lot of money. Should I have stayed at home?'

'I believe in Ireland for the Irish and Home Rule. Is that too much to ask?'

Garrett drew a long breath. Finally he said, 'You know, I used to think like that years ago. Then I went to America and grew up. Sorry to be blunt but frankly it's all words. The Irish and the English have been mixed up together for seven hundred years. The important thing is to get out and make your mark in the world. All the rest is talk. Once you've got your degree I'll take you in with me. You're a lad of mettle, Matt, and you're going to do well – once you get all these notions out of your head.'

Matt was silent for a moment but finally looked away, 'Once I graduate I'm going into the law, and then to work for Home Rule.'

During the following summer vacation Matt was invited by Fred to stay with his family at Ardnashiel. They travelled down to the west coast by train and as they got out at the station in Sligo town, Fred nudged Matt. 'There's Grace.' Ahead of them on the platform a girl was waving. As they approached Matt tried quickly to take her in. She was the same height as her brother and glancing between them Matt could immediately see the resemblance. She wore a plain brown skirt, short at the ankle, a little velvet jacket in plum red and, over the abundant dark brown hair which flowed over her shoulders, what looked like (and was) her brother's cricket cap. She held out her hand in a frank and open way and said abruptly, 'So you're the wild boy.'

Matt was taken aback.

'My brother's told me how you threatened to murder him and when that failed, how you tried to freeze him to death in the sea in the middle of winter. You're mad, the pair of you.' She said this in a completely calm voice and a sardonic look, and without waiting for a reply turned on her heel. 'Well, come along, the trap's outside, and the parents are waiting lunch for us.'

Fred turned to Matt and winked. 'See what I mean? Don't take any notice.' He raised his voice so she could hear. 'Most of the time she's quite rational! And almost polite! In any case,' he

went on in this loud voice, 'it was my idea to go swimming –
and we kept it up, didn't we, Matt?'

Matt had still said nothing. He was quite in awe of this girl
with her free and easy ways and her English accent, which to his
annoyance, he found slightly intimidating.

The trap stood outside the station, they heaved their bags into
it, and Grace, who still had not introduced herself, took the reins,
gave them a shake and the horse without further prompting took
the road out of town.

'When did you get back?' Fred asked after a moment.

'A couple of weeks ago.' She kept her eye on the road. 'Everyone
had gone out of town so there didn't seem any point in hanging
around any longer. Anyway, Paris in the summer is a bit of a hole.
But I suppose any city is.'

'What about next term? You going back?'

'I'm still thinking about it. I may try Rome, or Venice. They
say Venice in the winter is very atmospheric.'

'Really?'

Matt had not been included in any of this so far. Brother and
sister had resumed a conversation effortlessly that they might have
interrupted three months before. As for this talk of Paris and
Rome and Venice, it invested the girl with a glamour he found
very intimidating. In the meantime as they came in sight of the
sea the wind caught his breath.

The sky was clear, wide, miles high, with clouds far above and
the wind was like the breath of life, lifting the spirits. Forgetting
Fred and his odd sister for a moment, Matt rejoiced to be here
in this clean bare landscape. Mountains could be dimly discerned
in the distance across the immense sweep of a bay. The sea was
rich and dark with streaks of vibrant colour, aquamarine, ultra-
marine, cobalt blue – artist's colours – and glinting with white
foam caps. Matt felt liberated and couldn't help exclaiming, 'It's
wonderful here!' but the other two were busy talking and in the
fierce wind his words were carried away.

After nearly an hour's drive, along the cliffs for a while and
through a wood, the trap turned off the lane through gates and
drove for some time through woodland until a large square house
came into sight, grey stone and with a lawn reaching right to
the windows.

'You've caught us on a good day,' said Sir William as he was ushering Matt into the hall. 'The sky is clear but don't be fooled! We have the highest rainfall in Ireland.' The baronet, in knicker-bockers and tweed jacket, had a goatee beard, and a high bald forehead which gave him the air of a profound thinker and perhaps that was what he was. At this moment, however, he was hiding it well beneath an affable manner. His wife on Matt's other side, fussed round him. 'Fred will show you to your room. I expect you'd like to wash your hands – and then we'll have lunch.'

Meanwhile, Grace had disappeared round the side of the house to put the horse away and did not reappear until they sat down to lunch. The room they sat in had long windows to the floor which gave a view straight down to the sea and beyond towards distant mountains, blue-grey outlines beneath a wide empty sky. The space gave a sense of freedom and exhilaration, and Matt thought any girl brought up there might well have developed free and easy ways.

The table would have seated fourteen, so the five who sat down for lunch were spaced out and Grace was across at a diagonal and some distance from Matt. She confined her conversation to her mother and father and gave him not the slightest attention. In the meantime Matt was busy taking things in and quickly noticed some large roundels on the walls, perhaps two or three feet in diameter, coloured red and inscribed with flowing designs in gold. Eventually, taking courage, he mentioned them.

'Arabic inscriptions,' said Sir William. 'I bought them in Aleppo.' Seeing the mystification on Matt's face, he went on, 'In Syria, you know.'

His wife cut in. 'My husband is an explorer, Matt. He has travelled a lot in the Near East, Syria, Mesopotamia and Persia.'

'Thank you my dear – don't make me out to be grander than I am. To tell the truth, Matt, these are sacred inscriptions, and the Arabs had no business selling them to an infidel. But the calligraphy is exquisite; I could not help myself.'

'You mean – that is writing?' Matt was incredulous.

'Indeed.'

'Do you know what it means?'

'They are quotations from the Koran – the Arabs' holy book.

That one for instance,' he said pointing, and casually translated its meaning.

'So – you speak Arabic?'

Again his wife cut in. 'I will spare his blushes, Matt. My husband as well as being a traveller is something of a linguist and in addition to going all over the Near East he has been in Russia several times even as far as Kurdistan. He speaks Russian fluently . . .'

'As well as French, Spanish, German, Italian and Greek,' the girl cut in coldly and quickly, and glancing to Matt said, 'So now you know, wild boy. And that's enough boasting for one day.'

The parents glanced at one another after this interruption but said nothing and after a moment Fred said, 'There's capital swimming here too, old chap. We'll make ourselves a plan. Swimming first thing, then a couple of hours with the books, and after that – I say, do you ride?'

Matt nodded.

'There are some fine gallops along the sand.'

'There's nothing to equal a gallop along the sand,' his sister echoed abruptly. 'It's the only time I really feel free.'

'Free!' her father cut in tersely, perhaps still piqued by her rude interruption of her mother. 'I should say you do! You're as free as any girl alive today. I should think you would have found that out by now.'

At this moment a servant entered and bent over Sir William, 'Mr Scott is here, sir.'

'Ask him to wait. We have a guest and we're a bit late at lunch.'

Later as Fred led the way out he explained. 'Scott is the land agent. For the estate, you know.'

'Your father has an estate?'

'How do you think he pays for his travels? The farmers stump up their rents so my father can go gallivanting about the globe. Though, to do him justice, it's by no means a waste of time. If my sister had not so rudely interrupted her, my mother would have told you about his books. He's published quite a number – accounts of his expeditions and so forth. Member of the Royal Geographical Society and all that. Quite eminent in his way.'

'Does your father have a large estate?' Matt asked tentatively. They had arrived at the seashore by this time. The wind blew as fiercely as before, and they stood staring out to sea as it buffeted them.

'Well, it ain't small; sixty thousand acres to the best of my knowledge. Mind you, we had a bad time of it during the famine. My great grandfather nearly bankrupted himself and I don't think the estate yields that much even now. I must say the parents do the honourable thing when they can. They are well liked, as land-lords go.'

'Honourable thing? What do you mean?'

'At the land tribunal, when there's a dispute about the rent Pa always gives way. And he often lets farmers run on if they're having trouble paying.'

Matt said nothing. The only other great landowner he had ever known had been the Earl of Elphin and this scholarly explorer was about as different as could very well be. While he was looking away he noticed a small figure on horseback had appeared on the seashore half a mile below them and was flying past at a flat-out gallop on the silver sand, as swift as the wind.

'Atalanta.' Fred shrugged. 'She's the wild one, if you ask me.'

'Is she – is she always like that – I mean interrupting your mother the way she did?' It was not something with which he was familiar. Matt had been shocked.

'To tell the truth, no. I don't know what's got into her. She goes her own way – free spirit as she said – but she's usually polite enough.'

'She said something about Paris,' Matt said still watching the rider.

'She's been there all this year studying painting. In fact I was slightly surprised to see her at the station. I had no idea she was coming home. Maybe something's happened. Maybe she heard you were coming and wanted to meet you.'

'Meet me?' Matt glanced at Fred, who was grinning.

'Only joking.'

Later they sat down to afternoon tea in the drawing room. The girl was nowhere to be seen, but in the meantime Fred's mother engaged Matt in conversation.

'You come from the county Roscommon? Well, that's not so very far. I hope we may see more of you in the future. We've heard quite a lot about you from Fred. He says you're both keen Home Rulers.'

'That is correct.' Matt was still feeling somewhat on his best behaviour this first afternoon. 'We have a branch of the League in the college – a lot of students have joined.'

'You'll run into trouble from the Ulster Presbyterians,' said the father, sitting across from Matt with a knowing look. Matt knew nothing about Ulster Presbyterians, though the priest regularly harangued his congregation in Ballyglin on the evils of Protestantism.

Over the following days as he settled in to life in Ardnashiel, Matt pondered on this family.

Although he had lived in Ballyglin House for nearly ten years and had grown perfectly used to the comforts of a large country house, amply staffed by servants and with every convenience he could ask, yet here in Ardnashiel he still felt uncomfortable. The family inhabited the house in a way which Garrett and Bríd did not. Garrett had evicted the Earl of Elphin who obviously had been incapable of running his estate, had moved in with his family, had kept all the earl's furniture, even down to his plates and knives and forks. Garrett had done it on purpose deliberately to make a point, yet there was something slightly spurious about it. Here by contrast was a family which lived in its own house and these things, the pictures on the wall, the furniture, the beds, the knives and forks, were all theirs, had never belonged to anyone else, the accumulated treasures of many generations. This gave them a kind of authenticity.

There was another thing. Garrett was always telling Matt he had to get out and make his mark, to prove himself in the world, and he himself was a driven man, energetic, restless, always on the lookout for fresh ideas and schemes for business. Yet these people seemed to feel no such compulsion. They were comfortable where they were and did not feel the need to prove anything. If Sir William went exploring in Arabia or Russia, he did it out of genuine curiosity and scientific interest.

After tea Lady Langley took him on a tour of the garden which extended over a couple of acres and was enclosed within a series of high walls so that one proceeded as it were from room to room, through arched gateways. Here and there gardeners were at work, trimming borders or weeding flowerbeds and at this time of the year the garden was at its loveliest: massed banks of colour, rich blues, and golden yellows.

There was an orchard too, and beyond that kitchen gardens. Ballyglin House also had its gardens but Matt had never noticed his aunt taking much interest. 'I can't tell one flower from another,' she once confessed.

Then coming through the garden they came upon Fred's odd sister sitting on a little stool with a large board on her knees, painting in watercolour.

'Here you are, darling!' exclaimed her mother. 'We'd given you up for dead. Why didn't you come in for tea?'

'Didn't want any,' said the girl, not lifting her eyes from her work. There was an awkward hiatus, then when she still didn't acknowledge them, the mother, glancing brightly at Matt, said, 'Well, we'll leave you in peace.'

'See you later.'

As they strolled on, Matt couldn't help glancing back at the girl crouching over her picture.

She reappeared at dinner, however, and had changed into a long flowing gown.

'Grace – what on earth?' her mother exclaimed as her daughter entered the room.

The dress was like nothing Matt had ever seen before: open-necked, long and flowing behind her as she walked. It was a rich jade green, worked with silver designs, a fine thin fabric that seemed to follow the contours of her body, draped about her as if there were nothing beneath it – as if she had simply taken several yards of silk and wound herself up in it – and with a wide soft scarf in brick red twisted about the waist. Over this, half off her shoulders, hung a loose long coat, also silk, a pale rose and embroidered with flower designs which trailed behind her, swishing gently across the floor. Her dark brown hair hung about her shoulders and was cut in a fringe across the forehead. The fringe, and the short skirt she had been wearing when they met on the station platform that morning, had given her something of the air of a schoolgirl. This evening by contrast she had assumed an exotic, oriental character. Her mother in the meantime was in ecstasies, fingering the silk and examining the embroidery.

'Darling, why haven't we seen this before? Was it made in Paris?'

'Japan. Oh don't fuss, mother! If you want to know, it's a kimono.'

The mother quickly let go of the fabric which she had been examining closely.

'Steady on,' said Fred, coming to his mother's defence. 'How were we to know? We've never seen a "kimono" – whatever that is – in our lives, have we, Matt?'

Matt nodded, at a loss for words. The girl looked simply astonishing.

'How on earth did you afford it?' Fred went on. 'Must have cost a packet.'

'Coarse boy,' said Grace witheringly, 'it's none of your business.'

Then something happened after dinner. They had retired to the drawing room where the long windows stood open and as the sun was beginning to set Grace and her father had wandered out into the garden. But after a moment she re-entered quickly, and caught Matt by the sleeve.

'Come quickly. Quick! Quick! Or you'll miss it!'

Surprised by this sudden attack he followed her into the garden. She called over her shoulder, 'No, not you Fred, you've seen it. I want to show the wild boy!' She led Matt some way from the house and turned him round. Several miles away across the bay rose a range of mountains and at this moment, immediately before sunset, they glowed an intense fiery orange-red.

'Isn't it beautiful?' she breathed, still clinging to his arm. 'Have you ever seen such a sight? Who could ever want to live anywhere else?'

He turned, close as they were in the half-light, and looked into her eyes. He had never seen such an intensity of expression, such a look of ardent feeling and was quite rocked off his feet.

'No, don't look at me! Look! Look!'

Embarrassed Matt turned again to the mountains.

Eleven

Over the days that followed Matt was befriended by Sir William who produced books of drawings and watercolours he had done in the Middle East. As Matt turned these over his imagination was filled with wonder at the desert scenes, the camel trains, the caravans and desert encampments, the date palms. There were cities too, street scenes crowded with men in flowing robes and women veiled, with bazaars overflowing with carpets, brass pots, fruits in brilliant colours. Sir William would also open drawers and take out medallions, daggers, and other things he had picked up.

'I was interested in the remains of the Seleucid empire at first, but once I was there, I got more engrossed in the Ottomans,' and so on, none of which made much sense to Matt but which he drank up with an avid curiosity.

'The great thing about travel, Matt,' he said one day, 'is that it gives you a perspective on your own country. Helps you to a larger view, d'you see?' He looked into Matt's eyes with a kindly smile.

In the afternoon they went riding along the sand with Grace. She did not usually appear early in the morning, sometimes even skipping breakfast. One afternoon, however, Fred had to go into town and Matt agreed to go riding with her. Grace, as he had already long known, was a first-class rider and when she saw that it was to be just the two of them, she did not hesitate to challenge him to a race. Matt was staggered when she appeared on a large hunter.

'What's the matter?' she asked as she saw the surprise in his face.

'That's quite a beast. Do you think you can handle him?'

'Would you mind telling your grandmother to suck eggs?' she said briefly over her shoulder as she passed him out of the stable yard. He followed her down the track and on to the sand.

When they were close to the water's edge, she turned and pointed.

'You see that craggy point? Once you round that you'll find another cove—'

'That's where we go swimming.'

'I know. Well – you go on—'

'You know?'

'It's where the family always go swimming. It's secluded.'

'Oh – you've been swimming too?'

'Yes, why not?' Then, after a moment slyly, 'I know you go in with nothing on.'

He raised his eyebrows. 'Do you?' he said at last with difficulty.

'I saw you one morning. I was out with the dogs and caught a sight of you.'

She threw this out in a very careless tone, but there was a silence while Matt digested the news. She looked hard at him. 'Oh dear don't tell me you're shocked? I didn't come down on purpose, you know. Do you think I've nothing better to do?'

He shrugged, still trying to come to terms with what she had said. 'You should have come and joined us,' he said at last as coolly as he could, still holding her look and there was a moment, as if she were seriously considering this proposal.

'Ugh! Are you mad? It's far too cold! Only men would be crazy enough to swim in the sea so early in the morning.'

She burst into laughter. This broke the atmosphere, and she went on, 'At the far end of the next cove there is a fall of rocks so you can't go any further. See you there, wild boy!'

Without warning she whipped her hunter's side with her long cane and the great animal leaped forward. Matt urged his horse after her and they flew along the sand. The exhilaration was incredible, the huge freedom of the afternoon, the vast expanse of sand and the long curling line of breakers, mild and tranquil this afternoon: Matt could tell that his horse was enjoying it as much as he. The thudding of the blood in his veins blended with the thudding of the animal's hooves on the sand and the sense of all that power and energy working beneath him, working at his command, was exhilarating beyond words.

They rounded the point to the next bay and Grace was still ahead. Seeing the end coming up he urged his horse on and gradually began to overhaul the girl. When they were side by side, she glanced at him and there was written all over her face an exultation, a childish glee, something he had seen only once before in her face – that moment when she had dragged him out to see the last of the sun's rays reflected on the mountain. She's just a child, he thought, for all her airs.

Grace was still slightly ahead when they were forced to pull up and she turned the mare's head, her own face flushed with the exercise, her eyes sparkling.

'Is there anything like it? Don't you want to go on, just riding, and never stop?'

'Why do you always call me wild boy?' Matt said abruptly. 'I have a name.'

'I know,' she replied whimsically, walking her horse round in a little circle. 'I'm saving it up till I know you better.'

He pulled himself up alongside her. 'Don't you know me well enough yet?'

'Hmm.' She set her head on one side studying him. 'Don't think I do.'

'Tell me about Paris,' he said impulsively.

A cloud passed across her face and she looked away for a moment. 'Another time.'

There was an awkward pause.

'Did something . . .' Matt began tentatively. 'Is it – I mean, did something happen?'

She drew a long breath. 'You could say that.'

'Well, can't you tell me?'

'Don't know you well enough, wild boy!' She galloped off again down to the water's edge and allowed her mare to paddle in the shallow water among the small waves.

'I told you, don't call me wild boy!' he shouted.

Grace kept up this strange distant attitude to Matt. It puzzled him greatly, and he thought it must be something to do with him, that he was lacking in something; that she had an aristocratic edge, enhanced by her travel to Paris, while he must seem very rustic and untutored. The truth, however, was revealed several days later when some friends of Fred and Grace were invited to dinner.

After they had been sitting chatting in the drawing room and it had come on to bedtime, Sir William and his lady rose to say goodnight and as the others stood up, Sir William motioned them back into their chairs. 'No, you young people stay there. Fred and Grace will entertain you.'

There were five of them sitting about chatting aimlessly and it was approaching midnight when Fred said with a wicked look in his eye, 'I say, do you know what I found the other day upstairs? An Ouija board. What do you say? Shall we give it a try – commune with the other side, eh?'

The visitors perked up at this suggestion and in a moment Fred reappeared with this board which was large, round and in a rich dark red stain. About the edge were the letters of the alphabet in gold.

'Now, we all sit round the table. And we need a wine glass, a clean one, please. No spirits in it if we are going to commune with the other side.'

'Oh please,' said Grace with a weary raising of the eyebrows.

'What do we do?' said the other girl.

'We each of us place one finger on the glass –' which he had set upside down in the centre of the board – 'then we ask a question.'

'Well – what question?' said this other girl who was rather dim.

'I don't know. Gracey, what question?'

'Is there anyone out there?' she said prosaically. Matt could tell that she was not really sharing Fred's enthusiasm for the Ouija board. In fact, as he had long noticed, Grace had been subdued all evening, scarcely taking interest in their joking and contributing little to their lively chatter.

'Very good!' said Fred enthusiastically. 'Fingers on the glass everyone please!' It was midnight by this time, and the room had gradually got colder. Matt noticed that Grace shivered, and turned to her. 'Can I get you a wrap? You don't look warm enough.'

She shook her head briefly, not looking up.

'Now, everybody. Here we go!' Fred looked up as they all sat round with their fingers placed on the glass. 'Is there anyone out there?' he intoned to the ceiling.

'But I still don't understand – you don't mean—?' the other girl persisted.

'Hush!'

She giggled. 'This is silly.'

'Hush!' Fred insisted but he seemed perplexed. 'Nobody's answering. We'll try again. Come on everybody, concentrate!'

Fingers were placed on the glass again and Fred once more intoned, 'Is there anyone there? Is there anyone you wish to speak to?'

This time the glass began to move, dashing back and forth across the board and spelling out, 'Y-E-S.'

'It works. Keep your fingers on!' The others were all now exclaiming and furiously concentrating on the board. 'Who are you?'

The glass sped about the board. 'V-A-L-'

Grace leaped back as if struck by lightning. 'No!'

'Keep going!' Fred had got completely carried away.

'No! Stop, Fred!' Grace was white and Matt turned to her.

'Don't stop! It's working!' Fred was quite carried away, as the glass continued to spell out 'E-N-T-I-N.'

'Valentin—'

But he got no further because Grace with a gasp shot out of her chair and in a second dashed out of the room. Without thinking Matt went after her and in the darkened hall he found her, her face buried in her hands.

For a second he stood uncertainly before her, then without thinking and not really knowing what he was doing, he took her by the arms and folded her to his chest. Although she made a slight movement at first he persisted and she gave way, crying into his lapel.

'It's all right,' he murmured, 'it's just a stupid game. It means nothing.'

When she did not respond, he went on,

'What is it – can't you tell me?'

She shook her head still pressed against his coat.

'It's all right,' he repeated, not knowing why he said it. He had not the faintest idea what was going on and only felt the need to comfort her until she should be more calm. 'You're quite safe. Just tell me what's the matter. Does that word mean something to you? Valentin?'

She nodded. And he waited until she began, her voice muffled by his coat. 'Valentin, oh it's just Fred's stupid trick.' She drew a huge, shuddering sigh. 'I met him at the art class last year, at the *Académie des Arts*. I can't believe it, only last September, less than a year ago. We just fell in love – instantly. It was obviously meant to be, inevitable, written in the stars. We went everywhere together, almost from the first day. He asked me to marry him within weeks of our meeting.' She had cooled a little, and drew another shattering sigh, as if deflated. Without thinking Matt drew off his jacket and draped it round her shoulders. In the gloom of the hall he could just make out two chairs and moved them to sit down. Grace sat huddled beneath his coat and went on in a low voice drained of feeling. 'But he wouldn't tell his parents, or take me to meet them. I wanted him to come here, but he wouldn't. It was very mysterious. Anyway his parents found out about me and then it all came out. Even now I can't believe anyone could be so *weak*.'

'What do you mean?'

'His family lives down in the country, in the Charente, *la France profonde*,' she pronounced bitterly. 'It turned out that he had been promised since birth to a neighbour, a relation, not sure how distant, but a relation anyway. Promised since birth by both families because it would unite their estates. They had no objection to him taking a mistress – and that's what they thought of me at first, especially since I was a Protestant and therefore quite amoral! – but when they heard of a marriage, they came down on him in force. He was summoned home and browbeaten till he gave in. He and the girl had known each other since birth and both families had smiled upon them and given their blessing to the union. Val never had any choice in the matter it appears.' She paused. 'Of course he had a choice!'

Matt said nothing.

'I should have been married by now. The date was fixed, June the twenty-seventh.' Her voice cracked slightly as the tears started again.

'Really?'

She drew a shattering sigh, and was silent. Again he could feel as a mighty shudder went through her. Her frailness, her vulnerability pierced him to the bone. He pulled a handkerchief from his pocket, pressed it into her hand, and as she was mopping her eyes, he began thoughtfully,

'So that – just now – was a practical joke, by Fred? You had told him about – Valentin?'

'Of course. We tell each other everything.'

Matt was silent for a moment. 'What do you want to do now? The others will be wondering—'

'I couldn't face them tonight. Would you apologize for me?'

'Of course.'

'And Matt, thank you for listening. You're very kind.'

'That's all right,' he muttered. 'I'll see you in the morning.'

'Yes.' She felt for his hand and squeezed it. 'Thanks again.'

She disappeared into the darkness and Matt made his way back to the drawing room. It was the first time she had called him by his name.

'That was a mean trick.'

Matt stood in the doorway. Fred and his friends had in the meantime taken out a pack of cards and were engaged round the low table, the Ouija board forgotten.

Fred glanced up.

'At least she'll shut up about him now,' he said casually.

'There was no call for it, and if you were any kind of a gentleman you would not have played such a cruel trick.'

Fred stood up. 'Come off it, Matt! Do you suppose she's never played a trick like that on me before? She used to be a terrible practical joker; she just got a bit of her own medicine, that's all.'

'Oh is that all? Really? You reduce your own sister to tears – and call it a practical joke?'

'She'll get over it.' Fred, annoyed with himself, turned back to the cards.

Without speaking Matt lifted the rim of the little table and spilled the cards on to the floor. The other two spectators watched speechless.

'She'll get over it better after you apologize to her. And I suggest you do it now. She won't sleep for ages, I suspect, so you've got plenty of time. Go on, off with you now. You're my dearest friend, and I want it to stay that way.'

The two of them stood facing each other and Fred could see the force in Matt's eyes.

★   ★   ★

There was no repetition of this scene. It seemed very strange to Matt but the following day they all greeted one another as if everything were entirely normal. Nothing was changed except that Grace now called him Matt. He and Fred continued their swims, their studies, their riding. Sometimes Grace accompanied them, sometimes she sat in the garden with her watercolours.

'Won't you tell me about yourself, Matt?' she said as she dabbed a brush into the jar of water. He was lying on the grass beside her beneath an apple tree, his eyes closed.

After a long silence he said, absently, 'There's nothing to tell.'

'There must be something. Fred said you are an orphan.'

'That's true,' he said, opening his eyes and looking away.

'And you never knew your parents – at all?'

He raised himself on one elbow and turned up to her. 'Not merely do I not know them, I do not know anything about them. I don't even have a birth certificate, or my parents' birth certificates, or their marriage certificate – if they ever did get married. But I don't even know that,' he added bitterly.

'But surely your aunt and uncle must know?'

'They inherited me from another aunt and uncle – my life is filled with aunts and uncles! But my aunt – my other aunt – died when I was eleven so I can't ask her. She was the one who brought me up. She was good to me, very good, and so was my uncle Patsy.'

'Your uncle Patsy? He sounds sweet.'

'He taught me everything I know – in a way. When I was little I went everywhere with him. He's the nearest thing I have to a father. He is a father, really – to me.'

'Poor Matt.' She laid down her paints for a moment looking at him sympathetically. Matt roused himself.

'Please don't feel sorry for me! I wouldn't have mentioned it if you hadn't asked. I'm all right. I'm fine – in fact, I've been very lucky. I have everything I want and my aunt Bríd is more than a mother to me. I have nothing to complain of and I'll make my own way. It would be childish to complain!'

She was taken aback by his vehement tone. 'I won't feel sorry for you if you don't want me to,' she said mildly.

He relaxed and smiled, and after a moment threw himself down again on the grass.

'Anyway,' she went on eventually, 'Something tells me you are going to do well, whatever you decide to do.'

There was a pause while she continued with her painting.

'And you,' he said eventually, 'have you decided what you are going to do?'

She concentrated on the picture. 'I thought I knew. Everything seemed settled – my life, I mean. Then suddenly it wasn't after all. So at this minute I don't know. Probably go to Italy.'

'What do your parents say to you going off like this?'

She shrugged. 'They were a bit concerned at first. But my father is such a wanderer himself, he couldn't really refuse. He says I inherited it from him.'

'Italy.' Matt was silent for a moment. 'I couldn't even imagine it. You might as well tell me you are going to the moon.'

'A friend of mine went. She says it's smelly, hot, and there are mosquitoes.' She burst out laughing.

'What's funny?'

'You don't know her. She's never happy abroad. "Abroad"! She makes it sound like a prison sentence. Whereas I love it! I love the smells and the heat. I'll even put up with mosquitoes if I can see Florence and Rome.'

She had put down her paints again and was staring into his eyes. 'Think of it Matt! To see Florence! To see Rome! To stand on the Capitol Hill! I can scarcely imagine it!' Her eyes were shining and there was a breathless, entranced, smile on her face. 'Think of it!'

Something in Matt responded instantly to this and he sat up, unable to tear his eyes from hers.

Three weeks later he left for Ballyglin and Grace drove him to the station. As they waited on the platform they found themselves, after all their enthusiastic conversations of the preceding weeks, unexpectedly struck into silence. Matt looked away along the deserted platform; Grace was studying her shoes. He thanked her awkwardly, and asked her to thank her parents for their hospitality. She said she would, and again silence fell. It was only as the train was pulling in and slowing, with a rushing of steam and a clank of couplings and as Matt was gathering up his bag, that she said in a rush,

'Matt, thanks. You know what for. You really helped me.' She held out her hand. After he had got into the compartment and was leaning out as the train was about to pull away, he called,

'When you're in Dublin, come to tea!'

She waved. 'Thanks – I will!'

Twelve

On the train Matt thought over his stay at Ardnashiel. The memory of that night in the darkness with Grace when she had confided in him burned in his consciousness and she returned again and again to his thoughts – floated through them wrapped in a mysterious aura, a glamorous haze compounded of Paris and Rome and unrequited love. Grace had been to so many places of which he himself had only the vaguest idea. As for unrequited love! What were his tentative forays, his holding hands with Mary by the Fairy Ring, their first chaste kisses, compared to Grace's headlong plunge?

He arrived at Ballyglin House expecting to settle down to his law studies. The evening following his arrival, however, something arose which he hadn't anticipated. After dinner Matt strolled down into the village. It was late August and the sky was still bright. The green was deserted. Everyone was indoors enjoying their evening supper so, without thinking he turned into Mrs Carruthers' stores and bar and ordered a glass of stout. Near him in the evening light, half a dozen men were sitting with their drinks, talking quietly, but Matt, his elbow on the bar, one hand holding his glass, stared idly up at the bottles and tins on the shelves behind Mrs Carruthers' head.

Matt knew all the men sitting there. They knew him too and in old times would have called him naturally to join them. Matt however was no longer a poor lad like the others in the village. He was a university student, the adopted son of Mr Doyle who could buy, and in fact had bought, the whole village.

Even so, one of them, Micky, eventually called to him.

'Matt! Won't ye join us?' There was a cool, sarcastic note in his voice. 'We was just talkin' of Mr Doyle.'

Matt jerked round, shaken out of his reverie. 'Sorry, I never saw you there.' He sat down among them. 'You were saying – my uncle?'

''Twas nothing, Matt,' said Noel Gallagher. 'Micky meant nothing by it.'

Mick Carruthers, Mrs Carruthers' son, was an insolent fellow who, because he stood to inherit Mrs Carruthers' shop, thought himself a cut above the others and free to speak his mind where others might be more prudent.

'Nothing by what?' Matt looked deliberately into Micky's face.

'Well, now since ye've come into your millions, Matt, ye no doubt will not have time for your old school mates.'

'Who says I won't?' Matt looked round at them. 'What have I ever said to make you think that?'

'Take no notice of him, Matt,' said Noel. 'The truth of it is, we're all a bit upset on behalf of Sean here and the letter he's after gettin' this mornin'.'

'What letter?'

Sean Higgins was a shambling middle-aged man of few words, who contrived a living with a few acres of rented land and hedging and ditching, and other odd seasonal work; he had also managed to beget seven children of whom Mary Higgins was the eldest. Sean now produced a sheet of paper, much folded and grimy with handling and passed it over. 'I took it to Father Geoghegan this morning for him to read to me.'

It was a notice to quit the following November, following on his inability to pay the last two quarters' rent.

'Twelve pounds?' he murmured. 'He'd throw you out for *twelve pounds*?'

There was silence as the others allowed this to sink into Matt's consciousness.

'Twelve pounds, now, that would be pocket money to the likes of Mr Doyle,' said Mick with his eyebrow raised ironically as he looked at Matt.

'With your permission, I'll take this, Sean.' Matt said quietly. 'I think there has been a mistake. No one would throw you out of your house for twelve pounds. I'll speak to my uncle.'

'Easily said,' Mick went on. 'The old earl now, he would never do such a thing.' He looked round at the others. 'He was the easy-spoken gentleman entirely.'

Matt did not reply for the moment. He drained his glass, stood up, and then at the door, turned once more. 'I'll speak to my uncle, Sean,' and went out.

★   ★   ★

On his way up the lane he studied the letter again. It was actually written by Garrett's land agent Macnamara, who Matt knew well. When he got home he found Patsy in the stable smoking his pipe.

'Patsy, did you know Mr Doyle has ordered Sean Higgins out of his farm?'

Patsy looked troubled and after a moment nodded.

'For the missing of two quarters' rent?'

'Last year was a bad year, Matt. The oats was all lost and the price of butter down on the year before. The money just wasn't there.'

Matt stared at the letter again and shook his head. 'Twelve pounds? My uncle can spare twelve pounds. It's absurd.'

'Absurd?' Patsy shook his head. 'To the likes of Garrett maybe, Matt, but to a poor man with only a bit of land and seven children to think for, 'tis another story entirely. Still,' he drew a breath, 'Maybe this year will be better.'

'I'll speak to Macnamara tomorrow. This may be only his doing. I'm sure my uncle would never throw a man out for such a trifling sum.'

Patsy shrugged and said nothing.

But when Matt rode over to Mr Macnamara's house and questioned him, Macnamara assured him with some asperity that he was acting under Mr Doyle's orders.

'D'ye think I'd do it without express instructions, Mr Byrne? And maybe risk a bullet in my back one evening?'

'A *bullet?*'

'Ye've been away in Dublin with your studies, Mr Byrne. But down here, 'tis a different story. There was a landlord over in Ballyvaughan shot one evening on his way home. I have to watch my back nowadays.'

That night Matt wrote to Garrett outlining the situation and asking for an explanation. The reply came the following day but one.

Dear Matt,
Thanks for your note. I hope you enjoyed your holiday by the sea, and are now once again buckled down to your studies. We're all well here and will be coming down to

Ballyglin next week for a bit of a holiday ourselves. We'll discuss the Higgins business when I see you.
Best wishes
Garrett

As promised the whole family arrived the following week, in a great upheaval of carriages and carts filled with bags and boxes. His aunt Bríd spilled out with the children and she and Garrett were busy installing themselves in the house once more, making arrangements, ordering in food, and for half a day Matt was a mere bystander in his own home.

Before dinner that evening Bríd at last found time to be alone with Matt.

'Thanks so much for your letters, darling,' she said. 'I'm so glad you've found friends – and not so far from here either. And I was sad to hear what you said about Grace and the breaking off of her engagement.' She took his hand. 'Do you think you're likely to meet again? You said she talked of going to Italy,' she enquired gently, at last catching his eye.

Matt shrugged. 'It was just talk. Maybe I'll hear from her. I don't know.'

'Why not write to her? I'm sure she'd love to have a letter from you.'

He nodded. 'Maybe I will.'

After dinner, Garrett strolled out on to the terrace to smoke a cigar. Matt followed him.

'Sean Higgins?' Garrett knew what was in Matt's mind.

'I simply don't understand how you can evict a man for such a trifling sum. Twelve pounds? I thought that was what the Earl of Elphin did, not an Irishman like yourself.'

'Twelve pounds? That's half a year's rent, Matt. That represents twelve acres. Well, now, let's do the arithmetic. Sean Higgins pays twenty-four pounds a year rent on twelve acres. There are a hundred and twenty farms on the estate, half of Roscommon. Most of them are bigger than Sean's, say average size forty acres, average rent eighty pounds a year. That's eighty multiplied by a hundred and twenty. Nearly ten thousand a year, Matt. It's a lot of money to lose.'

'That's absurd! They're not all unable to pay.'

'Unable? Who says he is unable?'

'Isn't he?'

Garrett looked shrewdly. 'You think he hasn't the money?'

'Patsy says the oats was ruined last year and the price of butter's down,' Matt said coldly.

'Last year was bad, that's true. And maybe next year will be better. That's what farming's all about. Up one year down the next. The intelligent farmer puts money by in good years. Sean Higgins has not the first idea about farming. I've given him time enough to pay. If he can't make the farm work I'll put in someone who can.'

'So you'd see Sean go to the poor house? He's got seven children!'

Garrett said nothing, and at last Matt went on, 'I can't believe an Irishman who was brought up in the village would put a poor farmer out of his home for a few pounds.'

Garrett refused to rise to Matt's suppressed anger. 'It's business, Matt,' he said gently. 'I'm not a charity – though I pay a poor rate of £740 a year. If a man takes on a farm, it's a responsibility. You have to pay your way. Where would the world be if every-body started to be nice to each other and let them off whenever they got into difficulties? He's not a child. He took on the farm. Let him pay, or get out of the way of someone who can.'

Garrett took a pull at his cigar and looked away across the evening landscape, across the fields and woods. He seemed completely relaxed about the business. Matt watched him and said at last,

'I'll not let it stand here.'

'Oh?' Garrett turned in polite curiosity.

'I'll fight you.'

Garrett raised his eyebrows. 'In the courts? Have you any money?'

'If necessary I'll oppose the eviction.'

'Break the law, Matt?' He looked serious. 'You mean it?'

'I do.'

Garrett was silent for a moment then said quietly, 'Strong words. We shall see, my bucko.'

★   ★   ★

The following morning Matt rode down into the village and to Sean Higgins' cottage which stood a bare two hundred yards from the church. He found Mrs Higgins at home and behind her shoulder he could see several children including Mary.

'I was hoping to speak with Mr Higgins, Mrs Higgins.'

'He's away to the fields this morning, sir. But won't ye come in, and stay for a moment.'

Removing his hat Matt bowed his head and entered the low door. The children all disposed themselves about him, open-mouthed, at the sight of this smart young gentleman in riding breeches, and finely cut jacket and hard hat looming large in the small dark room. Matt was conscious of Mary watching him.

'How are ye, Matt?' she asked, and he turned a little embarrassed.

'Oh, well enough, Mary thank you.' He turned to her mother. 'I spoke to my uncle last night, Mrs Higgins—'

'Heaven be praised. We knew ye wouldn't forget us—'

'It's not such good news, Mrs Higgins, I'll be frank. At the moment he's not disposed to change his mind.' He saw the change in her face and hurried on. 'But I told him, I would not let it rest, and I am going to fight him all the way.'

Mary took his hand and squeezed it fervently. He went on awkwardly, 'There is a bit of money I could let you have—'

'No! We wouldn't be taking the money out of your own pocket, Matt.'

'Why are you taking such an interest in the family?' Garrett confronted him that evening when Matt again mentioned the family. 'Mary Higgins' bright eyes, is it?'

Matt said nothing.

'All right, Matt, since you're so upset, I'll tell you what I'll do.'

'What?'

'I'll pay passages for them to America.'

Matt took a moment to let this sink in. 'Sean Higgins is too old to start a new life. He hasn't the strength for it.'

'He has young sons. They will.'

'There's nine in the family. You went to America when you were young and single. It was easy for you.'

'Easy?'

'Well —' he corrected himself – 'easier.'

'Listen Matt, you're young and to be frank you don't know much. And what is worse, you're full of anger and passion. But that's not the way to run a farm, or a business, or a country. You need a hard head, a clear head. Now listen, because I am getting tired of this. Sean Higgins scratches a living of sorts, when he's lucky and there's a good season, out of twelve acres. If he's unlucky, if there's heavy rain in August, he and his family starve. Suppose I remit the rent this time? What about next year and the year after that? And what about all the other small farmers who would be clamouring at the gate? I'd have half the county out there once they heard I'd let Sean Higgins off his rent. The problem is that Sean's holding is too small and it's scattered about, a field here, a bit of land there and half the time he's applying for poor relief. He'll always be at the mercy of the weather or the market, or disease, or any of a hundred factors. What I plan to do over the next so many years, is gradually to amalgamate the holdings into large farms and let them to men who have studied scientific farming. That way they won't be always at the mercy of fortune. This is the way forward for Ireland. Otherwise the country will be forever on its knees. That is why Sean Higgins has to go. Like I said, I'll pay his passage to America or wherever he wants. He won't starve.'

Matt was about to speak, but Garrett who half turned away turned back brusquely, 'And Matt, you're intelligent enough and educated enough to know what I am saying is true. Enough now!'

'You have no feelings at all.'

'Feelings! What do you know of anything? You think I don't have feelings? You're still a boy, but I tell you this, Matt, it takes more than feelings to run a farm or a country! That's enough or you'll make me lose my temper.'

Garrett turned on his heel and Matt was left staring at his back.

'I won't let it rest!' he shouted, but Garrett went back into the house without turning. It still seemed inexplicable that a man born in the village could cold-bloodedly turn a family of nine into the street. And the image of Mary kept returning to his thoughts, Mary and those little brothers and sisters. The fact was that Sean was a shambling sort of fellow, old before his time, worn out with worry and toil, and the family was kept together by his wife and his eldest daughter Mary. As Matt pictured the family to himself in his imagination, pacing about in the park, his resolution hardened. None of Garrett's economic arguments made any impact on him at all. It was all theory. In a perfect world, no doubt farms would be of larger size, run on model lines, clean, modern, efficient. But this wasn't a perfect world and we had to start from where we stood. And if this perfect world was to be purchased at the cost of Sean Higgins' family then Matt was against it.

Thirteen

As Garrett poured himself a whiskey the bottle clattered against the glass; he was more disturbed than he liked to admit. There was something about Matt which got under his skin; the boy was too full of anger. Perhaps it was because Garrett saw himself in the boy, himself at that age. Perhaps it was that, and perhaps it was . . .

At that moment Bríd came into the room. Perhaps it was her? Instinctively he knew she would support Matt against him.

'What was that about?' she enquired. He stood looking out of the window for a moment.

'There's a family in the village won't pay their rent,' he said tersely. 'I gave them notice to quit but Matt has taken their side. We had an argument about it.'

Bríd said nothing and after a moment Garrett turned irritably. At that moment he wished he were back in Dublin. He should have remained there and given the orders at a distance. Then he wouldn't be embroiled in these rows. He could just sit in his office, give the order and the matter would be finished; he wouldn't have to be confronted with the messy reality.

'What did Matt say?' she began tentatively.

'And I think he may be sweet on the girl,' Garrett said pursuing his own thoughts. 'Ten to one that's at the bottom of it.'

'Girl?'

'Mary Higgins. I don't want him getting mixed up with village girls. I should have known.' He threw back his whiskey and set the glass down with a clatter in an orgy of irritation. 'I sometimes wonder whether I should have come back. I'd have been better off staying in America.'

'I remember distinctly what you said to me before we came back,' she now said. 'You wanted to come back to the old country and do some good with your money.'

He didn't reply.

'And you have,' she went on. 'There are many things you have done here for the people. Unlike the old Leighton family you have done some real good.'

'Bríd, that's all right but it's just decoration. Underneath nothing has changed. Everything just goes on as it ever did. There's a kind of inertia in this country that infuriates me. I feel as if I'm trudging through mud all the time. The whole place really wants a kick.'

'Who is this girl Mary Higgins?'

'Sean's daughter. It didn't take me ten minutes in the village before someone had whispered to me that Matt had been seen with Mary – up by the old Fairy Ring.'

Already Bríd was making for the door.

'Where are you going?'

'Where do you think? I must speak to him about this.'

As she went out, Garrett thought, 'That's it. Matt comes first. Her boy, her first born.' He poured himself another drink, a larger one.

At first Bríd could not find Matt but at last looking out of the window she saw him at a distance in the park coming towards the house. She went out to meet him.

'Hullo darling, are you well? It's a lovely evening, isn't it?' She slipped her arm through his and looked about her as if suddenly noticing it.

Matt looked up thoughtfully. 'What has Garrett been saying?'

'Well – it was about the Higgins family. What did you say?'

'Aunt, it's outrageous that he should throw a family of nine out of their home. I won't stand for it.'

She was alarmed. 'What do you mean?'

'I don't know yet. Maybe the Land League can organize a demonstration, or a boycott.'

'*Boycott?*'

'If we can organize the farmers, he wouldn't dare throw Sean Higgins out.'

It was quite clear that Matt was determined and in her alarm Bríd went in search of the only other man she could confide in, Patsy. She eventually located him in a barn with one of the labourers examining a cow. Patsy had his hand on the cow's back attempting to soothe her as the other held the hoof between his knees and worked on it with a knife. Bríd waited, watching with impatience.

He looked up and noticed her in the barn doorway.

'Bríd?'

'Is something wrong?' she enquired tentatively.

'Not at all – a stone merely, got jammed in the hoof,' he remarked mildly, and his tone, always so calm, reassured her at once.

The stone was removed at last and the cow sent off to join the herd in the byre.

'Patsy,' she began tentatively, waiting until the other man had led the cow out. 'Can I ask you something?' He noticed her strange tone immediately. 'Will you walk with me a little?'

'Surely.'

She slipped her arm through his and they strolled away across the park in front of the house. For a while she did not speak; he did not seem inclined to speak either and she was wondering how to bring the subject up.

'Patsy,' she began at last, 'you know, I feel guilty sometimes . . .'

'Guilty?'

'I mean – leaving you here after we went to Dublin.'

'I'm quite happy here, Bríd. I told ye, I have no taste for the city. What would I be doin' above in Dublin?'

'I feel I have neglected you,' she went on awkwardly.

'Neglected?' He turned to her. 'Bríd – there's somethin' on your mind, I can tell. What is it?'

'Oh Uncle Patsy,' she said in a rush, 'you were so good to me when I was little. I'll always remember it – and then you took in Matt too. I really owe you everything.'

Patsy stopped, took her hand in his, and looked into her eyes with a kindly patient look. 'Bríd, you know Nora had no child of her own, and you giving Matt to her to care for and watch over, was the gift of heaven itself. She never ceased to give thanks for it.'

'Really?' She searched his eyes.

Patsy nodded.

'But,' Bríd went on awkwardly, 'when I came back – broke my vow—'

'Of course Nora was unhappy, thinkin' you wanted to take Matt away from her, and you with all your dollars—'

'Oh God – and I did want to. It's true. The moment I saw

him I wanted him. Do you remember that first afternoon, it was a summer afternoon, and I came to the house? Can you imagine how I felt when Nora opened the door? How did I have the impertinence?' There was a trace of a tear in her eye. 'I honestly expected Nora to slam the door in my face. And then we were waiting for Matt to come home from school, and – I can still see it now – the door opened and the sweetest little boy there ever was came bursting in, and stopped as he saw me—'

She stopped, and turned her head away for a moment. Patsy strengthened his grip on her arm, and waited, as she held a tiny lace edged handkerchief to her nose. Finally he went on gently,

'Bríd, there's somethin' else. What is it?'

She drew a breath, blinked the tears from her eyes, and turned to him.

'It's this eviction in the village.'

'Sean Higgins and his family.'

She nodded. 'Matt is determined to be involved. I think he has been encouraging the others to resist.'

'I know. He told me.'

'He told you?'

'He tells me everything, Bríd.'

'Oh, I am so glad. My husband is so rigid, so certain in his views.' Patsy was silent. 'Is there anything . . . ?' she went on uncertainly.

'Anything I can do? What do ye want me to do, Bríd? I am Garrett's guest in the house. Am I to encourage the boy to oppose him?'

There was a long silence. Finally, Bríd went on, 'Patsy – you are happy here aren't you?'

'Oh, I'm happy right enough, ye've no need to worry. Though, to tell the truth, it all happened rather quickly, maybe too quickly, what with the shock of Nora's death—'

'I know! It was my fault, Patsy! I was so desperate to have Matt with me that the second Nora died I brought you both to live with us. I thought, you know, that you would be happy not to have to work any more.' She looked imploringly into his eyes.

He laid his hand on her arm again to steady her. 'Look, Bríd, with Nora gone and Matt livin' with you and Garrett, what kind

of a life would I have had on me own? And I after getting older?
'Twas for the best.'

'Really?'

He nodded, then drew a sigh. 'But as for young Matt –' he
shook his head – 'there's nothing I can do. He must make his
own way.'

'And there wouldn't be any good talking to Garrett?'

He jerked a little laugh. 'Me? Talk to Garrett? You know your
husband better than me, Bríd. You think he'd listen to me?'

After this there seemed nothing more to be said and they made
their way slowly back to the house. Even so, it felt comforting
to Bríd to have her arm linked snugly under his.

Mrs Carruthers' *shebeen* was crowded. In the dim light of the peat
fire and an oil lantern nearly twenty men sat about in front of
the fire on benches, their faces distorted into ghostly shadows by
the dim light.

Matt was excited so many had come and particularly surprised
to find Father Geoghegan among them. He would have been
astounded to know that it was he himself who was to dominate the
meeting. Everyone had their mug of spirits and there was a buzz of
conversation until Father Geoghegan called the meeting to order.

'All over the country the Land League is springing up, and
thousands are flocking to join. It's the tenants' best bet because
by joining the Land League you all join together to preserve your
livelihoods. Everyone knows that since prices fell last year times
have been hard and there's no sign they'll get any better. The
landlords' income has fallen as well and they'll be looking to get
their money back from you. If you wouldn't be put out of your
cabins the safest way is to band together and to demand a reduc-
tion in your rents.'

This was the burden of Father Geoghegan's speech. At first
there was enthusiastic support from everyone for the proposal
and a committee was appointed with a treasurer to collect a
penny from each man.

'If anyone does pay their rent why we'll teach 'em what it is
to betray their friends,' cried Liam O'Connor a farmer of about
sixty with a deeply lined face and a strong taste for drink. 'We'll
teach 'em!'

'And if anyone should be evicted let no man take their farm,' said Paddy Brannagh. 'Let it stand idle so Mr Doyle can get no good by it. Let it rot and he'll learn he can't be throwing honest men out of their homes and think to get away with it.'

'But the Land League will never have any success unless we all stick together,' said Matt.

'Aye stick together!' men joined in as the whiskey warmed them.

'And what'll we do with anyone who pays?'

'Burn 'em out! Ruin 'em! Traitors, they're on the landlords' side.'

'Friends –' Matt stood up – 'to be honest, I'm ashamed to stand here tonight among you, when it's my very own uncle – though in truth he's no uncle of mine – who thinks to evict Sean here from his home and his family with him. I've spoken to Mr Doyle, I've argued with him, but I know he has every intention of sticking to his word. In November when Sean's lease runs out, he plans to evict him. What I say is, let's stand together, let's oppose him. In the days of old when there was the Earl of Elphin, we'd expect such treatment. But my uncle was born here which makes it doubly shameful he should want to throw out a family he's known since his childhood days. I say we oppose him. Refuse to let my uncle near, or his agent, or his hired men – black Protestants from the north – or the Peelers, or the military – throw a wall of men about the house!'

Matt sat down as the cheers of the others rang in his ears. He could hardly believe that it was he himself who had just made this speech.

When Garrett heard about this meeting and the resolution that had been passed he was angry. What made him more angry was that he knew Bríd would support Matt in whatever he did and he did not want to antagonize her. Through all the years Garrett had never wavered in his love for Bríd – through all the vicissitudes, all the setbacks, the thousands of miles travelled, and the thousands of dollars laboriously amassed, she had been the focus of his thoughts. Behind all his work and effort, though he enjoyed the struggle, the thrill of adrenalin when he was locked in business negotiations and projecting fresh plans, there lay always the thought, 'I am doing it for her – making these dollars only to lay them at her feet.' Since she had presented him with two children, of whom he was intensely proud, he had thought at first that they would cement them even more strongly together.

But there was always Matt, and Garrett knew that when it came to a choice, he would come first in her affections.

It was this which hindered him from really having it out with the boy. In other circumstances he would not have hesitated to throw Matt out. He was nearly twenty and was old enough to make his way in the world. Garrett summoned Matt to his presence.

'This nonsense has got to stop.'

'I take it you're referring to the meeting?'

Garrett was silent, looking seriously at him.

'Nothing you say will make any difference,' Matt went on. 'The whole village is behind us.'

'Behind you! Do you think they would have been cheering so loudly if it had been anyone else? No, Matt – they were cheering you because they knew that through you they could strike at me!'

'No one said anything about striking anybody,' Matt said quietly. 'We're only concerned to prevent Sean and his family from being thrown out of their home.'

'So – do you seriously intend to break the law? You, a student of law? Did they never explain to you the sanctity of property?'

'The sanctity of property? What about the sanctity of the home?'

'The sanctity of property, Matt, since I am having to give you a lesson in law! A country's prosperity is wholly founded upon the sanctity, or if you prefer, the security, of property. Now, that land is mine and that cabin too, and the law gives me full right to do with it as I choose. If it were any other way, the country would descend into anarchy and ultimately into something much worse, into tyranny. Don't be under any illusions.'

'The Earl of Elphin himself could not have said it better,' said Matt with contempt. 'But at least the old ascendancy did sometimes understand the meaning of *noblesse oblige*.'

Garrett burst into a bitter, despairing laughter. 'You really don't understand anything at all. Why was the earl so hard up, why was his land mortgaged, every last foot? Because for a hundred years his grandfather and great-grandfather, and probably his father before him, had wasted their substance in riotous living in London – and never gave a thought for their tenants over here. Not once.'

There was a silence. Finally Matt said, 'I have given my word, and I will not go back on it.'

'Then be damned to you and get out of my sight!'

Fourteen

In the early light of an autumn morning there must have been twenty men gathered. Breath rose from them as they stood on the village green muttering among themselves. Most were dressed in long overcoats with pot hats pulled down low over their brows, and many had shillelaghs under their arms. Matt was among them. The plan had already been explained to Sean Higgins.

'When the agent arrives with his men we're going to form a cordon round the house, Sean. We won't let them touch you.'

Sean had listened rubbing his hands together, his shoulders hunched, and nodding nervously.

'It was the only way. My aunt even offered to pay the rent you owe, but Mr Doyle is determined to have you out. We shall see. He may have other thoughts when he sees the whole village is against him.'

Mr Doyle was at that moment in Dublin with his family. When Matt left the house two days earlier to travel down to Ballyglin, nothing was said. He had announced it the evening before, looking across the dinner table to see Garrett's response. There was none.

'It's wrong, and I intend to oppose it,' Matt reminded him.

'So you said,' Garrett replied dryly and continued with his dinner. Bríd looked anxiously between them. Afterwards when she wanted to raise the subject with Garrett he merely remarked, 'Let him get it out of his system. It's probably the best way.' And he wouldn't say more.

So now in the early morning Matt stood among the farmers in the cold damp autumn morning and waited.

It was nearly an hour later that they heard the tramp of marching boots and into the village came a file of red-coated infantry, rifles across their shoulders. An officer rode before them on horseback. A sergeant bellowed orders and the soldiers came to a well-drilled halt on the green for all the world as if they were on the barrack square and there was no crowd of villagers watching them.

Soon afterwards there were more tramping feet and a platoon of the Royal Irish Constabulary in their bottle-green uniforms, also with rifles on their shoulders appeared, and right behind them Mr Macnamara the agent on his horse with a gang of twenty men, remarkably like the villagers who were waiting for them. These were now outnumbered at least three to one.

At the sight of the military Matt had galvanized the waiting villagers. 'Take up your positions!' And by arrangement they formed themselves before the cottage. Its door was closed and barred.

Silence descended. The villagers looked at the formidable force which now stood arrayed against them across the muddy space of the village green. Mr Macnamara conferred with the officer in red and the leader of the men recruited to do the dirty work. Finally he turned his horse and addressed the villagers crowded in front of Sean Higgins' cottage.

'Sean Higgins? He scanned the crowd. 'Where are you?'

Sean stood forward. Matt was beside him.

Macnamara produced a paper from his pocket and proceeded to read it aloud.

'Sean Higgins, I have here an order from the county court for ejectment of the property. Your lease is expired and you are required to vacate this house. Are you ready to do so?'

Before Sean could answer, Matt stood forward. 'Mr Higgins is not ready to vacate his farm! It is the only livelihood that he and his family possess. If you throw him out he has no option but to starve. He refuses to leave and we, the assembled villagers stand firm beside him to resist the landlord's order! Don't we?' He turned as the assembled farmers cheered and waved their shillelaghs.

Mr Macnamara turned back to consult with the redcoats and the chief of police and there now took place a well-drilled, coordinated operation. The armed police and the platoon of redcoats snapped to attention and advanced on the little knot of villagers. With no hesitation they began to push the unarmed villagers aside with the butts of their carbines. To his bewilderment Matt watched the protest melting away with scarcely a gesture.

In a fit of desperation he stood in the way of one redcoat and as the man raised his carbine, Matt took him by the shoulders and thrust him aside. 'Come on!' he shouted, and his example seemed to galvanize the others. The affair now became serious, blows were exchanged, clubs raised, and a rowdy fight developed in the mud in front of the cottage. Matt was thrown to the ground, a man tripped over him, and another was thrown headlong aside. Then it became really angry. Men began to fight desperately. Matt got up and seized a constable by the shoulders, before another had struck him from behind with the butt of his carbine, and with an agonizing pain he was thrown again to the ground.

It didn't last long. The villagers were thrust aside and the workmen advanced on the cottage, the door was rudely broken in, the children came running out with screams of terror, Sean and Mrs Higgins watched as pieces of furniture began to be carried out, and very soon there was the extraordinary sight of Sean's household arrayed on the mud of the green. Other men were up ladders and pitchforking thatch off the roof. Matt got to his feet breathing heavily, a terrible pain in his shoulder, watching in bewilderment until a strong hand descended on his neck and he heard an order.

'Take that man into custody!'

Macnamara mounted his horse and surveyed the scene. 'Let this be a lesson to any man who thinks to defy the law of the land!' he shouted to anyone who might not have got the message. 'There is such a thing as the right of property!' he added, to remind them of who really owned the village.

Matt was led away in the midst of the file of constables. His clothes were muddy, his hands and face too, and he still had an aching pain in his shoulder. In silence he marched all the way to Boyle. It was mid-morning as they arrived, the town square was alive and life was going on as normal. This seemed strange to Matt after the events in Ballyglin and he felt conspicuous as they crossed the square to the castle. People turned to watch and seeing them he could see himself in their eyes. They arrived at an ancient blackened door studded with rusty iron bolts, and he was pushed through a smaller door set in the larger one. In a dirty, stone-flagged room, dimly lit from one barred and dusty window and smelling of stale tobacco, there was a conference between the officer commanding the constables and another at a desk, their voices echoing strangely, and finally a ledger was opened and Matt's name was entered. Then another ancient and dirty door was opened, Matt was pushed through, and a third door unlocked by a large and rusty key, and he found himself in a cell. The door was closed behind him and Matt was alone.

His first thought was whether anyone else had been arrested – though he thought not. He certainly had been the only prisoner on the march to Boyle. He sat on the bench, examined his muddy hands and wondered vaguely what was going to happen next. 'Making an affray' had been the words written down as far as he could see. Matt's law studies had taught him that this was something within the competence of a magistrate to punish – if he chose; alternatively he might send Matt for trial at the assizes, if he thought the event serious enough. Matt sat and considered these possibilities in a curiously detached frame of mind.

What lay behind this calm reflection was the realization of the immense power of the British state when they chose to exercise it, a power so great that Matt in his simplicity had scarcely been able to comprehend it. The 'sanctity of property' had been well and truly upheld that morning.

He thought of Sean and his family. Where were they at this moment?

His reflections were interrupted by activity outside the door. The ancient and rusty lock was being opened and in a moment the door opened and a constable appeared with a mug of tea.

'Here's a wet for ye,' he said in a kindly voice.

Taken by surprise Matt was grateful.

'There'll be a bite of dinner in a while.'

However, before the door could be closed again a priest appeared behind the constable and after a murmured word which Matt did not catch, came into the cell, as the door was locked behind him.

'I am allowed only a few minutes, my son, but I had to come to see how you are.'

'That's kind of you, father,' Matt said, sipping his tea.

'I heard what went on down in Ballyglin. You were arrested for opposing the forces of law and order in the execution of their duty.'

'Word travels fast,' Matt said calmly.

'These are serious matters, my son; a flippant tone is not in order,' said the other piercing him with a look from his grey eyes. This was a man in his forties in a dusty cassock, of medium height and spare build, with steel-rimmed spectacles, his hair cut *en brosse*.

'I am quite serious, Father. A man and his family – seven children – were evicted from their home this morning. That's serious enough, I should say.'

'The landlord was within his legal rights to evict his tenant.'

'Father, I don't know who you are, and right now I don't feel like discussing the matter. A family of nine has been thrust out of their home. That's all I know. I intend to fight it with every means I have.'

'Every means?' The priest studied him for a moment. 'I haven't long with you, my son, so I must be brief. I can see you are in some distress and I feel it is my duty to help. You are going to be released shortly from this cell. I shall be waiting for you. I have an important message for you which can more easily be conveyed to you outside.'

He got up and rapped on the door. It was opened and a moment later he was gone. Matt remained sipping his tea in some perplexity, astonished at this short visit by the priest.

Darkness fell.

The cell was lit only by a dim light which filtered through a gap above the heavy door. Matt lay on the bench, dozing, thinking of Grace and the sea at Ardnashiel and wondering whether he was ever going to see her again.

Later he heard heavy footsteps outside and a key in the lock and sat up. The door opened and for a moment Matt was almost blinded by the light from the lantern in the constable's hand. He motioned with his hand to come out and screwing his eyes against the light Matt followed him down the corridor and through a door into the guardroom where a man was sitting at a desk smoking a pipe. The constable said nothing but crossed the room and opened the outer door. He turned to Matt with a nod of his head.

'Be off with ye now.'

Before he had time to think Matt found himself in the street

and the door was slammed behind him. The air was refreshing
after the dank smell of the cell, and it was a relief to be free again
but he turned in bewilderment back to the door, wondering
whether the priest had something to do with this.

He had hardly gone a step before he felt a strong grip on his
arm which halted him dead where he stood. He turned in the
darkness and made out the shape of the priest by his side.

'Ye didn't have long to wait, you see?'

'Was it you?'

'I could see ye were in some distress, my son, and I used what
little influence I had – told them you were a parishioner of mine.
The outlook might have been grim, Matt – striking an officer
in the execution of his duty.'

'Well, I'm mighty grateful to you, Father, though I don't even
know who you are.'

'Father Murphy.'

'Father Murphy then, I'm grateful to you, but you must excuse
me. I must get back to Ballyglin.'

As Matt set off out of the town, the priest walked beside him.

'You seem an educated young man, of good family too, as far
I can see. What moved you to wish to protect this poor farmer?'

'Justice, Father. That's all.'

'Hmm. For the farmer. Or for all farmers?'

'For all Ireland. The landlord – my very own uncle – called
up all the forces of the British state – the military, the constabulary and brought in black Protestants from Ulster. The family
never stood a chance.'

'You protested against your own uncle?'

Matt said nothing as he tramped. Suddenly he turned.

'Father, I'm grateful for your interest, but you'll have to excuse
me. I've got to get back to the village and see what has happened
to the Higginses.'

Without speaking further Matt tramped on and it was late in
the evening when he arrived in the village. Everything seemed
quiet. The cottage was standing empty with its door open and
as far as he could see most of its thatch off. He felt suddenly
very tired and his shoulder still ached abominably. He crossed to
Mrs Carruthers' bar.

As he entered there were a dozen or more men sitting about

by the fire, in the light of one lantern. They stood up as he entered with enthusiastic cries of greeting.

'There y'are! Our brave boy! So they let ye out, Matt!'

'Where's Sean and his family?'

'Father Geoghegan has taken them in – they're in his barn for tonight.'

Matt crossed the green to the presbytery and the housekeeper directed him round to the back where he found the barn not far off across a yard.

As he stood in the door the whole family was revealed making themselves comfortable in the hay. Sean came over as he saw Matt.

'Father Geoghegan's after taking us in for the night, Matt. But after that – tomorrow . . .' He shook his head. His two teenage sons came and stood beside him. Matt's mind was made up in an instant. 'Tomorrow you're coming with me,' he said.

'Where?'

'To my uncle's house.'

'Mr Doyle's house?' Sean echoed in a wonderstruck tone.

'Why not, since he drove you from your own home. Anyway he's in Dublin so he can't stop me.'

'Matt . . .'

He turned to where Mary had been watching him.

'It's kind of ye to think for us and all, but it's been decided. We're to stay with my uncle in Ballintober, and then we're goin' to America, like Mr Doyle said. He's paid the money. I have it here.'

'*You* have?'

She nodded, and then Matt understood. The women had made the arrangements, since Sean was useless. Mary leaned in and spoke in a low voice.

'I have to, Matt. My father can't cope, and my brothers are too young. Someone has to take charge and it seems it'll be me.'

'Couldn't they go without you? Do you have to go?'

She nodded. He was still struggling to understand.

'So – when are you going?'

'On Friday we're going to Cork and there's a passage booked on the *Alberta* to Boston. After that – we'll see.'

He looked round desperately. The whole family were gathered

round him waiting for his every word. Even in his muddy torn clothes, he had never been so self-conscious, so aware of his privileged position. He felt responsible, but also helpless. Hoarsely, he muttered, 'Come outside – for a moment.'

And in the darkness, he took Mary's hand. 'Mary – I never thought it would end like this. Do you really have to go?'

'You saw my Da, Matt; my brothers are too young—'

'Not so young—'

'Too young anyway, Matt. There's else nothing for it. Believe me.'

He felt for her hands and held them silently.

'I don't know what to say – it's all been so quick.'

'I know.'

'Well, will you write when you arrive and tell me where you are?'

She shook her head. 'I'm not such a hand at the writing, Matt. Better leave it.'

For a moment there was silence between them, until at last suddenly conscious of the family just a few feet away inside the barn, he released her hand.

'I'll come down to see you off in the morning – and Mary . . .'

And for one brief moment he took her by the shoulders and kissed her. He turned and walked quickly away.

Fifteen

The following day he was sitting in a hotel bar, waiting for the train to Dublin. He had said farewell to Mary and after the upheaval of the last few days felt empty, deflated; she had been wrenched so unexpectedly from his arms that all his memories of her were shrouded in a painful aura. Mary was about to set sail for America; a completely new life was ahead of her and her family. It had come as a shock to Matt that Mary was suddenly the head of the family, with a heavy responsibility crowded upon her. And all this directly as a result of his uncle's callous business calculations.

He felt, though he knew not exactly how, that he had failed her. Should he have gone with them? How? He had no money of his own. The whole situation seemed to have been taken out of his hands, far beyond his capacities. Painful though it was, it seemed his life and hers were destined to be lived apart.

In this obscure way, feeling he had let them down, he found his eyes fixing on a man standing at the bar reading a newspaper. He was neatly dressed, dapper, in a suit and stiff white collar, a bowler hat and a gold watch chain across his waistcoat. He wore a gold pince-nez. As he studied him, Matt noticed the man giving him little suspicious glances. He looked like a commercial man, down from Dublin, but intuition told Matt that this was only a disguise. Matt had been taken into custody by the police. Wouldn't they be keeping an eye on him?

The man must be a police spy. Otherwise why had they let Matt out? They had let him walk free so as to be able to follow him. It was going to be like this from now on, he realized, always being followed, always looking over his shoulder.

Then a thought struck Matt like a blow on the back of the neck – what if Father Murphy too were a police spy? That strange visit in the police cell – was it a trick to implicate him? And this man watching him – had he been tipped off by the priest?

Matt felt like a man on the run. But before he could panic,

he thought again, and took a grip on himself. They had no right to follow him, no right to spy on him. He would confront the man, face him down, challenge him to declare himself.

Matt rose from his bench and crossed to the bar. Standing before the commercial traveller, he boldly looked down into his face.

It was Father Murphy.

'Gently, Matt.'

Matt gripped the bar to steady himself.

'Take you by surprise? Good. Don't say anything. I'll explain it all later. Now listen.'

It was the same man, yet it was not him. This was a Dublin commercial man. The priest in his dusty old cassock and his earnest shrewd manner was gone and here instead was a dapper travelling salesman with a pince-nez, neat fingernails and a gold watch chain. The man smiled.

'Take it easy. Matt. It's not as strange as it looks. And we don't want the whole town to hear about it, eh?'

He pulled out his watch and glanced at it. Then turned again to his newspaper. As he read it he spoke softly. 'The train leaves in twenty minutes. I suggest we meet on it. Third-class carriage. Off you go now.'

He turned again to his newspaper.

'Wait a minute. I don't understand—'

'I'll explain everything on the train. Off with ye now.'

He did not look up as Matt turned mechanically into the street. In a daze he bought a ticket to Dublin. He stood on the platform staring down at the rails, and wrestling in his mind. Who was this Father Murphy – if he was a priest – and how had he wrought such a startling transformation?

The train came into the station and Matt got into a third-class carriage – something he was unused to. Garrett and his aunt always insisted on travelling first class, and for the first time Matt found himself sitting on a wooden bench hemmed in among farmers and their wives and children. Meanwhile passengers were hurrying along the platform, looking into the compartment, and then hurrying on.

There was a whistle from the engine and a great rushing of steam; Matt felt the train was about to move at any moment.

He glanced out of the window then sat down again, confused. Where was the man – or was this another trick? Then Murphy appeared at the window.

'I'd prefer a smoker, Matt – do you mind? Come with me.'

He moved on down the train and Matt hurriedly followed him to another compartment. They had just climbed into the compartment when there was a roar of steam, the clanking of metal and Matt felt the train move under him. Murphy took out a box of cigarettes and Matt accepted one; Murphy lit them with a lucifer from his pocket.

'Fooled ye, Matt, did I?' he said cheerfully. 'Don't worry, you wouldn't be the first. I have to do it. The country is full of police spies and informers. It keeps them guessing. Well, ye've seen me, but do ye know what I look like, eh? Father Murphy, or Gerry Hanlon the Dublin merchant as my friends know me?'

Murphy – or Hanlon – drew on his cigarette and looked shrewdly at Matt through the smoke, his grey eyes slightly screwed up. Matt didn't know what to say to this stranger. Finally, he muttered, 'I'm grateful to you for getting me out, anyway. Why did you?'

'I heard what you did. Nobody asked you to stand up for that farmer. But you did. I admire that.'

Matt shrugged. 'It's a question of justice,' he said at last, throwing the cigarette out of the window.

'For the farmer?'

Matt nodded.

'And for Ireland?' Hanlon asked pointedly.

Matt looked up. 'What are you? Are you from the Land League?'

'Ah.' Hanlon paused. 'The Land League. Wasn't much use to ye was it? Not much use to Sean Higgins.'

Matt remembered the ranks of redcoats and the Royal Irish Constabulary massed on the village green. 'Words aren't much use when it comes to fixed bayonets,' he said listlessly.

'*They never are.*' Hanlon leaned forward, speaking intensely. 'Bayonets can only be met with bayonets. Force can only be met with force. It's not words which will drive the English out. Do you understand me?'

'Drive the English out,' Matt echoed. 'You mean Home Rule?'

'*Home Rule?*' Again Hanlon picked him up with peculiar

intensity. 'Home Rule?' he echoed. 'The British Parliament may debate Home Rule for a hundred years, and they'll still be here! There'll always be an excuse to delay it. But there are some of us who are impatient, Matt. We don't want talk, we want actions.' He leaned in closer, speaking intensely. 'Not Home Rule, Matt, independence! *Freedom!*' He hissed the words closely into Matt's face.

For a second Matt felt the mesmerizing power of Hanlon's words and the intense, glittering light in his eyes. It was as if Hanlon had read his thoughts; here for the first time was a man who thought exactly as he did.

'Freedom,' he echoed in a passionate whisper.

Hanlon leaned back, calmer now but still holding his gaze. 'If I thought you were serious, I could introduce you to men who think as you do. Men who don't just talk, don't just go to meetings, or march with banners; men who act.'

'I'm serious,' Matt responded instinctively. Everything that had happened over the last two days had fired him, worked him to an intense certainty; all his old feeling that he was alone, without family, adrift in the world, not knowing who he was, all of it impelled him to a fierce certainty, to go on, to act.

'You're a bold lad,' Hanlon went on, watching Matt carefully. 'I dare say there aren't many things frighten you? You're not a man to lie down under an insult, I dare say?'

'You can count on me,' Matt said with a calm certainty.

Hanlon waited, still giving him this cool, appraising look. At last Matt repeated,

'I said it, didn't I? Try me! Put me to the test!'

'Give me your hand!' Hanlon said impulsively. 'Damn it, Matt, you're one of us! You've that in your eye – I can always tell.'

Matt grasped the proffered hand and shook it firmly as he held Hanlon's look. It was a look of recognition. Matt felt a door had opened, a way forward now beckoned.

Hanlon took out a pocket diary. 'How can I get in touch with ye?'

Matt thought quickly. 'You'd better write to me at the university, Law Department.'

'It's Matt Byrne, isn't it?'

Matt nodded.

'Good.' Hanlon snapped an elastic band round his diary and stowed it in a pocket. 'I'll be in touch – when the time is right.'

They parted on the train and left the station separately. Matt walked across to Fitzwilliam Square and by the time he arrived it was six o'clock, nearly dinner time. The children were glad to see him, and a moment later his aunt came in and rushed to embrace him.

'Thank God you're back! Are you all right, darling?'

'Sure, why wouldn't I be?'

'After what you said—'

'Aunt, I wonder whether you could lend me some money? There was an emergency and I had to give the Higgins family all I have. They've gone to America.'

'But surely Garrett took care of that?'

'As far as I know he paid for the passage, that's all. Don't worry, I'll ask when he comes in.'

'Oh, Matt –' she led him to a chair – 'your uncle – you know – when you disappeared back to Ballyglin—'

She ground to a halt.

'Aunt, I made my position perfectly clear. Garrett had no right to throw that family out of their home. Surely you agree?'

'Morally I agree,' she began uncertainly. 'Of course, I know what is involved. Unfortunately he has the law on his side. Oh, Matt –' she sighed and took his hands in hers, looking down at them as she thought – 'I don't know what gets into him. He's not a bad man but somehow – sometimes – he just seems driven. Please don't think too hardly of him. You know – he took you in, he has given you everything. He looks on you as a son, believe me.'

As always when she spoke like this, all Matt's defences crumbled, and he could feel himself weak inside, unable to deny her anything.

'And as for the money,' she went on, 'of course I'll give you whatever you want. Better not to mention it to Garrett, though.'

'Where is he?'

'Out to dinner. It'll just be us and the children tonight.'

'Good. I always enjoy it when it's just us.'

'So do I.'

* * *

Garrett came in just as Matt was thinking of going to bed. He stood in the doorway and surveyed his wife and her son on either side of the fire where they had been chatting.

'The prodigal son returns.'

Matt stood up. 'The Higgins family have left for Cork.'

'I know.' Garrett came into the room, a large presence, and threw himself into a chair. 'And your shoulder – still aching?'

'How did you know about that?'

'Do you think I don't care about you? I asked Thornton for a report.'

'Thornton?'

'He was the one on a horse,' Garrett explained pedantically, 'in a red coat.'

'You know him?'

'Why shouldn't I? Since he was in charge of the operation, of course I spoke to him.'

'Your shoulder?' Bríd interrupted nervously.

'It's all right now, Aunt,' Matt hurriedly reassured her. He turned again to Garrett. 'Do you know the chief constable too?'

'I've been in public life in Roscommon for ten years, Matt. I make it a point to know everyone who matters. They threw you into the cells for a few hours to cool down then let you go. It seemed best.'

'Seemed? To whom?' He now made the connection. 'Are you telling me you asked them to arrest me?'

'Of course – if you made a nuisance of yourself. I thought a few hours in the cells might give you a chance to think.'

'And then . . .'

'Then they let you out.'

'All by your arranging?'

'To tell you the truth, I didn't want you to get a criminal record. Not if you are going into the law.'

Matt stood up. 'I don't believe it. You arranged everything.'

'I told you before, Matt, it is my property. The Higginses will be better off in America.'

Without thinking Matt dashed past him, out of the door and into the street.

It was a joke! Everything, the demonstration, the military, the constables, all arranged by Garrett! The protest had been a farce!

Matt felt stifled. What was the point of anything? Anything at all? How could he ever escape from Garrett's shadow?

Two days later, the porter stopped him as he was going past the lodge.

'Postcard for ye, Mr Byrne.'

The card, which showed a view of Sackville Street, read simply, 'Father Murphy will hear confession on Thursday at 10.00 in St Aloysius'.

He was about to enter the church when he was stopped by a beggar who was loitering on the step with a shabby tray of cigarettes and matches, a wreck of a man in a ruined soldier's red coat, bearded, in broken boots and battered cap.

'Won't ye help an old soldier, sir, what's seen service in foreign parts fightin' for Queen and country? God bless ye, sir.'

Matt was about to pass him when he turned for a second look and recognized Hanlon.

'Oh yes of course. Give me a packet.'

'Thank ye sir. God bless ye.' And in an undertone, 'Saturday night in O'Leary's bar in Dame Street, nine o'clock. Thank ye sir and God bless ye.'

Hanlon had already turned his attention to another passer-by. 'Won't ye buy a packet of cigarettes from an old soldier that's seen service in the four corners of the globe . . .'

As Matt walked away he remembered how Hanlon had casually taken the credit for getting him out of jail in Boyle. When Garrett had explained the truth Matt's faith in Hanlon had suffered a shock. The fact was, he now realized, he knew nothing about Hanlon himself. Who was he? As for this disguise there was something bizarre about it. What was the need? Suddenly, Matt was very uncertain about the business. Nevertheless on Saturday night he was in O'Leary's bar, which stood almost opposite the entrance to the castle. It was crowded with working men and the air was thick with tobacco smoke and the gas fumes from two circular gasoliers which hung overhead. Matt pushed through to the bar and ordered a pint. Soon afterwards Hanlon appeared at his shoulder. He was once again the Dublin merchant, gold pince-nez and all.

'You've decided to come as yourself tonight?'

Hanlon didn't answer this as he ordered a drink. He turned back, however, and it was clear he was displeased with Matt's flippant tone. 'You're new to the game,' he said severely, and then to the portly barman, 'Any of the lads here yet, Tom?'

'A couple of 'em.'

'Follow me.'

Hanlon pushed through the crowd, through a door and up stairs. At the top he gave two knocks at a door followed after a moment by a third. A few seconds later the door opened a fraction and a man inspected them, before opening wider.

'It's Gerry.'

Several men were seated about a table, pints of porter before them and smoking pipes. They had been leaning forward watching the door and now appeared to relax back in their chairs.

Matt was introduced to these men; one was a carpenter, with the smell of wood shavings fresh on him, and another, he was told, was a road-mender. They were of his own age or a year or two older. He did not remember the others, except for one. They were examining him suspiciously and he felt conspicuous in his neat suit and stiff collar.

There was a double rap at the door, a pause and a third knock. They all looked round but it was clear they recognized the new arrival as they relaxed back in their seats.

'Sam's quartermaster,' Hanlon told Matt. This was an older man; Matt had no idea, but he thought perhaps fifty or more. His face was well lined and it was clear he had seen the world, and suffered too. He was examining Matt with a penetrating glance.

'Sam was lagged for the Clerkenwell job,' Hanlon went on, 'and did fifteen years in Portland. But he's back in the old country now.'

Hanlon introduced him to Matt and soon after Tom appeared with a tray of glasses of porter and they sat sipping the black beer waiting for others to arrive.

'We won't wait for Mick,' Hanlon said, 'I saw him this morning and he said he'll be along later. And first, I've had a bit of good news. Mick McCaffrey is on his way home from the States.'

There was an approving reaction to this news. Hanlon nodded

to Matt. 'And I've found a new recruit – Matt Byrne from the County Roscommon. Matt's a student in college just now.'

However, there was some movement among the men present, and before Hanlon could continue, Sam Walsh interrupted.

'Not so fast, Gerry. Who is he, anyway?' He looked round at the others. 'We don't admit anyone. How do we know he isn't a police spy? Eh? A well-dressed lad like him, a college man? What is he doin' here at all?'

'Try me!' Matt cut across him.

Hanlon interrupted. 'Matt here was taken while trying to prevent an eviction down the country. I'll vouch for him.'

Walsh was suspicious.

'Look,' Matt interrupted, 'why would I be a police spy? Do I look as if I need the money? I live in Fitzwilliam Square – you'll find no more elegant address in Dublin. My uncle Mr Garrett Doyle is one of the richest men in the city. I want for nothing. So why should I be here at all and risk everything? My comfortable house and all the money I need? My college degree?'

'Ah – that's the question.'

'Well, here's the answer! Because I saw a man, his wife and their seven children thrown out by my own uncle – so-called. Thrown out and told to go to the States and be damned to them. And when I protested, I was taken and thrown into Boyle jail. Will that satisfy you? I've seen the military, I've felt their hand on my collar.'

'So there's no love lost between ye and Mr Doyle?'

'None.'

'And when they threw ye into Boyle jail, what did they do to ye?'

There was a pause. 'They kept me in all day, then threw me out.'

'Threw ye out?'

There was a silence and Matt was conscious that it didn't sound very much after all. Walsh too felt it because he now stood, and lifted one foot on to a chair.

'Listen, son.' He pulled up one trouser leg. There were weals, long-healed marks about his ankle. 'Ye see that mark? And that one? Them was from shackles I wore in the quarries at Portland hewin' rocks all day. Fifteen years I done, for the Clerkenwell job. And damn near swung for it, an' all, along with Barrett. And what have ye done? One afternoon in Boyle jail – and never charged? No man is admitted to the Vindicators until he proves himself.'

Matt looked round; all the others had their eyes fixed on him. 'And have you,' he began, 'have you all—'

'Every man here has blood on his hands,' said Walsh with chilling finality.

There was a long silence. Finally Hanlon turned to Matt. 'I'll vouch for Matt,' he repeated and turned to Matt. 'We'll swear him anyway. Are you ready to be sworn?'

Matt stood up. 'I am.'

Hanlon took from his pocket a long clasp knife and pulled it open.

'Take the knife in your left hand.'

Hanlon was holding the knife in his right hand so they were both grasping it together.

'Now raise your right hand and repeat after me, "That I of my own free will and without any mental reservation whatsoever will obey orders transmitted to me by the Irish National Vindicators, not to seek to ask more than is necessary in carrying out such orders, violation of which shall be death".'

As Matt repeated the oath after Hanlon his mind was casting about: Irish National Vindicators? Hanlon had not mentioned this name before.

'Matthew Byrne, I declare you to be a probationary member of the Vindicators, to live with us and to die with us in the sacred cause of Ireland.'

'Every man must pass a test,' Walsh said heavily.

At this point there was a thump at the door and Matt noticed how everyone jumped and looked round anxiously. Hanlon went to the door.

'Who is it?'

'It's me!'

'It's Mick,' said someone and the atmosphere relaxed.

Hanlon opened the door and what Matt took to be a cabbie came in, seemingly wrapped in three overcoats, a hat pulled down over his eyes and holding a whip. The cabbie wiped his brows with a large and dirty handkerchief; he was a plump man past sixty with a florid, lined face, heavy eyebrows and large moustache.

'Bring me a pint of porter for God's sake or I'll shrivel to dust. I'll atomize meself. I've a thirst on me you could photograph. Hullo Gerry, greetings to one and all. Sam, haven't seen ye in a while. Who's this, a new recruit?'

Hanlon introduced Matt. 'Now Tom,' he went on, 'where's Kevin Meany tonight?'

They all looked round.

'Why, did ye not hear about it, Gerry?'

'Hear what?'

'Kevin Meany was a traitor.'

'A traitor?'

'Meany led the Peelers to our arsenal. They took the lot.'

'What are you telling me?'

'Did ye never hear about it? 'Twas in all the papers.'

'God! And it's me that's been in the depth of Connacht. I never heard a thing. But Kevin?'

'A traitor, Gerry.'

'How did you know?'

'Mick here was spoke to by a police spy who mistook him for Kevin.'

'Would ye be Kevin Meany, says he,' said the cabbie. 'I was on me guard in a moment, Gerry. He's me brother, says I, just to lead him on like. Tell him there's been a change of plan, says he. The meeting's off, we'll send him further information when the time's ripe. And with that, he goes. And that very night there's a police raid. The Peelers took everything, pistols, guns, the lot. Well, thinks I, Kevin Meany, you have a heavy responsibility this day.'

Hanlon sat, his face grey. 'They took the lot?'

'Every last bullet. If we have a penknife between us, that's the size of it.'

'Christ! And Kevin Meany! Kevin! One of the boys! One of the best!'

'He was a traitor.'

'Are you sure now?'

'He confessed. We took him from his bed at five in the morning. Bring your beads, says I, you'll be needin' them. The cowardly traitor, his knees was like jelly. I swear on me mother's grave it wasn't me boys, says he. Save your breath to say your prayers, says

I. Didn't the police spy only tell us your name? What police spy, says he. Jesus, Mary and Joseph, I never spoke to the Peelers in me life. They knew your name, worse luck for you, says I. Your number's up, Kevin Meany, say your prayers. We took him out on the Finglas Road and shot him like a dog.'

Matt sat quiet, listening hard. There was something frightening about the way the cabbie had told this story, so cold-blooded, so casual.

'I never would have believed it,' Hanlon breathed. 'Kevin Meany. Christ, is there no trust in the world? And all our guns taken!'

One of the others struck in. 'But if he mistook you for Kevin, that means they know you too, Mick. They know you're one of us. They're probably following you.'

'They've got nothing on me.'

'The spy talked to you! He thought you were Kevin!'

'Christ, they could tear us to pieces!' Another man cut in, looking round at the others. 'The whole Directory could be shopped!'

'I tell ye they've got nothin' on me!' the cabbie shouted.

The others were all exclaiming, looking at each other with fear, doubt and mistrust painted all over them.

'They don't know me,' said Matt without thinking, and this for a moment defused the atmosphere of tension and hysteria which was now palpable in the room. They turned to look at him.

'That's right,' Hanlon echoed. 'They don't know Matt . . .'

Sixteen

As Matt was pushing his way through the crowded pub after the meeting, he unexpectedly caught sight of Fred at the bar. A chill ran down him and he was turning away when Fred called his name. Matt turned again and pretended to notice him.

'Drinking alone, old chap?' He tried to control his breathing. 'Doesn't bode well.'

Fred was slumped against the bar, a glass of stout before him. He did not look happy.

'Am I glad to see you, Matt. I've been standing here, confronting my future. For God's sake say something to cheer me up.'

'Your future – is it that bad? Anyway, where are the others?'

'Gone back to college. I'll have to go soon, too. I've been locked out twice this term already. Can't afford another fine.' In his slightly drunken state, he turned. 'Lucky Matt –' he lifted his hand to Matt's shoulder – 'living at home.'

Matt had relaxed by now. Evidently Fred had no idea why he should be in O'Leary's.

'So – your future?' Matt prompted him. He noticed over Fred's shoulder, Sam Walsh watching him as he passed through the crowd.

Fred stared into his beer. 'Time to grow up, old chap, face the world. The old man has been laying the situation out for me. Once I graduate I'll have to return home and get to grips with the estate.' He shook his head in a slightly bewildered fashion. 'There's just so much to learn. For one thing, I know nothing about forestry, and he's keen to increase our woodland. And something else: he believes there may be iron ore deposits on the estate and there's good clay too. The old man thinks we might start a pottery. The law degree will come in handy though, he says. And to tell you the truth, politics is beginning to bore me. A crowd of windbags in love with the sound of their own voices and more interested in making a name for themselves than doing anything for Ireland. In any case –' he paused, turning to Matt – 'I should have thought the same applied to you – didn't you say your stepfather had a few acres of his own? You stand to inherit, don't you?'

Matt shrugged. 'Why should I? I am not his son. Stephen will inherit – his real son. He has offered to take me into partnership with him – or give me a start in some other way. But I'm not interested in making money, Fred! I mean – not for its own sake. I want to act! I'm going into the law – start there at least. I don't know . . . I get so frustrated sometimes . . . I want to do something, you know, make a change. Anyway, finish your drink and I'll walk back with you. Don't want to be shut out again, do you?'

'Too true.' Fred drained his glass, and they left and made their way down the street in the direction of the college. It was refreshing to be in the open air after the smoky atmosphere in the pub. Fred drew a long breath.

'Well, thanks old chap.'

'What for?'

'Listening to my woes.'

'Fred, you haven't got any woes. You have a lovely family: your parents, your sister – all lovely. You've got a lovely house, and you've got your life's work cut out for you. What more can a man want? You don't know how lucky you are.'

A pause, and at last Fred murmured, 'You think so? Well, suppose you're right after all. Things could be a lot worse.'

'I should say.'

They walked on until they got to the college gates. Fred offered his hand. 'Thanks again old chap.'

'It's nothing. See you on Monday.'

Matt turned to make his way home.

This conversation made Matt very thoughtful as he made his way through the dark streets, through a crowd just emerging from a theatre, dodging across the street among the cabs and broughams. It was as if he and Fred inhabited different worlds. What would Fred say if he knew where Matt had been that evening? Fred had said politics was all talk but those men – the ones who had been in prison, who had returned from America, from Australia – they didn't just talk. They were prepared to act – and he was prepared to act with them. It was better than the milk and water approach of Home Rule and the polite, gradualist approach to Irish independence. And the Vindicators had given him an identity; from now on he had some sense of who he was. The opportunity to act might not come straightaway, they had told him, but it would come one day and on that day, he would be ready.

His mind filled with these thoughts he was surprised suddenly to find Hanlon and Sam Walsh blocking his path.

'Just a minute, boy,' Walsh said abruptly. 'In here.' He pushed Matt violently into a shallow shop doorway.

Matt was shaken out of his thoughts by this abrupt intrusion. 'What?'

'What's the word, me boyo. What were ye doin' just now back there?'

'Back where?'

'Don't act stupid, boy. We saw ye, talkin' with a feller. What was that about?'

'Nothing. I just bumped into him. He's a friend of mine.'

'Oh yeah? Just a coincidence, was it?'

'Yes it was! He's a student.'

'Just a student? And ye expect us to believe that? And just happened to be in O'Leary's tonight?' Walsh took Matt by the lapel and thrust him violently back against the door. 'What's your game, boy?'

'Will you take your hands off me!' Matt shouted and tried to thrust him back. He did not reckon with Walsh's strength, however. He was held in place with rocklike strength.

'Take it easy, Sam,' hissed Hanlon, 'Aren't I tellin' ye, Matt's clean. Would I bring him in if I wasn't sure?'

'Ye may be sure, but I'm not.'

'What do you want me to do, to prove I'm clean?' Matt said breathlessly.

'That's to be decided.'

'Well, make up your mind and tell me. Then you can set your mind at rest! Now let me go.'

'Let him go, Sam,' Hanlon echoed.

After a moment Walsh released Matt.

'Thanks.' Matt was getting his breath back. 'A fine welcome to the Vindicators, I'm sure.'

'Don't be funny, boy.'

'I'm splitting my sides laughing, can't you see? Gerry – you decide – what do you want me to do to prove I'm safe?'

'We'll let ye know,' Walsh answered for him.

'It's OK Matt.' Hanlon was more conciliatory. 'Relax. No harm done, eh? Only Sam here was worried.'

'We'll be in touch, boy. You can go.'

It was clear that Walsh was still very suspicious and Matt's heart was still beating fiercely after this encounter as he made his way home. They wanted proof? Well, let them name it! He was ready.

In the meantime he must behave outwardly normal. No more childish quarrels with Garrett. He settled down to wait until Hanlon should contact him again. After that last brutal encounter he was anxious to prove himself to the likes of Walsh.

He continued with his studies. One morning Fred told him that Grace had gone abroad again, this time to Florence and Rome, with a friend, to continue her painting studies. This gave her a glamour almost more than he could comprehend. She was twenty-one now, Fred told him, and free to do as she pleased. Matt wondered who the friend might be. 'From school,' Fred said: a girl, and this relieved him, but Matt then wondered what kind of fantasies they were that could conceive of the enigmatic Grace abroad with a man, free, in a way that Matt could scarcely imagine. Of course Grace was with another girl. Then Matt remembered the story of her 'engagement' which was not really an engagement, and he wondered whether she and this 'fiancé' had – he scarcely knew how to phrase the question to himself – whether they had 'done it'? Since childhood, 'purity' had been the watchword whenever relations between the sexes had been discussed. The friars, and Brother Ronan foremost among them, had again and again stressed the importance of 'clean living'. 'Will you serve the white maiden Erin, and you in a state of sin, boys? What would she say if you came to her, stained, impure? Resist the temptations of the flesh, boys. Hold yourselves ready, worthy of her sacred trust. And when you come to marry – for you will come to marry, boys – remember, "A pure woman is above the price of rubies." Will you come to her, bowed down by a weight of sin, your body soiled with abuse? The woman you have chosen to be your wife?' At school all the boys had suffered the pains of hell, racked with guilt, as they strove to control their natural impulses. 'A pure knight vowed to serve his lady, the white maiden Erin', Matt had prayed as a boy. 'Oh keep me pure to serve her', and though he was an adult now, much of this teaching still unconsciously coloured his thought. He wanted to keep himself chaste too for the day when he might take a woman for his wife – though that eventuality seemed indescribably remote. Yet when he thought about it, though he remembered this teaching very well indeed, the thought of Grace actually 'doing it', was furiously disturbing and the thought of her doing it with him was almost more than he could comprehend. He dreamed of her.

'It'll be Matt's twenty-first birthday in a month's time. We must plan something really splendid for him.'

'Have you talked to him about it?' Garrett looked up from the armchair where he was reading a newspaper. It was early on Sunday morning, and the room was filled with light. The children were all across the road in the garden. Bríd sat at her escritoire with a piece of paper and a pencil in her hands.

'I wonder whether we shouldn't take a room in the Gresham for the occasion?'

'Have you spoken to him about it?' Garrett repeated.

She looked up thoughtfully. 'I thought we could make it a surprise.'

'I don't recommend it. People never like surprises.'

'You mean you don't like surprises.'

'That too,' he remarked evenly. 'Even so, I should discuss it with him before you book the room. He might prefer something more modest – a quiet family dinner party? He's not a very demonstrative boy – he might find a big affair embarrassing.'

'Do you think so?' Bríd's notions of parties were modelled on theatrical first night celebrations, which began at eleven, were filled with too much eating, too much drinking, hugs, tears, oaths of eternal friendship, extravagant praise of each other's performances, and finished only when everyone was asleep sometime the following morning. 'It is a special occasion,' she said at last.

'Well, talk to him. It is his party after all. And Bríd, there is something else you could talk to him about, now that he is going to be twenty-one.'

She looked up as Garrett went on seriously, 'Matt is going to be – legally – an adult, in charge of his own life, able to make his will, go to law, or buy a house. Isn't there anything else you might want to discuss with him?'

She knew now what he was talking about. When she didn't answer, when she continued studying her piece of paper, he persisted.

'Don't you think it's time you told him?'

At last with a shake of her head, 'I can't,' she whispered hoarsely.

Abruptly he leaned forward. 'I think you should!' he said quietly with intensity. 'I know it preys on his mind and Bríd, he has a right to know the truth. All of it.'

'I will tell him,' she muttered quickly, 'I will – one day – when the time is right.'

'Make it right! It's your choice. But the longer you put it off, the more he will resent the delay when you tell him.'

There was a long silence while she sat full of thought.

'It's just,' she began at last, 'such a story, and I am so afraid he will hate me for abandoning him. I dread it. Suppose he were to blame me, to repudiate me? I couldn't bear it! And we are happy as we are!'

'You are! Is he?'

'I think so,' she faltered, 'I'm sure of it. I mean, we are so close. He looks on me as a mother in any case. It's easier to let things go on as they are.'

'Easier for you!'

Bríd did not answer. In truth she had no answer to give. The idea of unravelling all the long complicated story of Matt's birth was more than she could face. And the thought that she might alienate him was too dreadful to bear. All she could do was to let things drift on as they were and pray that nothing ever happened to drive them apart.

Garrett was studying her with a very serious look. He shook his head slowly and at last said carefully, 'I know that he is the most important person in your life.'

She made a small gesture, but he went on, 'It's all right, Bríd, I've always known it. Oh, there was a time, after Nora's death

– when you were grateful to me for taking Matt and Patsy in. I think you loved me then – I mean really loved me – really, really, loved me. I knew it at the time. I could sense it when I took you in my arms, when we made love. You gave yourself to me then truly, fully, unconditionally. And you have given me children, given me a son and heir, for which I will always be grateful. But I have long realized that deep in your heart it is Matt who comes first.'

Again she made a small gesture, but he held up a weary hand. 'No need to deny it. It's true. And I suppose I shouldn't complain.'

She was hanging her head. There was no answer to any of this.

'Grace is back, by the way.'

'Oh?' Matt looked up from his book. The bright summer afternoon flooded the library where they sat over their essays.

'Just had a letter from her.' He flapped it briefly. 'Says she's coming to Dublin. The parents have tickets for the horse show.'

'What's that?'

'At the RDS, you know.'

'No?'

'The Royal Dublin Society, you ignoramus. The number one event of the social calendar. And Gracey is such a snob beneath all her free and easy ways. She wouldn't miss it for the world. I say old chap, that gives me an idea. You wouldn't like to come too, would you? The parents take a box, and there's oceans of room. Bring your aunt and uncle – I told Grace about your aunt, and she's dying to meet her.'

Matt was thinking fast.

'They usually come to Dublin at this time of year, meet all their friends, all that. Viceroy's ball.'

'Ah.'

'Gracey was a deb, you know,' Fred went on slyly, 'white gown, three feathers in her hair, kissed the Viceroy. She would rather die than admit it, mind you. She's such a hypocrite; she loves all the trappings of privilege, and then comes out with all this Home Rule and bring back Gaelic stuff. I tease her about it mercilessly. Serves her right.'

Matt was thinking furiously. He had to see Grace again, he

would kill to see her again. But what would he say to her? What did they really have in common? He remembered those brief visits to Sligo, the wild deserted strand, the power and magnificence of the Atlantic. She belonged there: he associated her automatically with all that wild freedom and for a moment couldn't picture her in conventional surroundings.

'Fred – do you think she'd like to come to my twenty-first?'

'She'll go anywhere for a free drink. No seriously – she'd love it. Do you want me to mention it?'

'Wait, I ought to send an official invitation. Where will your parents be staying in Dublin?'

'With my aunt. She's got a draughty old place, round behind Merrion Square.'

'That's not far from us.'

'Indeed not.'

Garrett and Bríd faced each other over breakfast. The children were having theirs in the nursery; Matt had gone out. Garrett carefully folded the newspaper and passed it across to Bríd.

'Your old admirer.'

Puzzled, Bríd took the paper and read, 'Earl of Elphin to be Viceroy of Ireland.'

She was still studying the announcement, endeavouring to think through all the consequences, or indeed whether there were any, when Garrett went on, apparently inconsequentially,

'And this may amuse you.' He passed over a letter. It was from Sir William – an invitation to join him and his family at the Horse Show.

'Oh!' she exclaimed, dropping the newspaper, 'that will be Matt's friends. I've wanted so much to meet them. Yes, we must go! It will be such fun!'

Garrett had been watching her carefully. 'The Viceroy will be there. Honorary President of the Royal Dublin Society. It would be a chance to meet. I'm sure he'd like to see you again,' he added.

She couldn't meet his eye, looked away and there was a long pause. 'You might have said that first, Garrett. As a matter of fact, and contrary to what you might think, I would prefer not to see him again. All that – it's best forgotten about.'

'Oh yes you will, madam.'

Bríd was startled by his decided tone. 'Why?'

'Because he is a connection too important to lose. He feels guilty about you. That's good. It'll give us a handle on him.'

'What do you mean?'

'Well now –' Garrett leaned back in his chair – 'let us think for a moment. There's the contract for the North Wall Extension. And the Finglas Road tramway. That's two reasons to be going on with. I dare say I'll be able to think of more.'

'That's outrageous.'

Garrett sighed. 'Normal business practice, I'd say.'

'Well I want nothing to do with it.'

Garrett stood up abruptly. 'I remind you madam, that every stitch of clothes on your body, every mouthful of food you eat, every lump of coal on that fire and the nurse for our children is paid for by my "normal business practice".'

'That's not true. I brought my own money to the marriage.'

'*Did*, Bríd, *did*,' Garrett said softly. 'But I'm afraid you ran through that some time ago, paying for your darling boy at the university. And you have expensive tastes in clothes – something I applaud, by the way. I like to see a woman dress well.'

'I am not *a woman*,' Bríd said coldly.

'That's neither here nor there. We will accept Sir William's invitation, and you will make yourself agreeable to your old admirer.'

He got up and calmly left the room, leaving Bríd staring at the letter, filled with confused thoughts. Some part of her was indeed curious to see Harry again. 'I wonder whether he'll even remember me?'

Seventeen

The sun was shining the day Matt arrived with Bríd and Garrett and the children. Matt was in a pale-grey morning suit as all around him the elite of Irish society gathered for, as Fred had put it, 'the number one event of the social calendar'. Garrett had a pass which had been forwarded by Sir William and led the way through the lively crowds. On all sides people were greeting each other, long-lost friends, distant relations, business colleagues, but eventually the family found themselves at the door of Sir William's box.

The baronet was all affability and introductions were made. As soon as he saw Grace, Matt was stricken into silence and stood, awkwardly holding his grey top hat, as introductions were made. Before them spread the showground, and on either side voices rose in high-spirited chatter as people crowded in and out of boxes. The ladies took their seats, and a moment later Sir William had produced a bottle of champagne.

Grace had changed, he thought. She looked – what? – more grown-up? No sign of the schoolgirl who had greeted him on the railway station. Matt stole covert glances at her as she was introduced to his aunt. This was the girl who had poured out her heart to him one night in the dark, yet, today she seemed – he strove to explain it to himself – more sophisticated, distant. She held herself so gracefully, seemed so at ease, to have some repartee for every occasion. She was introduced to Bríd.

'My brother told me about you, Mrs Doyle. I have been on fire to meet you ever since.'

'Oh goodness!' Bríd exclaimed. 'Well, here I am – a little the worse for wear, but otherwise in good working order.'

'He told you that we saw you in London. I will never forget it. You were just wonderful. You filled the stage, I mean – your performance – you just *were* Beatrice.'

'Oh hush! You'll embarrass me!'

Grace recovered herself. 'Well, I'll say no more. But I couldn't meet you without telling you how much pleasure you gave us. Have you given up the stage entirely?'

'Entirely.'

'And never had any urge to revisit the past – I mean, your triumphs?'

'Never.'

Revisit the past? the phrase stuck in her mind. The past haunts me every day, every day I see Matt. At that moment, as if on cue, Sir William leaned in and said, 'The new Viceroy is here, you know. Over there – you can see him – in the Viceregal box.'

She schooled herself not to turn too quickly as all the others did. But Garrett had heard Sir William and she knew he was watching her. She glanced to him and saw the amused, curious smile on his lips.

Lord Elphin, as Honorary President of the society, had now the pleasant duty of declaring the proceedings open. From where she was sitting, Bríd could just hear his voice, and despite everything that had happened, it reverberated in her mind and a mass of memories were stirred as if someone had climbed into an old attic, had suddenly opened a window, and decades of dust been stirred into the air. Memories swirled about her in the sunny afternoon.

'The old earl died then?' Matt said beside her. 'I don't remember this one.'

'He was away overseas – I suppose,' Bríd said uncertainly.

'What a weedy specimen.'

Bríd turned to where His Lordship was finishing his speech. Poor Harry, he did seem much older, his face lined, his shoulders a little bowed. He was not at his ease in public events – but she knew that anyway. Harry had been a sensitive young man, unassertive. She tried to keep her voice even.

'I think perhaps the tropics did not agree with him. He may have been ill. It kills a lot of men, I believe.'

'And to think they have sent him to rule over us,' Matt went on, his voice dripping with contempt.

Garrett behind them, chuckled. Bríd turned quickly, but his face was a blank.

'I don't think he is going to rule over us – literally,' she said.

'Of course not, Aunt. He's just the symbol. The symbol,' Matt repeated, 'of the whole rotten, corrupt, system. And just look – the natives are cheering their new white master. How perfectly fitting. Conniving at their own slavery.'

The Viceroy finished his speech and there was a burst of polite applause. Now someone else announced the opening of the proceedings and a man on a horse had appeared and was cantering round the obstacle course, the fences, jumps, water barriers.

The sun was shining, flags fluttered from mastheads, Dublin's elite were turned out in their finery. It was a day to enjoy if ever there was one, so, amid all this innocent enjoyment, Bríd was horribly pained to hear the depth of bitterness in Matt's voice, and was hunting in her mind for something to say, when he turned away to Grace who had caught his eye.

Before Bríd could find the right words, however, Sir William too turned in to the party and announced, 'Now then, every-body, what do you say to a little lunch?'

In a moment hampers were being unpacked and for a while conversation slowed as they tucked into cold chicken, ham, fresh rolls, cress sandwiches, a pork pie and much more.

Grace, who was sitting across from him, looked up from her cress sandwich and whispered, 'Wild boy', with a wicked smile on her face. Matt was taken by surprise, flustered, but also flat-tered, and with a sudden relaxation, he smiled too.

'You were in Italy, I heard?' He tried to make it sound as offhand as he could, as if he himself had visited Italy many times. 'How did you get on?'

'Wonderful. I'm going back.'

'Going back?'

There was a movement among the party at that moment and a chair became vacant beside her. He moved quickly into it. 'But why?'

Grace looked about her, leaned in and whispered, 'Bored.' She mimed a yawn.

He strained to catch her meaning. 'You mean – with home?'

'With Ireland.' She mouthed the word, half whisper, half mime.

'But why?'

'Why? Just look around you.'

He understood her and for a moment said nothing. 'Where did you go?' he said at last.

'Rome first, then Florence and Venice. Venice was best. That's where I'm going back.'

'And you painted?'

'That's right.'

'I'd like to see your pictures,' he said impulsively.

'You shall. Come and stay.'

'Thanks.' There was something ridiculously easy about talking to Grace. Feeling more and more relaxed he went on, 'How long are you staying in Dublin?'

'Don't know. A week or so – ten days – partly depends on the parents.'

'Come out with me one day.' The idea came out of nowhere. 'For a picnic – just the two of us.'

She was startled but replied almost immediately. 'All right.'

'Will you – really?' He couldn't believe what he had just heard.

'I said it, didn't I?'

Matt relaxed, as if pounds of weight had suddenly been removed from his shoulders. 'There's just so much I want to say to you,' he exclaimed into her face and to his joy she replied immediately, 'And I too!'

Matt was suddenly stricken speechless, glanced up again into her eyes, could find nothing to say, smiled, and suddenly embarrassed, looked away. Fortunately Grace spared him further embarrassment by turning away to say something to her father.

Did she want to speak to Harry? That was the question revolving in Bríd's mind. Did she? She turned her thoughts back to their last meeting in London, on the little bridge in St James's Park that summer morning: Harry buttoned-up in his formal coat, with his top hat, his walking cane, Harry nervous, furtive. The huge disappointment when her romantic memory of him had come into collision with the mediocre reality. Ten years ago – oh how she had despised him! But ten years had passed and she was ten years older; perhaps now she could be more generous. Her first feeling, when he stood up to speak this afternoon and she heard the tones that she remembered so vividly, that first feeling was one of pity. Poor Harry! Her knight in armour, her gallant young soldier – and now this – beneath the dignity, the bearing and grave tone of voice that had become second nature through long years as an administrator, as magistrate and governor, she could see a prematurely middle-aged man, already a tremble in his voice, a hesitation as he fumbled with a piece of paper in his hand.

Bríd glanced across to Matt who was sitting beside that girl, leaning in, speaking with his quick, earnest manner. Matt, so quick to condemn, so scathing, so sarcastic, so certain in his views. What if he knew? What would he say? Bríd trembled. How could she tell him? He would be devastated, there could be no question. No, it was impossible.

But just as it was impossible to tell Matt the truth, so too grew the conviction that she must speak to Harry. Poor man, he seemed so lonely. He appeared to have no wife beside him, no consort to steady him; he desperately needed a little cheer in his life, it was clear. Later she rose on the excuse of finding the ladies' room and made her way through the crowd towards the Viceregal box. A policeman was on duty at the door. Still uncertain, but determined now, she turned away to a table, sat, tore a page from a notebook in her bag, scribbled a quick note and returned to the policeman.

'Would you see that is handed to Lord Elphin?'

The policeman saluted and disappeared inside. Bríd wandered away and stood watching the horseman as he made his circuit of the course, made his jumps, mistimed one and knocked off some cardboard bricks, righted himself and cantered on to the next obstacle. Her heart was thudding now in her throat.

'Bríd?' A polite cough behind her.

She turned, a huge smile on her face. 'Harry!' she exclaimed, putting into that one word every ounce of warmth, compassion, friendliness, and calm tranquillity she had, as she offered her hand.

There was a pause as they scanned each other's face.

'D'you know,' he began, his voice trembling slightly, and still holding her hand, 'I had an idea you might be in Dublin. Felt it in my bones, as it were – sort of – fate. When they asked me to come over again, it was the first thing I thought of.'

'Well –' she drew a breath but still smiling – 'and here I am!'

She turned back to watch the horseman and he stood beside her. It was easier this way.

'And how does it feel, Harry, to be back?'

'I am glad, in a way. Since mother died, I've been on my own, y'know, so I rather jumped at the chance when they offered it.'

'Your mother died? Oh Harry, I'm sorry.' She couldn't help turning to him again.

He looked down, prodding the ground with his stick in a way she so clearly remembered. 'Yes, poor mother, it was . . . well, cancer, in the end. She sort of . . . wasted away.'

'That must have been terrible for you.'

'I was glad to be able to be with her, y'know, look after her – I think she appreciated it.'

'I'm sure she did!'

He nodded without speaking, still staring down at his stick while Bríd remembered Harry's mother, the stiff-necked, arrogant snob, remembered how she had addressed her own son by his title over the tea cups. 'Elphin, have you asked Miss Flynn whether she would like another cup of tea?' She could hear it still. Well, she drew a sigh. *Nil nisi bonum.* Let her rest in peace.

At that moment a footman coughed behind them. 'My Lord, Mr Herbert was looking for you—'

Harry looked nervously round. 'Right away!' He turned back to Bríd. 'Look, Bríd – I . . . er . . . we must meet again.'

'We shall!' she replied cheerfully. 'Shall I write – in a week or two once you've got settled in?' She extended her hand. 'I won't keep you. You have your duties to attend to.'

'But we will meet again?'

'Of course. And I am so glad to see you again, after all this time, Harry. Off you go now.'

He hurried away after the footman and, as she turned back to the box, her head full of thoughts she saw not far away Garrett who had been watching her. He smiled slightly and turned away in his turn.

Later that afternoon Matt was wandering through the crowd with Grace. Everything she said he found irresistibly fascinating; and by a miraculous coincidence she seemed to find him equally interesting. All his ideas, his frustrated hopes and fears for Ireland she agreed with wholeheartedly. She had, it seemed, exactly the ardent, impatient temperament he had. Their eyes constantly met, a flash of recognition passed between them, again and again the electricity of sympathy crackled between them. Matt was intoxicated, couldn't believe his luck.

'You said you've never left Ireland,' she said at one point, 'and yet you have a wider scope to your thoughts, a clearer vision. I've travelled, I've been to Italy and France, but in a way I still feel trapped in Ireland, as if, wherever I go, I take it with me. Wish I'd gone to university, in a way.'

'Why didn't you?'

She laughed. 'They'd never have me! I'm such a dunce!'

'You're not!' he protested. 'You're very clever.'

'I could never concentrate. My teachers at school were always complaining about me. No concentration! Anything would distract me. A rainbow, the view across the bay. Anyway, all I wanted to do was paint.'

'What's wrong with that?'

'Nothing I suppose. It's just that I envy men like you, who can think deep thoughts.'

Ahead of them, as they wandered through the crowd, Matt noticed Garrett, who was in earnest conversation with a woman Matt had never seen. He stopped, transfixed by the unexpected sight.

'What is it?' Grace turned.

Matt didn't reply. This was not just any conversation. After all, Garrett knew thousands of people. No, this was an intimate conversation. The woman was pleading; there was anxiety and hurry written all over her face, and she glanced about guiltily from time to time. Garrett was leaning in, concentrating on her. He laid his hand on her arm, trying to explain something, trying to calm her perhaps. Now he too glanced about him, guiltily it seemed.

Matt steered Grace in a different direction. She looked up curiously. 'What's the matter?'

'Nothing.' He shook his head as if trying to dismiss the thought of what he had seen, but as they continued their walk he ran the scene over in his mind What had happened? Something – or nothing? Was it what it so manifestly seemed? He wrenched his mind back to Grace.

'Grace, while we are alone – about the picnic, you did mean it, didn't you?'

She nodded. 'Yes, why not?'

'Well, in that case – I mean . . .' He was flustered. 'Well – when? Would tomorrow be too soon?'

She laughed. 'Are you afraid we might run out of things to say?' She stopped as she saw the anxiety in his eyes. 'On second thoughts, I think the parents may have something arranged. Let's think – well, let's say Tuesday, and then if anything does come up I can easily let you know.'

'Tuesday it is! I'll call for you at ten, would that be too early?'

'Too early? What do you take me for? Just because you go for a swim at seven every morning, doesn't mean the rest of us are still in bed.'

There was a pause as they stared into each other's eyes. The image of Grace in bed had immediately drenched his consciousness. He searched her face, devouring her with his eyes.

'What is it?' she asked innocently.

'Oh – nothing. It was just something you said.'

'What?'

'Really, it was nothing!' He was embarrassed.

'Oh, you are an enigmatic boy. I can't make you out sometimes.'

'Make me out? What is there to make out?'

'Come on,' she said briskly, 'I think the parents will be wondering about us.'

Eighteen

Matt called in a pony and trap promptly at ten, a picnic hamper under his feet, and within twenty minutes they were jaunting along the wide rim of the bay, heading towards the great lion-shaped outline of Howth Head, which juts far out along the north side of Dublin Bay and is joined to the mainland by what is little more than a sand bar.

As they clattered along beside the bay, a sea breeze lifted the spirits – if any lifting were needed. Grace was in a skirt and a thin blouse with a light man's jacket over it, and constantly having to hold down a little straw hat, which the breeze lifted.

'Why don't you take it off?' he said at last. She did, and in a moment, undid a ribbon too so that her hair spread across her shoulders. She ran her fingers through it to spread it out.

'And to think of the trouble I went to, to put it up this morning. I needn't have bothered. It was only for the parents' benefit anyway. They wanted to inspect me before you arrived, make sure I was all shipshape. They can be surprisingly old-fashioned sometimes. What is it?' She had noticed the look on his face.

'Nothing!' He laughed. 'I just love hearing you talk.'

There was an awkward pause as she fell silent. Matt too had nothing to say, conscious of their being together alone for the first time. Through what seemed a long minute they listened to the iron rim of the wheels on the road and the steady pony's trot.

'Fred was telling me about the eviction,' she began at last. 'He said you were arrested. Is that right?'

He nodded, watching the road.

'Someone in the village,' she went on, 'and your uncle threw them out of their home?'

Matt nodded modestly, still watching the road.

'Tell me about it,' she said impulsively.

He turned abruptly with an intense concentrated expression.

'My foster-father owns a hundred and twenty farms in the county Roscommon. He has an income of over ten thousand a year from land alone and God knows how much beside in businesses in Dublin. For the sum of twelve pounds he threw a family of nine out of the only home they knew and sent them to America.'

'And you protested?'

'Anyone would have! It was iniquitous. Unjust. No one who calls himself a man would have stood aside.'

'What happened? Was there a fight?'

'If you can imagine a handful of villagers against a platoon of soldiers and the constabulary. We did what we could.'

'And you were arrested?'

'Thrown into jail.'

'Matt,' she breathed, and reached impulsively for his arm.

He shrugged. 'What's a few hours in a cell compared with losing your home?'

'It was very brave,' she said seriously, and he caught her look.

'Grace —' he took her hand impulsively — 'there has to be a better way! There has to be. Otherwise what's life for? I'm lucky, my foster parents are rich. They'll give me anything I want. My foster-father will give me a job if I want in one of his companies. Grace, I wasn't put on this earth just to ride on the backs of others. I want to change this country, to make her free! Free and just! I want this to be a country in which poor farmers won't be thrown out of their homes for the sake of a few pounds!'

Grace had been watching him, mesmerized by the blazing conviction in his eyes and Matt fell silent, suddenly self-conscious after this outburst.

After twenty minutes they were on Howth Head and the track led up and along the steep side. Above and below them stretched rough grass, heather just coming into bloom, and the brilliant gold of furze. Further down to their right, the steep slope finally collapsed into an irregular cliff, punctuated with rock falls and little bays. This was a popular spot with Dubliners but this morning Matt and Grace seemed to have Howth to themselves. To their right the vast expanse of the bay stretched away, glittering in the morning light, the dark mass of the city huddled low beneath the brilliant summer sky, and in the distance the grey outlines of the Dublin hills and the Wicklow mountains were visible. With so much to take in there seemed little need to speak.

Eventually they came to the far end of the peninsula, overlooking the lighthouse, and stopped again to admire the view.

One lonely ship made a thin line across the bay, its smoke drifting in the morning breeze. They sat watching this for some time, and at last Matt said thoughtfully, 'The Holyhead ferry. Goes every day, twice a day, and I've never been on it; never left Ireland.'

'You will. Why not? You only have to buy a ticket.'

'You were talking to my aunt the other day – about London. You saw her there.'

'It was a long time ago now, to tell the truth, only I do remember her on the stage.'

'She never talks about it much – not unless a visitor asks her. I know nothing about all that.'

'Well, ask her.'

'If I do, she turns the conversation away.' He glanced around. 'Shall we get down for a bit? Rest the pony?'

Up the slope to their left patches of grass appeared between banks of furze and purple heather. 'We could take our picnic up there – what do you say?'

Matt unharnessed the pony, and hitched her to the trap leaving her enough rope to graze on the grass at the edge of the track, then took out the hamper and they made their way up the slope, among the patches of gorse and heather until they found a convenient private space on the dry, springy turf. He spread a blanket and they sat. Above them was a clear bright sky, and spread before them a wide, wide prospect of the bay and the distant mountains. Grace drew a long breath.

'How I love the sea – don't you?'

He nodded. She sat, with her knees drawn up and her arms around them. Suddenly Matt was tongue-tied. There was something so precious, so strange, so fascinating about the woman beside him. They were alone together, not a soul in sight – the possibilities were infinite, and it was as if the open sky and distant view were a metaphor for his life – and hers too perhaps. They were together and all before them stretched this great vista of the future. It was a foolish thought and he didn't utter it, yet he didn't know what else to say. In truth he wanted to kiss her more than anything and couldn't make out whether she would allow it, or be embarrassed, or offended. In the end, as the silence between them lengthened, and without thinking at all, he touched her shoulder, and as she turned to him, kissed her lightly, a passing, glancing kiss. His heart racing, he waited for her reaction.

'You might have before,' she murmured seriously and then as she saw the look on his face, threw her head back and burst out laughing. She lay back on the blanket.

'I wanted to kiss you from the moment I saw you,' she said.

'Did you?' He leaned over her. 'You mean that?'

'Certainly. I must say, you are a most backward boy and you kept me waiting an awful long time. You had better kiss me again to make up for it.'

His heart was racing, his brain in a turmoil. He couldn't imagine girls ever talking like that, so boldly. He couldn't even imagine girls actually wanting to kiss, actually telling him to do so.

He kissed her and for several minutes they seemed to wrestle on the blanket. She pressed herself up against him in a way he had not expected. For some reason he had imagined girls would be like statues, chaste, white and still, while he imprinted a kiss on their lips. Instead of which this girl was like an animal, like a cat, writhing, wriggling beneath him. And when he drew back briefly, she gave a little gasp, staring past him into the vast heavens.

'Oh God, Matt,' she gasped, 'you are a very attractive boy,' and with a wriggle, she twisted herself so that she was above him, as he lay back on the blanket. For a moment she was looking down at him with a small, wicked grin on her lips.

'I'm not a boy,' he muttered.

'Prove it.' She was staring into his eyes. He frowned, as an abyss seemed to open before him and the earth to shift on its axis. What on earth could she mean? He soon found out because a moment later he felt her hand at his trousers, feeling the straining, pressing urgency of him.

'Do you mean it?' he gasped.

'Have you got one of those – things, you know?'

'What things?'

'Oh, it doesn't matter, I've got something. Turn round.'

In a delirium of excitement and confusion, feeling that things

had got completely beyond his control, he did as she said. A
moment later, she murmured, 'All right.'

He scarcely dared to look but he could see that she had shuffled out of her skirt; he caught a glimpse of stockinged legs.

'No need to say anything, Matt.'

Their eyes were locked as he lay over her and he could feel
her guiding him into her. Suddenly, he felt himself sliding in,
being engulfed, overwhelmed by a sweetness he could never have
imagined, beyond all imagining. At the same time, she groaned,
and he felt her legs clutching him, as she arched her back. 'Oh!'
she cried aloud and then, as he moved in her, 'For God's sake
don't stop.'

It was beyond his will to control what was happening anyway.
He cannoned into her as if his life depended on it, carried
away like a paper boat down some steep rapids through high
mountain forests, leaping, dashing over rocks beneath a rainbow
spray, slipping between gulleys and then at last shooting right
over the edge.

It didn't last long and as he poured himself into her, she was
clutching, gripping, groaning. For long minutes they held each other
as the sweet languor relaxed him. I did it, he thought with inde-
scribable relief, and then, his brain restless, what have I done? The
world had suddenly changed; obviously they would have to get
married. And he hadn't calculated on marriage for a while. Yet we
must marry. She must be my wife. It was perfectly clear. I must
rearrange my plans, that's all. Besides she will have a child. My child.

'I'm hungry,' she said, after a while, and sitting up, reached for
her skirt and pulled it on. Matt tried not to watch as she buttoned
up the waistband. 'What have you got in that hamper?'

He opened it, astonished that she could be so relaxed about
what had happened, and for a while they made a lunch of cold
chicken and ginger beer. He could find no words, but she was
as carefree as a child. 'What's this, caviar?' she said, opening a pot
and sticking a finger in it. 'I must say, your people do pretty well
for themselves. Fred told me about it.'

A question was welling up in him, an awkward question but
one he was impelled to ask, and at last he began, 'Grace – don't
think me silly but – have you . . . have you . . .' He swallowed. 'I
mean – have you done it before?'

'Gentlemen don't ask such questions,' she said, her mouth full of chicken.

'I suppose –' he couldn't leave the question alone – 'I mean, you said you had been engaged . . .'

'Can you give me some more ginger beer?'

'Yes of course.' He hurriedly filled her glass.

He was silent, still thinking furiously until at last he said the only thing he could think of, the thing which now loomed huge, inevitable: his future – and hers, clear before him. 'Grace, will you marry me?'

'You bet.'

He was speechless at first but later, as they lay back on the blanket, his arm round her shoulders and her head resting on his chest, as he stared up into the limitless blue of the heavens, as little clouds moved slowly, very, very high, he couldn't stop talking. Everything poured out, all his hopes his ideas, his theories.

And later she talked too about Venice and Rome and Florence. 'We'll go together on our honeymoon,' he said, 'and you can show me round and tell me all about them.' And then, as he pictured this, he went on, 'To think, from now on, everything I do, for the rest of my life, everything, all the big things, all the small things, I am going to do with you. And everything you do, will be with me. I still can't believe it. This morning when we set off, did you know this would happen?'

She was silent at first. 'Not exactly. I thought it might happen, you know, sooner or later. But then, I knew that from the first moment I saw you.'

'From the first moment? On the station platform?'

'More or less.'

'Grace –' he sat up – 'are we going to tell your parents? What will they say, me being a Catholic?'

'It doesn't matter what they say. But anyway, they'll be happy about it. They like you.'

'Oh God, I do love you.'

That evening they drove back into the city in a haze of dreamy contentment. At the door, she said, 'I'm going to break the news now. What about your people?'

Matt thought about this as he returned through the streets to Fitzwilliam Square. Garrett might well be glad to be rid of him.

As for his aunt, she was always so solicitous for him, fussing round him. What would she say to his wife?

But his overwhelming thought, the thought that went round and round in his mind was: 'I am no longer alone.'

'We can make it an engagement party as well as your twenty-first!'

This was Bríd's first reaction.

'The cards are printed.'

'Well, that doesn't matter – we'll announce it during the party; it'll be a surprise.'

Matt's attitude to this party had completely changed. Originally he had been backward, uncertain, and would have preferred a small private dinner party at home with the family – as Garrett had said. But now, with Grace by his side, everything was changed. It was impossible to exaggerate the effect that afternoon had had on him; it added a foot to his stature. He was now a man of some consequence in the world. He could walk down the street with his head held high; no longer just any university student he was a man – that was what it was, he now realized. Grace had made him a man; he owed everything to her. As to the afternoon when she had so shamelessly seduced him – though he did not remember it in those terms – the memory of it burned in him with a white hot flame. Even now, a week later it would make him swerve in his walk, as if a mighty wind had blown. A mighty wind, he murmured to himself, has blown and everything is different. Everything about his life was changed.

Bríd was determined that no expense should be spared and, as she had promised, a room was taken at the Gresham. Menus were planned, food ordered, a band hired. Invitations went out; there would be two hundred guests. They would dance till dawn. 'Why not darling?' Bríd said, 'You're only twenty-one once.'

'And you only get married once,' he thought, his mind ablaze with the thought of Grace.

The day following their trip to Howth he received a note from Grace saying that she had broken the news to her parents, and why didn't he come for tea that afternoon and be, as it were, formally introduced?

They sat with their tea cups and absorbed the situation. Sir William and Lady Langley were so friendly, so kind; they were delighted, they said for Grace's sake. It had looked at one time as if she were to go roaming round the world indefinitely, and they were so relieved when she didn't get married to that Frenchman after all. But having Matt and Grace in Dublin would give them an excuse to visit more often. Fred too shook him by the hand and told him he couldn't have asked for a better husband for his sister, and thank God Matt would have the responsibility of keeping her under control from now on. There was not much Matt could say to any of this, but he kept expressing his thanks to her parents and promising that he would take care of her and that he was the luckiest man that ever lived and so on.

All the time he kept repeating to himself, Matt and Grace: people will say, 'Matt and Grace'. There was just a ring about it, it seemed inevitable; it had clearly been ordained from the first, just destined to be. And to think that she was his, he was still trying to absorb the strange wonder of it. When he was leaving that evening, he stood with her at the door, and didn't know what to say, wasn't even going to kiss her, just wanted to look at her, and say 'Was that us? Really us?'. He was suddenly shy, taking her hand timidly and wanted to say thank you, but it sounded silly, so he didn't say anything. She seemed to catch this, because in the end all that happened was that she reached up and kissed him lightly on the cheek. 'See you tomorrow.'

Through these days he did not think once of the Vindicators.

Nineteen

Invitations were for nine; there would a midnight buffet, waiters would circulate with champagne, the band would play.

Bríd and he had discussed the guest list. Some of them were fellow students, but there were also friends of Garrett and Bríd and also of the Langley family, so Matt thought he knew probably less than half the guests. In fact, he realized, the whole thing was completely out of his hands. Coming of age, like getting married, was a public event which touched the principals only peripherally; many others were owed their night's entertainment.

So as he stood, self-conscious in white tie and tails at the door with his aunt and welcomed guests, there were many – if not most – that he did not recognize. Quite a lot of them seemed to be friends of Grace; like a fool it had not crossed his mind that she might have friends. What a simpleton he was! Obviously she had friends, might have picked them up on her travels, in Paris or London. For a moment he was stricken by this thought; they seemed cosmopolitan, travelled and, like her, had English accents.

Grace was, for a second, unrecognizable and came as a real shock to Matt. He had almost to look twice: here in the doorway, then advancing towards him, came a vision in white, in a real lady's gown, off the shoulder, and cut to do justice to her figure, sculpted round the bust, tight-waisted, and with a fashionable bustle. Her hair was put up behind her head revealing her neck, and she wore jewels too, jewels in her hair, around her neck, her arm. Most of all, the occasion lent an added sparkle to her smile and her eyes shone with the prospect of an evening of dancing and fun. This was no girl, but a woman – as he now knew well. The moment he first caught sight of her as she arrived with her parents, his heart stopped with wonder and he felt almost as if he were greeting a stranger. This, and the presence of his aunt at his side, imposed a formality on their greeting. Grace seemed to pick this up – or it may have been her own consciousness of the impression she made – whatever it was, there was a slightly distant manner between them at first.

She immediately turned to someone he did not know, seemed to relax and called, 'Bobby! How are you? I'm so glad you made it!' Turning back to Matt, she said, 'Have you two met? Matt, this is Bobby Shaunessy; we knew each other in Paris,' and immediately turning back to him, went on, 'Did you ever hear from George?' and a conversation sprang up.

Matt was kept busy beside Bríd greeting people but couldn't help glancing over his shoulder at Grace a little later; she was now in conversation with a different man, whom he also did not know.

'Grace looks lovely tonight.' Bríd leaned in with a complicit smile. 'You're so lucky, Matt.'

'I know,' he whispered fervently, and a little later couldn't help glancing back.

Later he was called upon to open the dancing and he led Grace on to the floor for the first dance. The assembled guests watched as they circled the floor in a waltz. He felt no qualms, no inhibitions, no self-consciousness. He was in his rightful place, Grace was smiling happily; tonight there was a glow in her skin, and a light in her eyes. They danced together well, without awkwardness, as if they had been doing it for years and as they finished there was a polite burst of applause.

Then everyone was dancing. The girls had dance cards and, although Matt wanted to spend the evening with Grace, as the host he spent much of his time circulating and being introduced by Garrett and Bríd to men and women he did not know. Garrett assured him at one point, 'These are men you want to know. Matt. Every one of them can be useful to you. Make it a point always to gather about you useful men.' At that very moment Matt found himself face to face with the woman he had seen in such earnest conversation with Garrett at the Horse Show.

'Matt,' Garrett took his arm, 'This is a colleague – and old friend – Mr and Mrs Haynes.'

The woman took his hand with a warm, motherly smile. 'I've heard a lot about you, Matt.' After a few moments of conversation she leaned in again. 'I wonder –' she glanced about her at the dancing couples – 'whether your fiancée could spare you for a dance? We old ladies need all the dances we can get.'

The two older men chuckled at this witticism, Matt bowed and stuttered that the honour would be his, and soon afterwards they were circling the floor. He was struggling to make sense of the situation. Most importantly he was wondering whether the husband, whom he recognized now as the man he had seen once asking Garrett for a loan, had any idea of his wife's conversation with Garrett.

There was something ripe, mature, about this woman. She was old enough to be his mother and had – what was the phrase? – abundant charms. He was keenly conscious of this as, in the crush of other couples, her bosom was pressed against his. She smiled in a knowing way, a complicit way and made small talk with a dry wit, commenting on the other couples, and when she had been bumped against him for the third or fourth time, glanced behind her. 'Sure, some of these people today don't know how to dance at all, Matt,' she said, giving him a huge smile. There was something distinctly unsettling about this familiarity from an older woman and it aroused a fastidious, puritanical streak in him. She was too free, too forward.

When he finally got free of Mrs Haynes and was looking about for Grace he glimpsed her in the midst of a crowd of friends, some girls, mostly men. She seemed so popular, they all seemed to be hanging on to her words, laughing with her, and all in English accents. She didn't seem to know any Irishmen at all – but then he rebuked himself. Fred and Grace were themselves as Irish as he – if three hundred years of descent counted for anything at all. And if they had English accents, that wasn't their fault. And why was he having to explain this to himself anyway? It was because that fellow – Bobby was it? – had just led her on to the floor at the very moment when he was himself about to ask her to dance. Bobby had taken her in his arms and they were circulating among all the other guests, away from him, as he watched them with burning eyes. Bobby was saying something, whispering in her ear, and she burst out laughing.

'So you're the lucky fellow, eh?' A man was at his elbow also watching the dancers. 'Where did you meet her? Paris?'

Matt was disturbed in his thoughts. 'Through her brother,' he said briefly.

'By God but she's a cracker, say what you like. The things she got up to. Ask Bobby.'

The man chuckled. Matt tried not to hear, his eyes following the dancing couple.

'Ask Bobby what?' he said, without turning his head.

'Well, I think in the old days – it's just gossip, mind – in Paris, they were very close. Very. She didn't want to marry him, mind, but –' he leaned in – 'she was a very popular girl, know what I mean?' He gave Matt a significant look.

Matt turned to him in a fury, 'I am not interested in your gossip!' and walked away. But soon he had turned and was watching them again.

He waited for the dance to end. It seemed to go on for ever and when at last it did end, there was an announcement about the buffet and Grace and this Bobby moved off together into the other room where the buffet was laid out. Matt couldn't understand it – why hadn't she waited for him? It was crazy. It was his place to escort her to the buffet, to hand her things, and instead this arrogant fellow, who seemed to have assumed some sort of proprietorial right over her, was taking her arm and escorting her. The crowd was so thick now that Matt couldn't get close and even if he could he didn't know what he would say. 'Excuse me, but it is my right to escort this young lady'? It sounded ludicrous, juvenile. And that was it: these men were older than he, they had a more assured manner and they thought they could elbow in and take over his fiancée. His pulse was racing, he could feel the palms of his hands sweating. And what was she doing? Had she completely forgotten him?

Bríd was at his elbow. 'Are you going to take me into supper, darling?'

'Of course,' he muttered hoarsely. She had noticed which way his glance was turned, and as she slipped her arm through his, went on lightly, 'Grace seems to have so many old friends to catch up with.'

Together they made their way through the crowd and finally reached the scrum about the buffet table. Waiters on the other side were filling plates. Matt looked about for Grace but couldn't see her. With an effort he turned to Bríd, 'What would you like, Aunt?'

While she was pointing things out to the waiter, he glanced

round again and with a shock he saw Grace with this Bobby at a table, leaning forwards over their plates, their heads almost touching. He couldn't believe it. What did she think she was doing? Now another man joined them; he had a bottle of champagne and was filling their glasses. At that moment Grace looked round, saw Matt, and waved cheerily with her fork. But she quickly looked back as the men were explaining something to her, something to do with champagne, because the man with the bottle refilled their glasses and said something, and they all three emptied their glasses at once and then burst into laughter, and someone else had to pat Grace on the back as it seemed some of the bubbles had gone up her nose. She was coughing and reached into her vanity purse for a handkerchief, and was still laughing as she dabbed at her eyes.

As he watched she now tore the corner off the menu standing on the table. She scribbled something on it and stuffed it down the front of her gown.

Matt could see nothing. It was if a red cloud had descended before his eyes.

'Excuse me, Aunt,' he muttered, setting his plate down with a clatter, and crossing to where Grace was sitting with these men.

'What exactly do you think you are doing?' he said hoarsely.

'Matt! Come and join us!' she cried, 'Bobby, make room there – bring a chair for Matt!'

'Thank you, I have no wish to sit down. Grace, may I have a word?'

She looked up in surprise.

'*Now!*' His eyes were burning. 'I wish to speak to you now.' He was stuttering with emotion.

As she rose hurriedly, upset by his tone, he grasped her arm and dragged her a yard or two away.

'What was that?'

'What?'

'That paper – or whatever it was – that you pushed down the front of your gown?'

Grace was confused and upset by his tone. 'That? Nothing.'

'Well if it's nothing you won't mind me seeing it.'

His face was livid, his eyes blazing.

'Why are you talking like this? Come and join us – I want you to meet—'

'I asked you a question!'

She reacted now to his tone.

'And supposing I don't want to answer?'

'Ah.' It was as if this were the answer he had expected. His tone changed; it was level, controlled. 'And is it this way you are with every man you meet?' He was cold now. 'Like a whore, laughing and touching and—'

'*What*? Let go – you are hurting!' She wrenched her arm away from his iron grip. 'What did you call me?'

'What else should I call you? Fooling and playing with every man you meet – is that what I am? Just another of your conquests?'

'Are you mad? They're—'

'You don't have to tell me – I can see very well with my own eyes.'

'You called me a whore,' she said in astonishment as if she had only just heard it.

'And what else should I call you? The way you are carrying on? You're here as my guest, and already you're making assignations.'

One of the other men rose and came to her side.

'Grace – is anything the matter—'

Matt pushed him very hard in the chest so that he staggered back. 'Stay away!'

Grace watched this in astonishment. There were tears in her eyes as she turned to where Fred was watching them, along with several other people.

'Fred,' she choked on the word, 'Take me home.' She looked back at Matt, her voice filled with tears. 'How *dare* you talk to me like that! How dare you! How *could* you!'

She turned and pushed her way through the crowd, and was lost to view. Fred gave him a strange look and followed her. The other men at the table were watching him with very strange looks indeed, and in a daze he slowly looked round at them and then again at the door where Grace had disappeared.

'Look here—' The man whom he had pushed was straightening his jacket, but before he could say anything, Matt burst out, 'Shut up!' and forced his way through the crowd after Grace.

By the time he reached the street door she had gone. He looked about him in bewilderment.

A moment later Garrett was beside him. 'Matt, what's the matter? What's going on? You'd better come in. It's time for the speeches—'

'She's gone! What have I done?'

He dashed out and down Sackville Street through the late-night crowds, but after a while slowed. He began to cool. What exactly had happened? He tried to unscramble that brief scene. He had called her a − but what was she after all, fooling and laughing with all those men, when she had come as his guest? Then everything began to unravel. The afternoon at Howth − she had been very free and easy, hadn't she − as if he were just another of her conquests, and when he had asked her whether she had ever done it with a man before, she had just laughed it off and wouldn't answer.

Matt tramped the streets, seeing nothing. How could he have been so stupid? Did he really think it would be so easy for him? That he was really destined to be happily married − to have a beautiful wife that men would admire? Did he really think that could happen to *him*? As for what had happened on Howth, she had been using him, just as she had used so many others, no doubt.

But if that were the case, where did it leave him? Alone. Again. But that was something he had always known. Always known he was destined to be alone.

For most of the night he wandered the streets. Sometimes standing beside the river, standing on the Halfpenny Bridge staring down into the water. Why not take a header? He could almost do it. Then he turned into a pub − by this time he was up near Christ Church in the Liberties − a poor working-class pub, and drank a whiskey, and then another, not noticing the looks the other men were giving this toff in his white tie and tails, and at last staggered out, not knowing where he was going, only wanting to escape, to hide, and worst of all, to hide from himself.

It was dawn before he found himself in Fitzwilliam Square, his throat dry, and with a headache. He couldn't go in. He dreaded confronting Garrett and Bríd. What could he say? He stood on the opposite side of the square staring across. His life had changed for ever − but in what a way! How could it have happened like this?

When he did eventually go in, there was nobody about except a housemaid, setting breakfast. He walked past the open door up stairs to his room, and threw himself on his bed. He couldn't sleep. How long he lay there he didn't know, but there was eventually a knock.

'Matt? Are you in?'

It was his aunt. After a silence from him, the door opened a little and she looked in, saw him, came in without speaking and sat on the side of the bed. She sat beside him where he lay fully clothed, and took his hand. 'We can talk later. Is there anything you want?'

This reaction, so unexpected from her, almost broke him up, and he could feel tears smarting at his eyes. 'Aunt,' he spoke with difficulty, 'I don't understand . . .'

'Hush – don't say anything. Do you want a drink of water?'

He nodded.

Much later that morning there was another knock and Bríd looked in to where he still lay. He had fallen into a light sleep, but had woken again.

'It's Fred,' she whispered. 'Do you want to speak to him?'

Without speaking Matt went down to the door.

'He's outside. Said he didn't want to come in.'

Without speaking, Matt went out to where Fred was standing a yard or two away on the pavement. For one moment they stood facing each other, then Fred struck him hard in the mouth. As Matt staggered back clasping his cut lip, Fred came after him and punched him hard in the face again, and then again, and Matt fell backwards.

'Get up,' Fred hissed. As Matt staggered to his feet, Fred struck him again with all his force and again Matt fell backwards. Fred stood over him, nursing his fist. 'Don't ever come near our family again.'

He turned and walked away.

Twenty

Unexpectedly it was Garrett who confronted Matt as he returned indoors and went up to his room to wash the blood from his mouth, where his lip was cut against his teeth. Matt had no words to say, no thoughts to think. But as he was dabbing his mouth, Garrett appeared and leaned against the door jamb. They watched each other in the mirror.

'You'll have to face the fact that you've caused a huge scandal,' Garrett said at last. 'Huge. Everyone you know, and pretty well everyone I know, heard what happened, or worse, an improved version of it. Also all her family and friends. It's lucky for you the vacation is coming up. By the autumn things may have calmed down. Though it's not the sort of thing people forget in a hurry. You've got a lot of explaining to do.'

At last Matt said, in a low bitter voice, as he continued to dab at his mouth, 'She was laughing and joking and drinking – like a whore.'

'That's an ugly word, Matt.' Garrett shook his head seriously. 'It's no word to throw across a crowded room. You've been too long in the hands of the priests. Just because a girl likes a drink and a laugh it doesn't make her a whore. It was a party for heaven's sake; what do you expect her to do? And who is this fellow Bobby?'

'I don't know! I've never seen him in my life – or any of the others crowding round her, all wanting to talk to her.'

'Well, didn't you ask?'

Matt didn't reply for a second. Then at last in a low mutter he went on, 'There was this other fellow who knew her in Paris – said she was wild.'

'Wild?'

'It just enraged me.' He was silent again as the memory of Howth Head suddenly flared bright. Matt knew only too well how wild Grace could be. 'Everyone seemed to know her better than I.'

'So you take the word of this man you've never seen in your life before against the girl who has agreed to marry you? What else do you know?'

Matt could only think of the sight of her with the other men all laughing and joking. He was silent.

'Well, it's a bad business,' Garrett said at last. 'You got hold of the wrong end of the stick, it's clear, and you've come out of it very badly. I like the girl myself. You could have done a lot worse. Very good connection – respectable family.' He shook his head. 'You could have done a lot worse,' he repeated. 'Are you going to write to her?'

'And say what?'

'Well you could start by begging her pardon. Even if you never see her again, she's entitled to that.'

'Pardon? You didn't see her! What's a man supposed to do? Was I just going to stand by and watch her flirting and ogling these fellows?'

'I think you're a fool.' He drew a sigh. 'But I dare say there are other girls out there. You need to broaden your mind. Maybe you should travel after you've graduated.'

He turned and left the room and Matt was left confused and angry.

Through the following days Matt roamed round the city his mind filled with thoughts too black to utter. He felt like a wounded animal dragging itself through the forest, friendless, confused, no longer knowing where he was, and seeing no way out of the hell he was in.

Then, on almost the last day of term, when he had gone into college to pick up his things, the porter leaned out and said, 'Mail for you, Mr Byrne.'

It was a postcard, and Matt recognized the words.

'Father Murphy will hear confession . . .'

On the following afternoon he arrived at the church expecting to see a beggar at the door. He was not, and Matt entered the church and took a seat in the last row of pews. He sat for a long time staring at the stained-glass window at the far end over the altar, and being here in the dim light, with the little red glow of the host over the altar, the smell of stale incense, the confession booths dimly visible between the columns, it all reminded him of Garrett's words: 'You've been too much in the hands of the priests.' Was that true? And if so, in what way? In what way were the church's teachings mistaken? About Grace? About purity? Grace was certainly not pure – but he hadn't minded that on Howth Head. In fact it had come as a wonderful revelation. He had never known anything like it. But had it been a snare, a trap? How? He had immediately asked her to marry him and she had consented. Surely that redeemed her – and him.

He felt a movement beside him and glancing round saw Hanlon, on this occasion dressed as Hanlon.

'All well, Matt?'

'Well enough,' Matt said briefly.

'There's been developments,' Hanlon said significantly. Matt waited for him to go on. 'The new Viceroy – no doubt you've heard?'

Matt nodded.

'The Lord Elphin – from your own part of the country at one time.'

'I know.'

'Yes. And now, installed in the Viceregal Lodge in all his splendour.'

'I've seen him. A feeble specimen.'

'Oh, you've seen him?' Hanlon was genuinely surprised.

'At the RDS.'

'Ah. To be sure, Matt, you move in higher circles. That's good. Very good.'

Matt sat, half listening, and wondering when Hanlon would get to the point.

Hanlon glanced round the empty church, leaned in and lowered his voice. 'The Directory have come up with a plan, Matt. The time for action has come. And they feel that you're the man for the job. Besides Sam had his doubts about you – you remember? Said you had to prove yourself. Well, now's your chance. Can you guess what that action might be?'

Matt waited.

'You're a bold young man,' Hanlon went on in a low voice, leaning in even closer. 'There's not many things you're afraid of,

I dare say. What would you do for Ireland, Matt?' He paused. 'Would you kill a man?'

Matt thought only for a moment.

'I would,' he said in a low voice.

'I thought it!' Hanlon hissed exultantly in Matt's ear. 'I told the lads, I told Sam, Matt's our man! Matt, the Vindicators have decided to execute the new Viceroy. And you're the man to do it — you can get nearer to him than any of us.'

In a flash Matt saw a way out of the stultification, the frustration, the confusion. One clean act, one clean break! And everything would be changed for ever.

'One of our men at the castle got hold of the guest list for the Viceroy's ball, and he can arrange to have your name added. There's hundreds of guests, it's easy enough to add one. Think of it, Matt, at the Viceroy's ball! Jesus, the effect. It'd be talked of for a hundred years!' He leaned in again. 'You see, Matt, I'll let you into a secret. Our friends in America have been nagging us, they think we've gone to sleep. It's kind of embarrassing, not having anything to report, you see. But with something like this, they'll have to sit up and take notice, won't they?'

'I'll do it,' Matt said doggedly. 'You make the arrangements.'

He got up and walked out of the church without looking round. Thank God he had found a purpose. But his thoughts immediately reverted to Grace. Later that day he stood on the opposite side of the road to her house. The blinds were down. And when a servant girl emerged up the area steps, he darted across and asked about the blinds.

'The family's gone down into the country' was all the reply he got, or needed.

Some weeks later, he was at the breakfast table alone with his aunt. As they ate, she was engrossed in a letter.

'What's it about?'

Bríd looked up from her letter. 'It's Uncle Patsy . . .'

'What does he say?'

'No, the letter is from O'Flaherty.' She passed it across. 'Patsy has been taken ill.'

Matt quickly scanned the few lines. 'The doctor's been to see him—'

'I must go down,' Bríd said quickly.

'I'll come too.'

That afternoon they were on a train together. Garrett and the children remained behind; they would be down in a few weeks anyway for their summer holidays, and hoped that by that time Patsy might well be recovered.

However, from the moment Bríd saw him, she realized this was not likely. Patsy was clearly on his deathbed.

'Uncle Patsy –' she sat on a bedside chair pulling at her gloves – 'It's terrible to see you like this, so low. I had no idea. Why didn't you let us know before? I'd have come down.'

He picked at the coverlet, looking up with a benign, resigned manner. 'I didn't like to trouble ye, Bríd,' he murmured, barely audible.

'Trouble? What trouble? You know I'd have come like a shot.'

'I know ye would.'

'Oh dear, this is terrible,' she repeated and then rallying, 'Well, now that we are here, we can look after you.'

'Ye needn't worry, Bríd. There's Mr O'Flaherty and Mrs Milton have been caring for me like one of their own.'

'I'm sure.'

Bríd glanced up and Patsy now noticed Matt. He smiled, a small painful smile. Matt was staring down at him, shocked to see how Patsy had seemed to shrink, to retreat somehow into himself, and into the bed. It was immediately clear that he was not destined to rise again. For the first time in his life Matt knew himself to be in the presence of death. 'We'll take it in turns to sit by you, Uncle Patsy,' he said at last. And Patsy nodded slightly and murmured 'That'd be nice', but with an air almost of indifference, as if he were past all help and they and perhaps everyone had become an irrelevance. 'Mrs Milton—'

'Yes?' Bríd said quickly.

'Mrs Milton takes good care of me, Bríd. Ye've no need to trouble yourself.'

She writhed her fingers together. 'It's no trouble, God knows. But why didn't you let us know sooner?'

That evening Bríd sat by him, and later Matt took over. According to O'Flaherty, the doctor said it was a matter of days only, just a matter of waiting. There was nothing that one could identify, only a general wearing out, a slowing down, and a growing indifference to life itself.

The next few days were warm; bright summer days, when the window stood open and the curtains scarcely moved in the faint breeze. Mornings, afternoons, whole days when there was no sound but the droning of a fly, the distant lowing of a cow, or an occasional clash of saucepans from the kitchens. As Bríd sat at Patsy's bedside she was reminded of one summer in London, when she'd had rooms with Mrs Walters in Buckingham Street, and the Maestro had lain in bed as she nursed him back to health – but here she stopped. There was to be no nursing Patsy back to life. Her only role was to ease his passing as best she might.

The priest called, she left them alone together, and afterwards there was a whispered conversation outside the door. The priest shook his head gravely and spoke of the consolations of his faith. Bríd had never remembered Patsy as a particularly devout man but he had known Father Geoghegan ever since she had been a girl and no doubt they understood each other well.

''Twill be only a short time in purgatory.' He patted her hand as he took his leave.

That evening, while Bríd sat with Patsy, Matt strolled down the *bohreen*. When he reached the village he found the Higgins cottage still standing empty, the thatch half gone, the little windows thick with dust, the paint on the door peeling.

'There's no one there, sir,' said a woman's voice, and he turned. A peasant woman, her shawl round her shoulders, and holding a jug, had been passing. 'That house has been empty these three years.'

'I remember. Sean Higgins and his family had it, that were thrown out by the master and went to America. Did you hear what became of them?'

'Why shouldn't we? His daughter Mary writes to Father Geoghegan and he reads it out on Sunday. She's married now herself and has a little boy. And her brother Mick is in the polis. She says Sean died, though. He could never get used to Americky, she says, and missed the old place.'

Matt said nothing, looking over the cottage and remembering Mary his first love. For a moment he had wanted to go with them to America. And if he had, he would have been married to Mary now and her son would be his son too. And I never would have met Grace, and never insulted her. Then he thought, But if I had married Mary, would I have said something stupid and insulted her too? How could I trust myself ever again?

'Thank you,' he said and the woman went on her way. He couldn't remember seeing her in the village before but he didn't come down so much as he used to. He was losing touch. He walked across to the presbytery and knocked.

When the housekeeper answered, he apologized for calling so late and wondered whether Father Geoghegan might be at home.

'Wait here,' she said, and a moment later he was shown into a little parlour.

'Sorry to intrude on you so late in the evening, Father, but I was told you had heard from the Higgins family and wondered if I might be permitted to see their letters?'

'Matt, isn't it? We haven't seen you in a while.' He hauled himself from an armchair, and shook Matt by the hand. 'My, but you've grown into a fine young man, a handsome young man. Sit down, and take a glass of sherry.'

In a moment he had produced a sheaf of letters and as Matt sipped at his sherry he could see there was too much here to read at once. In the end he asked whether he might be allowed to take them away for a day or so.

That night alone in his room he started to read Mary's letters. She hadn't wanted to write to him, yet she had kept up a correspondence with the rest of the village. Mary had known something he did not and had been too tactful to say it.

Her handwriting was neat and even, though devoid of personality, a hand trained in the National School, written along ruled lines.

'. . . Eventually we came to Boston. Which is a very big harbour, and so many ships and from every corner of the globe, from Africa, and China too, and when we finally came near the quayside we couldn't even moor as there was no room. We had to make fast against another ship and make our way over that ship to get on land. It was a most strange experience to stand on dry land after two weeks at sea, you have no idea, the ground seemed to rock beneath our feet at first. Poor Father had been very unwell on the ship and had lain most of the time and never rose from his berth but we are hopeful that now we have arrived he will recover.

'Well, you can imagine we had no idea what to do or where to go. But then this man came up to us, with a paper in his hand and asked were we from Cork on the *Alberta*? And when we said yes he led us away along the quayside, which was so crowded we could hardly squeeze through, and then into a side street, still very crowded, and with street cars on rails it was all very bewildering, until we came to a house. It was called the Ancient Order of Hibernians, and he said they were there to help families that had just come from Ireland. We were so relieved that we all burst into tears! . . .'

Matt sat and read into the small hours, and when at last he snuffed out the candle and lay in the darkness, the myriad images which Mary had conjured up in her letters went through his mind.

During the days that followed, the last few days of Patsy's life, Matt sat with him and read the letters aloud.

'And you that was sweet on her once, weren't ye, Matt?' Patsy said after a long pause.

Matt did not answer, and Patsy murmured, after another long pause, 'Ah well, 'tis no matter, with her gone to Americky and married over there.'

'Yes,' Matt muttered.

''Tis all one,' Patsy sighed.

Inevitably, as it seemed to Bríd, there was one afternoon when Patsy seemed troubled, and looking up at her seemed to question her.

'Did ye ever tell him, Bríd?'

'Tell?' Nervously, she affected not to understand.

'Tell Matt.'

She hesitated. 'It never seemed the right moment, Uncle Patsy. But I am going to tell him,' she added nervously.

'Ye must tell him,' he murmured.

'I know,' she said desperately.

'He's a good lad but he doesn't know where he's going – or who he is. He was always on to me about it – askin' did I know anything of his parents.'

It suddenly crossed her mind that Patsy himself might say something. She panicked. 'It's quite all right Patsy, you mustn't worry yourself about such things. I'll tell him when the time is right.'

But the troubled look on his face disturbed her and later when Matt took over she hovered outside the door trying to hear what they were saying to each other. The door, however, was too thick and she in the end stole away downstairs, full of trepidation. For the next two days she lived on a knife-edge, frightened for what Patsy might say.

Then, one morning, Matt called down,

'Aunt! I think you'd better come! And tell Mrs Milton too!'

As she raced up the stairs and into the room, Matt was half on the edge of the bed, holding Patsy in his arms, who was heaving short half breaths, his face contorted, his eyes wandering about the room, not seeming to see anything, and then, just as she entered the room, she saw the life go out of his eyes, which remained open but the body slumped back in Matt's arms and it was all over.

Matt laid him gently back on the pillow.

'He's gone,' he said in a tone almost of relief. And a moment later to his own surprise burst into tears.

'We were just talking –' Matt could scarcely speak – 'just chatting and he suddenly seemed to start up, just like that, and I thought he was going to do something or say something. That's when you came into the room, Aunt, and I took hold of him to help him, but then he just seemed to . . . he just went,' he ended lamely, the tears running down his cheeks.

Brίd clung to Matt and they stood together looking down at Patsy. Then she reached forward and closed his eyes.

'Poor Uncle Patsy,' Matt murmured, staring at the lifeless body. 'He's gone. He's just gone,' he repeated and wiped a hand across his eyes. 'He was very good to me.'

'He was very good to me,' she echoed.

'I could tell him anything, Aunt. He was my father – truly. He was my father,' he repeated.

She nodded her head, still clinging to Matt her arms about his waist, his arm about her shoulders.

'Did he say anything – before he died?' she murmured.

'We were talking about Nora, and things we used to do in the old house when I was little.'

In the midst of her distress Bríd found time to feel relieved that after all Patsy had said nothing about her and Matt.

That evening Garrett and the children arrived and the day but one after attended Patsy's body to the graveyard and saw him buried with Nora. There was a wake, but in the august surroundings of Ballyglin House it was a subdued affair. Matt remembered the wake for Aunt Nora years ago – another matter.

Twenty-one

On the day after the funeral Bríd was in Patsy's room tidying things. Matt was drawn in too and together they pulled out his few suits of clothes and one or two old things: his pipes, a bit of spare cash.

'We never had much when I was a girl,' Bríd murmured, turning over these coins. 'It doesn't seem much does it, at the end of a life, some old clothes, a pair of spectacles, a pipe or two, a few coins.'

As she was talking Matt had turned to a chest of drawers and opened one at random. Here he found a metal box, dented, scratched, paint chipped off here and there. He placed it on the top of the chest of drawers and opened it. There were a few papers, a couple of letters and a medal. He took this out and examined it.

'The Connaught Rangers,' he murmured in surprise. 'Did you know about this?'

'Patsy in the army?' Matt passed it to her and she turned it over in her hands. 'He never mentioned it. I wonder why he never said anything.'

But while she was examining the medal, Matt had taken out two letters.

'That's funny.'

She looked up.

'They're addressed to Aunt Nora.' He turned them over. 'Unopened too.' The letters were date stamped. 'They must have arrived after she died,' he said at last. 'But why did Patsy never open them?'

'Let me see,' she said sharply.

Surprised at her tone, he passed them across and Bríd examined them for a moment.

'Probably don't mean anything,' she muttered and stuffed them in a pocket.

'Aren't you going to open them?'

'What?' She looked up in surprise.

'Aunt,' he repeated. 'Aren't you going to open them?'

'I told you, I expect they were just bills. They're not important now anyway. Patsy won't need them where he's gone.'

'Bills? They were postmarked Dublin. Who did Nora know in Dublin?'

'Heaven knows.' Bríd's voice was shaky.

By this time Matt was thoroughly alert. 'Aunt, let me see the letters.'

She shrugged and would have turned away but Matt stood before her, suddenly bigger and stronger than she. 'Aunt, you're hiding something. What is it?' She couldn't meet his eye. 'Aunt,' he repeated gravely, as if addressing a child. 'Let me see the letters.'

There was something in him at this moment that she could not oppose; she pulled them from her pocket, thrust them into his hand and with a half sob sat on the edge of the bed, pressing a handkerchief to her nose. Matt remained standing in the middle of the room, clutching the letters and staring down at his aunt in mystification.

'What on earth is the matter? Aunt, do you know what is in these letters?'

She nodded, her face hidden in her handkerchief.

'Well, what is the mystery? Why did you try to hide them?' She did not reply.

After a moment Matt examined the letters again and ripped open the earlier of the two.

It was from a firm of solicitors.

> Dear Mrs Byrne,
> Further to your letter of November 28th last, I enclose a statement from Handley's bank. Since the fund is so large now we venture to enquire whether you have any instructions regarding investments, or whether you are content to leave the matter in Mr Archer's hands.
> I remain in the meantime,
> My dear Madam,
> Your very obedient servant, etc

Together with this note was a bank statement. Matt drew a sharp breath as he saw the amount at the bottom of the page.

He opened the second dated six weeks after the first.

> Dear Mrs Byrne,
> We do not appear to have received a reply to our letter of February 3rd last. Miss Flynn has written to us enclosing a letter addressed to yourself but, as you know, the terms of the agreement preclude any contact between you. We await your instructions regarding this matter and beg to remain in the meantime,
> My dear Madam,
> Your very obedient servant, etc

These letters begged so many questions that Matt scarcely knew where to begin. He looked again at the bank statement. This was a very large sum of money. It appeared too that the money was coming from a Miss Flynn in London. Far more important than this, however, was the mention of an agreement. For long silent seconds he stood staring first at one letter, then at the other. Bríd remained on the edge of the bed, sobbing softly into her handkerchief.

At last he looked up. 'Aunt, what *is* the matter?' He crossed to her. 'Why are you crying?'

She did not reply, only shook her head slightly.

'And what is this.' He held out one of the letters. 'Miss Flynn – that was you, wasn't it?' She nodded. 'According to this you were paying £30 a month into an account in Dublin for Nora.' Still stunned by these revelations, and her inexplicable response, at last he knelt by her. 'Aunt – that's a lot of money.'

She nodded without looking up. Matt struggled to make sense of it.

'That's very generous,' he repeated at last, still trying to make sense of it. 'Very generous. You were successful in London – and you wanted to help Nora and Patsy when things were tight at home? But why does it say that any contact was precluded by the agreement? What was this agreement?'

He remembered the last conversation he had witnessed between Nora and Bríd, the angry exchange in the rain – but it didn't make sense. If Bríd had sent so much money, why was Nora so hostile? He remembered suddenly all the moments they had been together – Nora's hostility, Bríd pleading with her. It made no sense.

The silence seemed to drag out and drag out. At last under the force of his attention she turned to face him. 'Can't you guess?' she whispered, her face wet with tears.

For a moment they were staring eye to eye, then she buried her face in her hands. 'Oh God, this is a moment I have dreaded. Dreaded! Though I knew it would come in the end. Oh dear.'

She reached for his arm and gripped him strongly, then looking up she drew a long agonizing breath.

'You often asked me about your mother and I was always unable – or afraid – to tell the truth—'

'*My mother?*'

He pulled instinctively back, staring at her and for another silent moment they stared one another in the eyes. 'You mean . . .'

She nodded, a shy smile now creeping into her face and then seeing the delighted smile which had broken out on his own face opened her arms and in a frenzy of joy they embraced.

'Mother!' he exclaimed. 'Of course! You were always my mother – always! But why did you never say?'

'Where shall I begin? It all seems so long ago now. Another world. If I look back on myself at your age – Matt do you realize, by the time I was twenty-one I was already a well-known actress in London. I had my name up outside the theatre.' She shook her head. 'I had to grow up fast, you have no idea. Very fast. Sometimes I look at you and you seem still a child. No – forgive me, I didn't mean that – you are a fine young man – but compared with me – I was already very worldly – and that's not a boast, honestly.' She looked down. 'They talk about the purity of Irish womanhood. Believe me, I wasn't very pure, and yet I did everything for the best! I'm sorry, I am rambling. Honestly I don't know where to start. Well, there was a man, of course. I was seventeen. What did I know of the world? Yet I wanted to know! Matt, I had a hunger to see the world. I wanted to go to London above all, and this man – well, he took me there. And when we were there –' she paused, and hung her head – 'it wasn't his fault—'

'What wasn't his fault?' Matt reached forward for her hand. Nothing made any sense so far.

'I had conceived a child – you! And we should have been married but then his father –' Bríd wiped away a tear – 'that scoundrel, I will never forgive him – he's dead now, God forgive me – he tore this man away – wouldn't let us marry—'

The tears were flowing more freely now. Again Matt interrupted her. 'Please don't go on, if it's too painful.'

She shook her head, wiping her eyes, and looking up for a moment, drew a gigantic sigh. 'No, I must, it's only fair to you. So this man – your father – was forced to go away, and went abroad, and I was left alone in London. I had nothing and I was expecting a child – you. So a very kind priest got me into the Convent of the Good Shepherd in Fulham – it's a place in London – and I had my baby – you, Matt! But then – you see, I had no money. Matt, I had nothing! And I had run away from the village and couldn't go back, so,' she hesitated, 'I wrote to Aunt Nora—'

'Aunt Nora!'

Bríd nodded. 'She was really my aunt, Matt. My mother was Uncle Patsy's sister. We met in Dublin and I asked her to care for you just until I could earn some money.'

'Earn some money? How?'

'As a singer in a pub at first and then on the stage. But Aunt Nora said she would care for you on one condition only – that I must hand you over and never see you again or return to the village.'

Again she broke down. Matt waited.

'What could I do? Everything she said was true. I was eighteen and had nothing, Matt, and Nora could give you a safe home and proper care. I had no choice.'

'So you—'

Bríd nodded. 'I handed you over and promised never to come back. I could send money, that was all.'

'And that was the agreement?'

She nodded.

'And Garrett, he's not my father, is he?'

She shook her head. 'I had known him in the village and he had asked me to marry him, but I refused. Then we met later in

America and married there. You see, I had promised never to return but I thought if I were married to Garrett I could—'

She faltered.

'You mean you broke your promise to Nora?'

She nodded. 'I wanted to see you so badly.'

Matt reached for her hand and there was silence. She was staring down and he watched her, filled only with a huge pity and love. What were his sufferings compared with this?

There remained one question unanswered and Matt trembled as he finally summoned the courage to put it. She looked up at him shyly and for a long moment there was silence as they stared into each other's eyes. He knew she already understood.

'My father?' he enquired, almost in a whisper.

There was fear in her eyes and she tried to draw back but he held on to her hand. 'It really doesn't matter, Matt. It was a very long time ago. He went away and I've never seen him since,' she went on hurriedly.

'It doesn't matter?' He wouldn't let her go. 'But surely it does matter. It matters very much! You must understand that? Mother, I have the right to know!'

'No!' she burst out hurriedly and would have withdrawn her hand, but he still held it firmly. 'It doesn't matter! Really, it was such a long time ago. He's nothing to me – or to you.'

Matt remained calm. 'Mother,' he said quietly, 'You must tell me. You owe it to me.'

'No Matt! Please let me go!'

'I don't understand why you can't tell me.'

'I will tell you – one day. You see, he doesn't know.'

Matt was stopped by this and released her hand. 'Doesn't know about me?'

She nodded.

'But how? Surely if you—'

'It all happened so quickly. I had only just found out that I was expecting you when his father came and took him away. I never told him.'

'But why?'

She shook her head. 'I don't know.' She was thinking hard. 'I suppose, I thought since he was deserting me, leaving me with nothing, I didn't see why I should.'

'But if you had told him he might not have left you. He might have married you if he knew you were going to bear his child?'

'I wasn't going to use you to blackmail him!' she flashed out. 'If he didn't want me for myself so be it!' There was suddenly a look of scorn and pride in her eyes.

He was slightly rocked by this and there was another long silence as he struggled to put it all together.

'And you never thought to tell him after I was born?'

She shook her head. 'He's nothing to you or me, Matt,' she said at last in a low voice.

There was another long pause but still Matt said quietly, 'I have to know.'

She hunted round for an answer, and at last said, 'Perhaps one day . . .'

He wouldn't press her any further; he could see she was quite drained by what she had told him and he too felt exhausted. She wouldn't tell him, but he knew that sooner or later she must tell him. He wouldn't let her rest until he had the truth out of her.

He did not sleep well that night, running his mother's story over and over in his mind. Where was the right in it? Bríd appeared to have acted in the best interest of the baby – himself. Yet he had been brought up in the belief that his mother was dead, whereas all the time she was walking about the earth and thinking of him. He had longed for his mother and she had longed for her son. Yet even when she had found him again she couldn't bring herself to tell him who she was. Why?

Because he was illegitimate. She must have thought that as an orphan he could more easily carry his head high than as a bastard. Matt couldn't decide what he did think. He was still recovering from the shock of that revelation. No doubt eventually he would be able to think more clearly. But not yet.

Then as always his thoughts reverted to Grace. What would she have said when she had heard the truth? But even before he thought this thought, another came to him. His own mother had born a fatherless child and she said herself she hadn't been very pure. It was the very accusation he had thrown at Grace. Now, after hearing Bríd's story, how did it reflect on Grace? The answer was, what Garrett had already said: Matt had been very cruel.

He had sympathized with his mother; why had he been so harsh and unforgiving with Grace?

Bríd did not sleep well that night either, though it had been a tremendous relief to be able to unburden herself. At last the truth was out and henceforth they could be what they truly were to one another – mother and son. She felt there was so much to catch up on; now she need no longer hide behind the impersonal mask of an 'aunt': now she could wholeheartedly be to him what she had always longed to be – a mother – and she was ready to unload the full weight of her love on to his young shoulders.

Yet there was the question of his father. Matt was going to want to know him and he would pester her until she told him the full story. But what about Harry? This was almost more difficult. What would he say to a son? As she turned these things over in her mind she decided she must see Harry again and try to decide what – and how much – to tell him. She knew nothing of Harry's domestic arrangements. He might well have a family of his own already, though there did not appear to be any wife at his side that afternoon they met at the RDS.

Matt's remorse was increased a thousand fold two days later when a letter arrived forwarded from Dublin. The moment he saw the Sligo postmark his heart almost stopped. He thrust the letter into his pocket and didn't get a chance to open it until he was in his room.

I shouldn't be writing this to you (it began bluntly, without any Dear Matt) but I will anyway. You behaved unspeakably to me and I don't think I could ever bear to see you again, but thinking it over I believe you are entitled to an explanation of what you saw. Maybe it looked worse than it really was. Not that that is any excuse for your conduct which was inexcusable.

All right, here goes. The man you saw me laughing so uproariously with is called Bobby Shaunessy. I had sent him the invitation after your parents (or whatever they are) asked us to invite anyone we wanted. I thought of him, among others, though I hadn't seen him since Paris.

So why was I so pleased to see him?

Bobby had a room over mine in the Rue du Bac. He was studying at the Sorbonne. Well, one winter two years ago I became ill; it started as flu then seemed to get worse. I suppose I was a bit run down and depressed over the business with Val, and hadn't been eating properly and so on, but the result was I got a really bad attack of flu and was utterly prostrate for several weeks, couldn't get out of bed. Bobby had the room above me and we already knew each other slightly. Well, during this time it was Bobby who looked after me. My own mother couldn't have done more. He was completely selfless and I will be eternally grateful to him for what he did. And in case you're thinking he had some other motive, I might as well tell you, Bobby is not made that way. I mean he's not interested in women the way you are. So all your fears were quite groundless. We've been very close ever since and we write regularly, though as I said I hadn't seen him since Paris. As for the note I scribbled down, it was simply the address of a mutual friend I hadn't seen since Paris.

Matt, how could you bring yourself to call me what you did? Did you imagine, after what happened on Howth Head, that I could even think about another man? What we did together that day was the most important thing that ever happened to me. You may think, because I laugh at you or tease you, that I don't take you seriously, that I am being flippant. I was never more serious in my life. I was ready to give you everything – in fact I had given you everything. I pledged myself to you that day; as far as I was concerned, we were already married. All the rest is just ceremonies for the benefit of parents and relatives. And you weren't man enough or adult enough to accept what I gave you in the same spirit.

Ah well, what's done is done. Maybe all men are immature – though I don't believe that. I just hope that you understand what you did and are sorry. And perhaps you will be more gracious with another woman.

Grace Langley

Twenty-two

Matt was on a train heading for Sligo. There was no point thinking about it; he just had to go. If she were to disappear to Italy again before he had a chance to beg her forgiveness, his life would have no meaning. He had not packed anything, just stuffed some money into a pocket, gone to the station, and bought a ticket – and not even a return ticket. He had no idea what to expect but he did not intend to return without doing everything in his power to bring Grace round. He didn't care what it took for he had never been more sure of anything than that Grace and he were destined to be together. The more he thought the more convinced he was. It was written in the stars.

It was late on a summer's afternoon when the train drew into Sligo town and the station was deserted. He came out of the station to where a jarvey, in a caped overcoat and pot-hat, was half asleep in the sunlight on an old sidecar, and threw himself on board.

'Ardnashiel.'

The jarvey roused himself, looked about in surprise that he actually had a fare, and gee'd the horse into motion.

'And as fast as you like.'

There seemed little chance of that, from the skinny old nag between the shafts who seemed content to amble along the dusty road out of the town.

'Damn you,' Matt nudged him fifteen minutes later, 'can't you make her go any faster?'

'Faster, is it?' said the jarvey coolly, 'if I was to make that horse –' he gestured to her with his whip – 'to go faster, sure the car would shake itself to pieces. 'Tis the devil of a road. Though, if ye'd care to make it three and six,' he added after a moment, 'I'd take the risk.'

'I'll make it five shillings, if you'll only give her a prod!'

'Done! And spoken like a gentleman!' The jarvey duly urged on the horse and she did actually improve her speed for a few minutes before lapsing back into her previous leisurely amble.

'Confound the beast!' Matt was beside himself. 'She'll fall asleep if she goes any slower!'

''Tis the time of day,' the jarvey confided. 'She's never at her best in the afternoon.'

Matt threw himself back, and stared away out to sea, as they ambled along the coast road, and finally after what now seemed to him half a century arrived at the gates of the demesne.

'Put me down here.'

He leaped lightly to the ground and handed the jarvey his fare.

'Will I wait for yer honour?'

'No.'

'God bless yer honour.' The jarvey turned his car and headed back into town while Matt stood for a moment at the gates, alone in the bright and silent afternoon. Far away, barely discernible, the sea could be heard, falling in lazy rollers along the strand as Matt set forward down the lane through the woods, his head full of conflicting thoughts. He had no clear idea of what he was going to say but was possessed only by a rooted determination not to leave until he had effected a reconciliation, let it take what it might.

The house appeared before him, silent in the sunlight, and Matt wondered whether the family might even be at home. But as he drew nearer he noticed several windows open and curtains flapping idly in the breeze.

Then he was standing at the door and his heart was beating painfully as he finally raised his hand to the old bronze knocker and gave it a firm double knock.

There was a long silence while he could hear only his own heart beating until at last footsteps sounded, the door was opened and a man appeared. Matt remembered him as the butler. They looked at one another.

'I'd like to speak to Miss Langley.'

The butler came forward a step and looked out, clearly surprised to see no vehicle or companions. Matt stood dishevelled and alone, raw and desperate. The butler took a moment to answer and obviously didn't remember Matt from his visits. This was clearly a gentleman but . . .

'If you would step inside, sir, I will enquire whether she is at home,' he said with all the dignity at his disposal, as if Matt had come for a fifteen-minute morning call.

Matt entered the hall, and stood looking about him at the familiar furniture – the pair of chairs where he and Grace had sat in the darkness and she had told him the story of Valentin – a large oriental vase on a side table, a pair of portraits facing each other.

Then a door opened abruptly and Fred appeared. He crossed quickly to Matt, wrenched the front door open and, without a word, took Matt by the arm. He would have thrown him bodily from the house, if Matt had not resisted.

'I only want to speak to her—'

'I told you,' Fred said in a huge, suppressed, anger, 'never to come near us again. Now get out.'

Matt wrestled himself free. 'I will speak to her, if only for a minute!'

'She doesn't want to see, or hear from, or about you. Ever. Get that into your head and leave this house.'

Again Matt shook himself free and was about to speak when Fred went on quickly, 'If you don't leave the house this instant I will ring for help and you will be thrown out.'

'Fred, she must hear me!' Matt cried out, 'she must!'

But Fred had turned and shouted, 'Mick! Fetch Liam and Sean! There's an intruder!' He turned and seized Matt again by the arm, and was about to force him through the door, when Matt broke free and walked out.

'Fred, I beg you! Just tell her I'm here! Let her decide!'

'She has decided, and so have I! Clear off and never bother us again!' he shouted at the top of his voice as two men now appeared in the hall behind him.

Matt and Fred now stared at each other for a second, both breathing heavily, until Fred slammed the door in Matt's face.

Matt stood, his mind empty, staring at the door. He drew back a few paces and scanned the front of the house. She was in there somewhere, he knew it.

'Grace!' he shouted up at the empty windows. Silence. 'Grace!' again. He waited, then in a desperate cry, 'Grace!' a third time. The curtains flapped, and in the silence somewhere far away the sea could be heard turning in those long lazy rollers along the strand. He turned along the front of the house to the corner. The garden lay serene in the afternoon sunshine. 'Grace!' he shouted. At this moment the front door opened again and Fred reappeared. 'If you don't take yourself off, I'll have the men chuck you out. I've warned you.' He disappeared inside with a slam of the door.

Matt stood for a long time, unwilling to give up, until at last, wiping his eyes, he turned slowly, and made his way back towards where the track wound through the woods. And it was as he made his way through the woods that he found Grace in his path. She was in the old riding skirt she had worn when they first met, and a blouse open at the neck. She wore no hat and there was something tired and careless about her, her hair put up anyhow. She did not look well.

'Don't come too near.'

He was brought up short, and they stood facing each other as Matt searched her face.

'What have you come for, Matt?'

'You know why—'

'I think there must be something wrong with me,' she interrupted in a low voice. 'I seem destined to be rejected and humiliated by men. First Val – and then you.'

'No!'

'When we first met, you and I,' she continued, ignoring him, 'I thought that all the hurt I had suffered from Val was going to be put right by you. You would heal my wounds and make me whole again.'

'I will! I will heal your wounds! Only let me!'

'I thought I knew you,' she went on in this low voice, drained of feeling. 'That you were superior to other men, that you were going to distinguish yourself in life, that you had ideals and would work for a noble cause, that it would be a privilege to be by your side. And then suddenly – in one moment – you were someone else, a boor, stupid and ignorant – a peasant. I will never forget that moment, Matt, not as long as I live. I was in love with you. I loved your voice, the way you turned your head, I loved everything about you. I had made up my mind, chosen you for my own. And when I had done that, Matt, I was ready to give you everything. I did give you everything.' She swallowed, as if her control was slipping. 'And you threw it in my face with an insult I can neither forget nor forgive.'

There was no answer to this.

'Goodbye, Matt.' She walked past him back down the track towards the house.

He started after her

'Grace. Please! Just give me a chance. We can make it whole again. Believe me! I will dedicate my life to making it whole again.'

But she ignored him.

'Grace!'

At last he stopped and watched her as she disappeared round the bend in the track.

It took him two hours to walk back into Sligo town and by that time it was nearly seven o'clock. There were no trains for Boyle until the night mail at eleven. He lay on a bench, cradling his head on his arm, seeing nothing, only hearing her words ringing in his mind, 'Goodbye Matt, goodbye Matt, goodbye Matt . . .'

He still had not eaten when the mail left at eleven, and it was after midnight when he got off the train at Boyle. It was an hour's walk to Ballyglin, and nearly an hour after that to Ballyglin House, so it was at some godforsaken hour of the night that footsore and very hungry he made his way into the stables and threw himself down on a pile of hay in the barn beside them.

His sleep was disturbed by Liam at six, and he opened his eyes blearily, very sore and stiff, as Liam prodded him with his boot.

'Holy Jesus, Mister Matt! What—'

Matt struggled painfully to his feet. 'I got here late last night and didn't want to wake you,' he said humbly.

'Jesus! Mister Matt –' Liam stood back – 'look at the state of ye! Sleepin' in the stable! Why ever didn't ye ring the bell?'

Again Matt only shrugged. 'Is the family awake?'

'Mr Doyle is, and takin' his mornin' tea this minute. You'll find him in the kitchen. But get yourself inside – have a wash and change your clothes, man.'

Without saying anything Matt crossed the stable yard and made his way across to the kitchen door. Here the household was well awake and there was the rattling of frying pans and women's voices. He walked in and found Garrett at the great table in the centre of the kitchen, as Liam had said, sipping a cup of tea. Matt stopped as Garrett looked up at him.

'Matt? What brings you here at this time of day?'

Matt turned to the cook. 'Mrs Milton, could I beg a cup of tea off you?'

He sat exhausted in a chair opposite Garrett. After a moment, gesturing idly, he went on, 'I was with a friend up in Sligo, and only caught the last train to Boyle . . .'

Garrett was never the man to be fobbed off.

'A friend up in Sligo,' he repeated slowly. 'You mean you went to see Grace?'

Matt nodded.

'You had a letter from her didn't you?'

Matt nodded again.

'Well, that's something. What did she say?'

'Goodbye.' Matt stared down at the table. 'She never wants to see me again.'

'Hmm.' Garrett sipped his tea. At that moment Mrs Milton placed a cup in front of Matt.

'Mrs Milton,' Garrett looked up mildly, 'you'd better give the lad his breakfast. He looks done in.'

Garrett watched as Matt tucked into a plate of rashers and eggs. Large hunks of brown bread and butter sat in a side plate. 'Well,' he said at last, 'you did the right thing, whatever she said.'

'Did I?'

'At least she knows how you feel about her. Just give her time. There is no one else, is there?'

'I don't think so.'

'Well,' Garrett repeated. 'Give her time. She'll come round.'

Matt looked up.

'Just don't give up, Matt. That's all the advice I can offer.'

But afterwards, thinking over the scene with Grace, Matt could see no hope. Grace was going to Italy; when would he ever see her again? She was bound to meet people – people of her own sort, he thought bitterly, Protestants with English accents, gentry who had never been brought up in a small farmer's cabin, who had never seen the inside of a cabin except to visit it on some errand of charity!

A terrible bitterness swamped through him; he felt what he had felt before – that he was good for nothing, except for some wild deed – Grace had been right about that – some act of destruction, some breaking out, for good or ill.

During the remainder of the summer Matt tried to forget his own troubles in the noise and activity of a family with small children. Garrett wanted to teach Stephen to ride, and one day they went to the horse fair at Ballinasloe. Rachel, who was five, hung on to Matt's hand, which always gave him a thrill of paternal tenderness; he loved her passionately, protectively, and often thought, what if she were my daughter? What if I had a daughter? And then his thoughts turned again to Grace, and the whole weary cycle revolved again in his memory. They could have been married, they would have had children of their own, he would have had a son and a daughter . . .

Looking down at her, he thought too, Rachel loves me; it is my responsibility to behave well for her sake, not to disappoint her, not to let her down. What if she knew what I had said to Grace? The thought made him go quite cold. But then Garrett would appear and Rachel would detach herself from Matt's hand and run screaming, 'Papa!' and be swept into his arms . . .

Bríd's worry about Matt was like a rock in her middle, weighing her down. In the past she loved it when the family came down to the country for the summer holidays but now all she could think of was the sight of Matt looking so unhappy. It made her ill to watch him. She knew it was all a consequence of the terrible misunderstanding at the party (she insisted to herself that it was only a misunderstanding) and she knew too that Matt had disappeared off to Sligo to see Grace. And now he was here looking like his own ghost. Clearly things had not worked out well. The worst of it was that she couldn't discuss it with him. Garrett knew more than she did; he had boldly broached the subject, told Matt frankly what he thought. Bríd knew that if she tried to open the discussion, Matt would close up, and most likely walk away. The most she could do was to express her sympathy by little signs, sympathetic gestures, touching him, smiling, giving him little gifts; reassuring him that she was on his side, come what may. What was worst of all was that, at the very moment they had discovered each other as mother and son, this had erupted and seemed to have forced them apart. Matt walked alone and there seemed no way at the moment whereby she could approach him.

The big matter constantly haunted her. Should she tell Harry first? Or Matt? Should she tell them before they met, or let them find out face to face? Which of them would be best able to take the news? Harry she thought, simply because it would not come as a complete shock to him and also because he was older. With Matt, on the other hand, as she turned it over in her mind it seemed that the delighted way he had taken the news that she was his mother, which had so surprised her, was an augury for the good. After all, to be told that the Viceroy was your father could be no bad thing; it was likely too that Harry would want to do something for his son – in due course after he had digested the news. On the whole, she felt the outlook was bright and, so long as it was handled with tact and diplomacy, could work out very satisfactorily for everybody.

Eventually, as the first hint of autumn was in the air, as the mornings began to have that crisp intimation of the revolving of the year towards the dark, the evenings shortened and the trees turned to red and gold, Matt began to think of college again. It was his last year, and the following summer he would graduate and begin to think about his future. Because of what had happened, however, he was unable to believe in any of it – what did it matter whether he graduated or not? – and he returned to college like a sleepwalker.

On the first day back at college, he was crossing the court-yard when he saw Fred, and without thinking ran across to catch him up. Then slowing, he tried to gather his thoughts, steadied himself, and at last touched Fred on the shoulder.

Fred looked him over, but said nothing, his face impassive.

'How is Grace?'

'What's it to you?' Fred said coldly.

'Fred! Please, just tell me! Is she well? What is she doing now? Has she gone to Italy?'

Fred watched him grudgingly, clearly weighing up in his mind what to say. Finally through clenched teeth he muttered, 'She hasn't gone to Italy, and she's very well.'

He turned away, but Matt followed him. 'And is she still at Ardnashiel?'

Fred did not answer.

His mind still full of Grace, Matt did not take much notice of a postcard which the porter had handed him when he arrived earlier and which he stuffed into his pocket. 'Father Murphy will say Mass . . .'

Twenty-three

That evening they met at St Aloysius and Matt went with Hanlon (who was dressed as Hanlon this evening) to Donovan's, a pub Matt did not know. Their way led over the river, down one evil-smelling dark alley lit by a distant street lamp and then another, then through the deserted open market, kicking their way through discarded cabbage leaves, rotten fruit and broken wicker baskets. Hanlon at length pushed open a door. The pub was already crowded but the drinkers were hushed as Matt heard the voice of a man raised in song. He and Hanlon stood in the thick crowd, the strong smell of pipe smoke in their nostrils, waiting till the singer had finished. Matt knew the song – a slow lament, the story of a man doomed to travel far to a new land,

My bonny bark floats light and free across the surging foam
It bears me far from Inishfail to seek a foreign home
A lonely exile driven 'neath misfortune's cruel frown
From my own home and the friends so dear in sweet King William's town.

This was no professional singer, only an old man with a glass of beer in his hand, his eyes closed and his face turned upwards as he sang. And as the song drew to a close, there was no burst of applause but rather a low murmur of approval before talk started up. Soon afterwards as Matt and Hanlon pushed through the crowd, he heard a fiddle launch into a spirited reel.

Throughout the evening entertainment continued to come from a variety of fiddles and tin whistles, of flutes and the elbow pipes. Other singers too would take the floor in a spontaneous and improvised concert. Not all songs were of despair: others were in a patriotic and martial style – *The Boys of Wexford, The Battle of Aughrim.* They reminded Matt of evenings spent in *shebeens* or at wakes in the village, of the ancient Gaelic songs he had known since his childhood.

Hanlon was among friends and Matt recognized most of them

from the meeting in O'Leary's. They were working men, with the smell of brick dust, or plaster, or wood shavings fresh on them, bags of tools at their feet or slung over a shoulder. Consequently, as a 'Varsity Man' as Hanlon called him, and in his well-cut suit, Matt rather stuck out. Hanlon was rather fond of this phrase 'Varsity Man', Matt had noticed, and used it on every occasion he could. It had begun to irritate Matt and he was conscious that Hanlon was doing it on purpose; he began to think that perhaps Hanlon didn't like him very much. In the meantime, there were pints of porter in every hand, the air was thick with tobacco smoke and the talk was continuous and deafening in the crowded pub.

'Where's Mick McCaffrey?'

'Don't know Gerry, but he'll be along, don't worry.'

Matt was looking about him as he sipped his pint.

The music now stopped and a comedian was introduced. The roar of talk subsided as men turned to listen.

'Boys, let's give a warm welcome to an old friend, Ireland's King of Comedy, Sammie Rogers!'

A small man in a loud check suit got up, a man with a lively, rubbery face and rather red nose, wearing a spotted bow tie and a red carnation in his buttonhole.

'There were twenty kids in our family and we worshipped me mother; we put her on a pedestal. We had to, to keep me father away from her!'

A big laugh.

'Me uncle, now, he was a terrible hypochondriac. Somebody told him mercury was good for you, so he had himself injected with mercury. On a normal day he was five foot eight. When it got a bit warm he shot up to twelve foot. One day it went down to freezing and the cat got him!'

There was a touch on Matt's sleeve. Beside Hanlon was a stocky, serious man around fifty, thinning on top.

'Mick, this is our new recruit, Matt Byrne – Matt, this is Mick McCaffrey, just back from the States––'

'OK, let's talk,' the other man cut in and led the way across the crowded bar away from the comedian. Hanlon turned to McCaffrey.

'We're planning a job Mick, and we need a shooter. Can you help us?'

McCaffrey was looking away as if he hadn't been listening to Hanlon.

'I brought in a load earlier this year, Gerry; what happened to them?'

'The Peelers nabbed 'em, worse luck.'

McCaffrey shook his head. 'Shooters don't grow on trees, Gerry. How did it happen?'

'Don't ask me, Mick! Sure, wasn't I down the country at the time? Kevin Meany split on us.'

'Kevin Meany? What happened?'

Matt could see that McCaffrey was displeased, and that Hanlon was having to explain, leaning in and speaking in an urgent tone.

'The traps raided our arsenal and took everything, Mick. That's why we're here.'

'Are the traps after ye, Gerry? I have to be careful.'

'Not so far as I know. Anyway, Matt here is clean.'

'Hmm.' MacCaffrey was thinking as he looked Matt over. 'All right I could let you have a Colt, brought it from the States last week. Four pound.'

'When can you let us have it?'

'When d'ye want it?'

'The sooner the better.'

'Wait here.'

McCaffrey disappeared and Matt turned to find the comedian still in full flow.

'Casey was coming home from the pub one night and he thought he'd take a short cut through the graveyard. Well, there was a freshly dug grave and didn't Casey only fall right in and fall fast asleep? Well, he wakes up the next morning and looks out of the grave. Begob, says he, 'tis the Day of Judgement and I'm the first up . . .'

Matt turned away and took a long draught from the glass in his hand. His head was beginning to buzz.

Hanlon was talking and Matt was conscious that he was justifying himself and wondered why.

'Mick's our main man. Been in the States, like I was tellin' ye. 'Twas him tellin' me our friends over there are lookin' for results. Between you and me, Matt, we need Mick – understand? He brings in the tools – and 'twas him that went to Australia in the *Catalpa* and rescued all them Fenian boys six years ago. Did you never hear about it? Brave lads, afraid of nothing, and dedicated to the cause.'

Some time later, McCaffrey reappeared, pushing through the crowd; he was holding a parcel wrapped in newspaper.

'Hullo Mick, let's have a look.'

They squeezed along one of the benches against the wall. Hanlon took the parcel from McCaffrey and unwrapped it beneath the table. Inside was a gleaming, oiled pistol.

'Forty-five. Newest model, six-shooter. The best.'

Matt was staring down at the pistol, the gleaming shining metal, the neat intricate design, the elegant ivory handle. Hanlon wrapped it again quickly and shoved the package into Matt's lap.

'You take care of it, Matt. You'll be safe.'

He pulled some money from his pocket and counted it out to McCaffrey.

'What are ye planning, Gerry?'

Matt spoke before Hanlon could say anything. 'The execution of a tyrant,' he said calmly. 'The tyrant of Connacht. The Earl of Elphin.'

'The Earl of Elphin – ye mean the new Viceroy? Jesus, that'd make a splash. Could ye do it?'

'Matt here could,' said Hanlon. 'He's got connections. Matt's on the inside, a Varsity man, hobnobbin' with the quality.'

McCaffrey lifted his glass. 'Well, here's to you Matt, and Death to Tyrants!'

'Ireland for ever, boys!' Hanlon added.

As he drained his fourth pint, Matt was dimly aware of the comedian's voice: 'Father Murphy was up in the pulpit giving us hellfire and brimstone. Stand up all those who want to go to heaven, says he. We all stood up. Sit down! Now stand up all those who want to go to hell! Casey stood up. Casey, says Father Murphy, do ye want to go to hell? No, Father, says he, but I didn't like to see ye standin' there all by yourself . . .'

But then a strange thing happened. Unable to believe his eyes at first and through a half-drunken haze, Matt saw Fred across the pub in company with several other students Matt recognized. Slumming again. His first thought was, I mustn't be seen here; making a hasty farewell, and clutching his parcel, he escaped by another door.

In the open air and the sudden silence that descended after the deafening noise in the pub Matt stopped and drew a long breath. Why had everything gone so horribly wrong? They had been sworn friends, fellow swimmers in winter waters, shoulder to shoulder. And now – he looked down at the parcel in his arms, like some misshapen baby he was cradling. Confound everything! He set off through the dark streets, his brain addled with the drink, a tear smarting in his eye.

> Dear Harry,
> I hope you are back now and have enjoyed your summer holiday. A cruise round the Scottish islands! You were mentioned in the paper and it sounded most enjoyable. We went down to Roscommon as usual and relaxed in the garden. The family are all well. Harry, we didn't have much time to talk last time. Would you like to meet again? It would be so pleasant to be able to bind up old wounds and start again as friends. Could you meet me in the park? I will be sitting on a bench by the road opposite the lodge. Any afternoon, just name it and I will be there.
> With very best wishes,
> Bríd Doyle

As she posted off this short note, the doubts still revolved in her mind. Would a middle-aged man want a son fathered on him like this? Suppose he refused to believe Matt was his? This was why it was so important to break the news to him before introducing Matt – supposing he wanted to meet his son. Yet underneath it all, she felt sure Harry would be glad to know. After all they had once been in love, and she knew he had never forgotten that. On the other hand, if ever word got out that the Viceroy had fathered a bastard . . .

They met on the park bench opposite the Viceroy's Lodge. Autumn was in the air, and a thin haze hung over the park; the trees were resplendent in gold and russet, and exuberant voices could be heard in the distance where a sports match was being played. Otherwise the park was nearly deserted. Harry was neatly dressed as always, buttoned-up in top hat and frock coat. He sat beside her his hands clasped over the handle of his walking stick. To her, for whom the passing seasons were so fraught with images and sensations, with feelings and memories, it seemed strange that for him the seasons did not appear to exist.

She turned to him: poor Harry, he seemed sunk into a dismal and lethargic middle age with a drooping moustache, older than his years, and very lonely.

It didn't take them long to come to the point. Bríd let him do the talking for the moment.

'I've never been able to marry again,' he said, resting his hands on his walking stick and staring away across the park towards the huge granite obelisk of the Wellington Monument. There was a long and embarrassing silence as they both stared at the monument; Bríd held her peace until he should be ready to speak. 'Felt guilty, you see,' he went on at last. 'About you – and about Stella too. I'd got you into trouble, left you in the lurch, Bríd.' She was about to speak, but he waved aside her objection with a flap of his hand. 'Oh yes I did. I treated you badly. No point in denying it.' He stared away again. 'Then there was Stella dying in child-birth. Shan't forget that in a hurry – still think of it – twenty years ago, y'know.' He paused and sighed. 'I just bring bad luck to everyone I meet. Better not to get involved.'

'Harry –' she rested a hand on his arm – 'you mustn't be so hard on yourself. You seem so – down. And you're still young – it's not too late, you know.'

He shook his head slowly. 'Oh sometimes I look at a woman. I'm being introduced to women all the time, attractive women. In my position, you understand, they're interested, mothers introduce their daughters, and so forth. But I look at them and think – would I betray her? Or her? And if I married that one, would she die in childbirth? Better to leave things as they are.'

There was another long silence as Bríd was thinking furiously.

'Things aren't as bad as you think, Harry,' she began uncertainly. He didn't seem to hear her, still resting his hands on his walking stick and staring away through the trees. She knew now she had to tell him. It would be too cruel to let him go on thinking himself a failure, when all the time he had in fact a fine handsome son.

'Harry,' she began again, 'I never meant to rake up the past but something has happened, and I cannot keep it from you any longer. I wonder whether you can guess what that might be?'

He was silent, waiting.

'You know, Harry,' she went on awkwardly, 'once many years ago, we were very much in love.' She placed her hand over his as he started. 'It's all a long time ago my dear, and much has happened since but,' she paused again, 'do you remember those days? The Fairy Ring? And then that afternoon when it began to rain and we took shelter in the little hut?' She paused, watching him carefully. He was looking down. 'And then, how I ran away to you in London—'

'How can I forget?' he burst out. 'I remember it every day! Anything can start it, a glimpse through a window, the turn of a woman's head, a scent, a flower. Don't you think I haven't reproached myself a thousand times for what I did? Don't you think I'd do anything to wipe clean the stain—'

'We were very young,' she murmured, still watching him.

'There was no excuse for what I did! I betrayed you! Yes, I did, Bríd, and I shall never forgive myself.'

'Harry,' she interrupted hurriedly. 'You have no need. We both of us have moved on, we have made our own ways in life, and we neither of us have anything to complain of. I certainly don't reproach you, honestly.'

There was a pause.

'But Harry – you see, there was something else. Can you guess what it might be? Something good that came of it, after all?'

He was genuinely mystified.

She reached again for his hand. 'All those times we made love, Harry and—'

He turned to her, shocked. 'You mean—?'

She nodded. 'You have a son,' she breathed. 'We have a son.'

He stared into her eyes for a long minute, as she read volumes of meaning in his look, minutes, as Harry was trying to make sense of this news and its implications. She held her breath; was it possible he might not believe her? All her doubts returned: why should a middle-aged man suddenly want to have a child fathered upon him like this? Bríd was filled with fear.

Harry was still speechless. 'A *son*?' he whispered at last. 'But that's . . . well . . . he must be – what – he must be twenty? – twenty-one, twenty-two? I can't be sure. But he is a man, grown up. What is he like? Is he like you, is he like me? Tell me, for God's sake, what is he like? Does he know about me?'

'Harry, before I answer, tell me one thing. Are you pleased at the news?'

'Pleased? How can you ask the question?' There were tears in his eyes. '*Pleased?* You tell me I have a son of twenty or so, and ask me whether I am pleased? I, who never thought to have a son of my own?' He gazed about him in stupefaction. 'A son! I can't believe it!' He reached into his sleeve for a handkerchief and covered his eyes.

Bríd laid her hand gently on his shoulder. 'Harry you shall meet – as soon as you like. And we can keep it quite quiet, there will be no publicity, everything can be as discreet as you like.'

He looked up.

'My dear,' she went on, 'you are the Viceroy and perhaps a little discretion is best.'

'But I will meet him? Soon?'

She nodded.

'And Bríd – does he know? About me?'

It was her turn to look down now. 'Not yet. I have promised to tell him about his father. You see, Harry, although I have known him most of his life, he has only discovered recently that I am his mother. The story is too complicated to go through now but I will tell you everything one day, I promise you.'

Harry's son was at that moment sitting on the edge of his bed with the parcel on his knees. He unwrapped it and disclosed the pistol. It was new, clean, freshly oiled. He picked it up and turned it over in his hand, examining it, the ivory handle, the revolving chamber, the safety catch, the bullets. It was heavier than he expected. He aimed it at a picture on the wall opposite and drew back the trigger, feeling the tension of the spring as he increased the pressure, then quickly let it go. That would be something wouldn't it: to take a pot-shot at the picture? That would wake up the household, for sure. He turned the pistol over in his hand again; there was something mesmeric about it: the power, the implied violence. What couldn't a man do with this in his hand? He was a god; with one shot from this everything could be changed for ever. And that was what Matt wanted. To break out, to smash, to change everything forever. As for himself, as for what came afterwards – what matter? He was of no account in himself. What was his life when weighed against the cause? What was his life worth, without Grace?

Twenty-four

This time they were to meet in another pub, *The Earl of Lucan*, at midday. When Matt walked in he could not see Hanlon for a moment but as he walked through the bar, looking about him, he realized at last that the shabby labourer sitting smoking a broken clay pipe and reading a newspaper was in fact Hanlon. This elderly man with a large spade beard, with the wrinkles of his face etched with dust, with his battered bowler hat and his moleskin trousers tied with string was Hanlon. Matt bought himself a drink and sat near him.

Hanlon shifted his pipe, peered into it, pulled out a box of lucifers and with some ceremony relit it. He puffed a moment, then folded his newspaper, looked up and at last noticed Matt.

'Lovely day.'

'It is. The trees in the square are very lovely.'

'What's a fine young gentleman like you doing in a place like this?'

'I come down sometimes to see old friends.'

'And how's life agreeing with ye?' Hanlon went on, still in character.

'Never better.'

Hanlon glanced casually round as he scratched the back of his neck. He now dropped the act.

'There's no point taking unnecessary risks,' he went on in an undertone as he raised his glass. 'I've been talking to Sam about it. The Castle ball was never a good idea. It's all very well to take a pot at him in the ball itself – but you'd never get away alive. You'd swing for it.'

Matt wasn't sure of this. 'There has to be a gesture, a blood sacrifice. That's all they understand.'

'True again. But we need to find another way.'

There was something about the man which irritated Matt. Matt wanted to be left alone to do it in his own good time.

'I've been scouting round,' Hanlon went on, 'and the best place is undoubtedly in the park. I was down there yesterday. Saw his lordship taking the air on a park bench, just like anyone else. And talking with a very elegant woman too.' He raised an eyebrow. 'His floozy, no doubt. I could have done the job right there and then, if I'd had the weapon. So. It's just a question of keeping an eye open. We'll spend a few days watching his movements and once we have a clear idea of his coming and going from the Lodge then we're in a position to make a move.'

'It need only take a second!' Matt interrupted. 'Just one decisive step, to walk up to his carriage and pull the trigger – I could be away across the park – you could have a trap waiting for me – and I'd be away towards Chapelizod in no time. They wouldn't have time even to see my face!'

'There's no hurry! It's better to wait till the nights start drawin' in and maybe do it after dark – for safety, like.'

'Safety!' Matt grunted with scorn. 'That's all you think of!'

'And with good reason!' Hanlon whispered in a suppressed hiss. 'How many fools have gone to the gallows and all because they couldn't wait! We take our time, get to know the lay of the land, and when everything is made sure, we strike.'

This was Hanlon all over, talk, talk, talk.

'You can leave it to me,' Matt said in a low voice.

'I'd rather not leave it to you, Matt. No disrespect. An operation likes this wants a bit of planning. We need some assistance. What's the use of you running out and putting a bullet in him and then getting caught? A little planning can help things run smooth, see? We can keep an eye on the Lodge, find out his movements, then we can plan the operation and strike at the best moment. Make a neat job of it. That way we'll live to tell the tale. You'd be no good to Ireland dangling at the end of a rope, now would you?'

'Better men than me have died for Ireland.'

'God rest them, Matt, and you've a heart of gold to say so. But I know what I say. We'll go up to O'Leary's, talk it over with Sam and see what would be the best way to handle it.'

'To hell with it! What do we want with the others? Isn't it dangerous to bring others into it? Don't you think that pub isn't packed with informers? You want us to be sitting round talking it over with all and sundry? I've got a better way. I'll go down there this afternoon and put a bullet in his Lordship neat and easy. I'll be gone before they know what's happened.'

Hanlon leaned in and lowered his voice.

'The history of Ireland is packed with hot-headed fools who thought it would be neat and easy! That's why we've still got the English on our necks after seven hundred years! Matt, you've been sworn and you're under oath to obey orders!'

Matt was silent, staring down. Hanlon looked at him shrewdly. 'Don't worry, you'll do it. But Sam calls the shots; we'll leave it to him to make the decisions. I'll leave you a message when I can get the lads together and we'll talk again.'

Hanlon rose, folded his newspaper and, stuffing it into his pocket, shifted the pipe in his mouth and shuffled out of the door.

Matt sat alone, angry with himself. Why had he allowed this man to give him orders? Why didn't he just go down to the Lodge and wait for the Viceroy to come out? Why not do it now? Why not?

In a moment he knew what to do. He didn't need advice from Hanlon or Walsh or anyone else. It was a simple job, and he would do it – now. It was his duty and Hanlon was just stalling for time. Hanlon was just a play-actor, a coward like them all, full of wind and talk, but useless when it came to action.

That night around ten, he put the pistol into an inside pocket and went out of the house. His mind was made up – though Hanlon was right about one thing: it was safer to do the job by night. After all, he had only to break into the Viceroy's Lodge in the park; with the pistol in his hand, no one was going to quarrel with him. In any case, it would only be a couple of footmen, it would be easy, he was certain. If necessary he could take them out too. His mind had hardened; let the cost be what it might, there was a burning need in Matt for action. He had to do something, to wipe out the memory of Grace, something to settle his fate one way or the other.

With his mind full of these thoughts, he was brought up outside the Shelbourne Hotel. A man and a woman had just emerged and the man hailed a cab which was stationed further along the pavement. The cabby gee'd his horse into motion and with a jingle of bridle and a clatter of hooves on the cobbles, came up to them. But in that moment Matt had recognized the voice: it was Garrett, and as Matt came closer he saw in the lamplight that the woman with him was the same woman he had seen pleading so earnestly with Garrett at the RDS – Mrs Haynes, with whom Matt had danced at the ball, the wife of that businessman who had been in difficulties. Matt started forward just as Garrett was opening the cab door and Mrs Haynes, gathering up her skirts, was climbing in.

'Garrett!' His voice rang in the night air. Garrett looked round. 'What are you doing?'

Garrett recognized him, leaned in to the woman, whispered something and closed the door. He gave the horse a hard slap on the rump to send it off and as the cab pulled away he turned to Matt. 'What do you mean shouting like that?' he said severely.

'And what do you mean, betraying my mother? You had the audacity to lecture me the other day. And here you are – out with this—'

'Hold your tongue, you fool!'

'Hold my tongue? You may not respect my mother, but I do. I owe everything to her—'

Garrett cut across him. 'You have no idea what you're talking about. And this is certainly not what you think!'

'Oh isn't it?' Matt waved his arm. 'I think it is. And I won't stand by and see my mother betrayed!'

Garrett was beside himself. '*Betrayed?* You think I'd betray your mother? Have you *any idea* of what it cost me to win her?' he shouted. 'You're a boy! You whine incessantly about your Grace – what has she cost you so far? Do you realize, I had to travel half way round the world to win Bríd, when she was obsessed with the memory of that *jackeen* of an Englishman, that anaemic, undersized runt! I nearly drowned to save you – for her sake! I nearly drowned trying to save your aunt Nora – for her sake! I made a million dollars only so that I could lay them at her feet! And you think I would betray that? Betray what cost me fifteen years of incessant labour and fighting, of scheming and planning to achieve? You have no idea! What would you do for your Grace? Eh? Eh? Fight for her? Risk your life for her? Give her everything you possess? Eh? Pah! Don't talk to me! You gave up too easily! You've done nothing to win her! I tell you honestly, Matt, you don't know what love is.'

Garrett stalked away into the night leaving his words ringing in Matt's ears as he stood stock-still on the pavement. 'Don't know what love is'? Was that what Garrett thought? And was it true? What would he do for Grace? What sacrifice would he make? Would he make a million pounds to lay them at her feet? Would he fight for her, risk his life for her?

He felt the pistol under his jacket. He had been on his way to commit a murder. Was that the way to win Grace? His head swam. *By murder?* Garrett's words had unwittingly set Matt straight. Murder was not the route; that was not the way to win Grace – it was the coward's way! Matt had given up too easily, as Garrett had said. If Garrett had travelled half way round the world to win the woman he loved, what would not he, Matt Byrne, do? If only she would give him the opportunity!

And what had Garrett told him once before? That he was not to go creeping through the world but was to face it openly, squarely, honestly. Matt stared about him. What had he got himself into? Murder? Suicide? It was all madness.

Was this how he was to break free, as he had thought? By murder? By suicide? Matt clutched his head. Had he really sat in that church and told Hanlon that he would put a bullet in the Viceroy? What madness was this, what evil?

And that murder would surely have been a suicide even if he had never been caught, he thought as he became calmer. What would his life have been thereafter? And where did it leave the Vindicators? Matt was sworn to live – or die – with them. And where did it leave the plot on the Viceroy's life?

Oh Grace, if only she would give him the opportunity!

Twenty-five

It was only a few nights later that Matt's opportunity came.

He was on his way up Dame Street heading for O'Leary's Bar. The theatres would be coming out soon and the streets were busy, men crowding in and out of pubs, or careering up and down in half-drunk jollity. Matt, cold sober, pushed his way among them. His mind was focused on the meeting coming up. He had decided to inform them that he was henceforth having no part in the plot. He realized now that he hated Hanlon, and could scarcely bear to listen to his self-importance, his play-acting. As to what they would say, he did not care.

His mind full of these thoughts, he did not notice at first what looked like a drunken brawl erupting from the very doors of O'Leary's bar. Voices were raised and then oaths; arms were raised, fists were flying, men were lunging and grappling with each other and then, in a whirlwind of violence, a man was knocked to the ground and kicked in the stomach. The man cried out and as Matt came up he recognized the voice.

It was Fred. Without thinking, Matt plunged into this sea of fists and bodies and before he knew it had received a crushing blow to the side of the head which sent him flying. He shook his head, and waded back in, trying to pull the men away from Fred who was still on the ground and receiving the most vicious kicks. There must have been four or five men in a frenzied attack as if they were a pack of hounds and Fred the helpless fox. Even as Matt grappled with one and then another, he was horribly aware of the others really laying into Fred, who now had his arms about his head, trying to protect himself. Fred had rolled over and was raising himself when he received a violent kick in the face and doubled up with a cry. In the midst of this frenzy Matt looked about and shouted for assistance. The street was crowded but no one was coming to his aid; some watched in amazement safe at a distance, others crossed the road to avoid trouble. Matt redoubled his efforts and again and received a thudding blow to his head which sent him staggering away as stars danced before his eyes. Again he hurled himself in and managed to land a blow on one of them, before getting a nasty kick himself. His head ringing, and with a stinging pain in his right knee he was making a last attempt when it seemed they had lost interest in Fred, who now lay still, and had turned on him instead. Matt had his back to the pub wall as they closed in on him, faces glistening with sweat, manic eyes glinting in the distant lamplight, inflamed with drink. There was no reasoning or arguing with men in this condition so, in utter, final desperation he launched himself at them, kicking and lunging, lashing out, butting with his head: everything – a human flail – and after a moment it seemed they were retreating, breaking up, drifting away, laughing, jostling, and were lost in the crowd.

Scarcely able to breathe, staggering for a moment as he regained his breath, looked about him to see what had become of the men, he saw Fred still lying where they had left him. He ran back and knelt over him. Fred was unconscious. Matt looked up at a stranger who happened to be passing.

'Stop a cab!' he shouted in such an authoritative voice that the man hastened to do it. In the meantime Matt was examining Fred's face which was smeared with blood. Fred was still unconscious when a sidecar drew up and the jarvey helped him get Fred up on to the seat.

'He's still alive, I'm sure of it.' Matt was close over him, holding him, propping him up on the seat, Fred's head on his shoulder. It seemed to take for ever before they arrived, rattling and bumping over the cobbles, getting snarled up in traffic, but at last they arrived at the hospital, there were lights, a door opened and a porter was helping him to lift Fred down and get him on to a stretcher. Then he was being carried in and Matt followed, limping painfully.

In a brightly lit room, Fred was eased off the stretcher on to a table and a nurse was wiping his face. Shortly after, a doctor arrived in his waistcoat with his sleeves rolled up and began examining Fred who was still unconscious.

'Hmm, broken ribs by the sound of it, and he's lost a couple of teeth. It's lucky he didn't lose an eye – that's a nasty bruise on his cheek. Let's hope there's no internal bleeding. It's always touch and go with broken ribs. Nurse, administer morphine. Five per cent solution.' He turned to Matt. 'Do you know how this happened?'

Matt was nursing his own knee which was now in severe pain. 'He's a friend of mine,' he gasped, still short of breath. 'I found him by chance this evening in Dame Street just as he was set on by a gang of thugs. I have no idea how it started.'

'It's well you got him here quickly. It could be serious. Nurse, strip him. I shall need to make a more detailed examination.' He turned to Matt. 'If you'd wait outside . . .'

Matt sat in an outer vestibule through the night waiting for news of Fred. It never occurred to him to seek treatment for his own bruises, and after he had exhausted all explanations of how Fred had come to be involved in such a brutal fight, his mind gradually focused on those passing him. As people came and went, he watched them in a curiously detached frame of mind. Finding himself so unexpectedly in this strange night-time atmosphere among men and women to whom it was not strange at all, he began idly speculating about them. Some were hospital staff – nuns going off duty, wrapped in their capes and chatting to each other as if oblivious to the suffering around them. Occasionally a doctor would pass him in a hurry. From time to time an accident victim would appear: someone with his head cracked; someone raging with drink, his face smeared with blood; a wretched, ragged woman with what appeared to be a broken arm; and one horrific case where a man was carried in by four men and screaming with pain.

Through all this, Matt sat nursing his knee and wondered how Fred could have got caught up in such a vicious fight. He finally concluded that this was the consequence of Fred's 'slumming'. He had always had a taste for rough dives, and this time things had come unstuck. As Matt thought about it, it now seemed inevitable; Fred was always ready to pick a fight. Matt remembered their bout with the gloves on his first day in college.

At some time in the early hours, the doctor reappeared, pulling on his jacket and Matt leaped up.

'We have done what we can. He has three broken ribs and a fractured jaw. Fortunately his eye is safe. However, he is going to be in for a month or so and then he'll need to take it easy for a while longer. Can you contact his family?'

Matt nodded. 'Can I see him?'

'He is unconscious. Come back in the afternoon. He may have come round by then.'

It was dawn as Matt left the hospital. By this time he could scarcely walk as the pain in his right knee had become more and more intense. By the greatest good luck a cab had only just discharged a fare and he was able to drag himself into it. His knee had swollen and by the time he reached his own home he could scarcely move for the pain. The family were not yet up, and he was admitted by a housemaid who had been laying the breakfast table. He dragged himself up to the drawing room and found a telegram form on Bríd's escritoire.

'Fred in St Lawrence Hospital not serious better come Matt.' He addressed it to Lady Langley and when the butler appeared, still tying his cravat, told him to take it to the post office the moment it opened.

'And tell my mother I have been out late and am going to sleep for a few hours, will you?'

Finally, he crawled up to his room, pulled off his jacket and boots, and threw himself on to his bed.

It was impossible to sleep at first; the pain in his knee was intense and he was aware now of bruises on his face and chest. He rang for the maid, but a few minutes later Bríd appeared. As she came through the door and saw him, she sprang forward.

'Matt, my darling, for heaven's sake, what have you been doing?'

'What—'

'You look terrible!'

She yanked at the cord for the maid and when the girl appeared rapped out instructions, 'A can of hot water, bandages, and some iodine—'

'I'll tell you everything. It's just that a man kicked me in the knee. I can't move.'

'For God's sake, lie back, and let me see.'

She managed to ease his trousers off as he lay on the bed, and together they examined his swollen knee. Then as the girl returned with the water, Bríd was able to wipe and clean his face.

'You've got a terrible bruise on your cheek, and you've cut your mouth – Polly, tell Mr Dunne to send for the doctor.'

She turned back to Matt. 'This is serious. Thank God you're here.'

As she worked on him Matt told her how he had come across Fred in the street and had attempted to fight off the gang of men who attacked him and had at length managed to get Fred into hospital.

'I sent a telegram to his parents. I ought to go and see how he is.'

Later that morning the doctor arrived and examined the knee. Eventually he bound it up tightly and put a dressing on the cut on Matt's cheek.

'You won't be walking anywhere for several weeks. I'm not sure how serious the injury is. We can only wait and see how it improves.'

After he had gone and Matt was actually undressed and in his bed, Bríd sat facing him. For a moment they were silent. Matt was a little sheepish and didn't like to look at her.

'Matt,' she began at last, 'I don't know how you do it, I don't really. I have never known a man for getting into scrapes the way you do.'

'Mam, it wasn't my fault. Fred was being attacked! What was I supposed to do?' A pause. 'Anyway, I've got to get over to see how he is. He's on his own in hospital.'

'You sent the telegram early this morning didn't you? They're bound to be there tonight at the latest. Don't worry.'

'I do worry! He was hurt much worse than me. He was uncon-scious. It was a wonder they didn't kill him.'

'Why were they attacking him?'

'No idea.' Matt winced. 'It's the knee. It's killing me.'

'The doctor left some laudanum. Take a few drops.'

The effect of this was to put him to sleep.

When he woke the next morning, the pain was still great in his leg.

'For heaven's sake, how long is this going on for?' he wondered. It was impossible to get comfortable and he could only sleep lying flat on his back.

The doctor called again in the afternoon and felt round the knee.

'It'll take weeks to heal, I'm afraid. It's hard to tell whether anything is broken, or whether there is a fracture. You're just going to have to rest.'

'Rest! You mean, lie here?'

'For the time being.'

'We can bring your books up, darling,' said Bríd, who was standing beside him. 'You can carry on your studies. I'll write to the professor and explain the situation.'

'I need to get to the hospital. I have to know how Fred is.'

Later that afternoon there was a visitor. Matt could hear voices below and then steps ascending. Bríd opened the door and ushered in Lady Langley. She was looking very serious. Bríd brought a chair, and her Ladyship sat facing Matt.

'You sent me a telegram,' her Ladyship began immediately. 'Of course I came to Dublin immediately. At first I found my son still unconscious but he regained consciousness this morning. He is very weak and has no idea how he came to be in hospital. I assume you do know.'

'Yes. I took him there. Is he recovering?'

Again she ignored this. She was still looking very serious. 'I take it you had a fight?'

'Fight? No—'

'I would not have come here but for Fred's condition. The police have been notified and they will be here, I expect, to question you. I regret to say you have been a source of un-happiness and trouble to my family since we first knew you. Now exactly what happened?'

'Trouble?'

'You know what I mean,' she said coldly. 'As if you were not satisfied with what you did to Grace, you have to attack my son too.'

'I didn't attack him!'

Lady Langley said nothing but clearly did not believe him.

'This is absurd!' Matt went on. 'I was walking up Dame Street and I saw a fight in progress outside a pub. Fred had been attacked by a crowd of men. There must have been half a dozen of them. I went to the rescue.'

'Six men – and you went to the rescue?'

'Yes.'

'You expect me to believe that? Why on earth would anyone want to attack my son? And why would you want to attack so many?'

'Matt!' Bríd interjected.

'I don't know. He must have been in O'Leary's and got into an argument.'

'This is simply a lie. Obviously my son would not go into a low bar and certainly would not get into an argument with common working men. I have never heard such an outrageous slur. I suggest you hired those roughs and laid in wait for him. You wished to hurt him for defending my daughter's honour.'

Matt was by now very aware of her hostility 'Why do you think I sent the telegram?' he said quietly. 'Why did I take him to the hospital?'

'I imagine you went farther than you intended and were frightened of the consequences. You hoped to cover yourself and attribute the horrible wounds Fred has sustained to others, by pretending to be his friend.'

'I can't believe what I am hearing. Look – my knee is so badly hurt I can't even get out of bed. Do you think I did this to myself?'

'My son is a fighter. I have no doubt he fought back gallantly when you attacked him.'

'You think Fred did this to me?'

'Clearly. Who else?'

Matt looked up in bewilderment to Bríd who was standing beside Lady Langley. 'Mam, what can I say?' He looked back to Lady Langley. 'Did Fred tell you I attacked him?'

'Fred has no memory of the attack.'

'No memory? None? But he is conscious? He can talk?'

'He can talk – with difficulty.' Lady Langley was not pleased to say this.

'I don't understand. He is conscious – but he doesn't remember what happened?'

'That is what I said.'

The more desperate Matt sounded, the tighter and more rigidly controlled Lady Langley became.

'Well,' Matt groped on, 'Will his memory return?'

'Apparently it will – eventually.'

'That's something, anyway.' Matt lay back against the pillows and, as if this were a signal, Bríd touched Lady Langley on the shoulder. She glanced up then rose. 'As I said, the police will be here to take a statement.'

After she had gone, Matt said, 'Mam I have to write a letter. Can you get me a pen and paper?'

> Dear Grace,
>
> Before you get this, I expect you will have heard from your mother about what happened to Fred. She will have told you that Fred has no memory of the fight – which, in view of what happened to him, is not surprising. I'm praying his memory will return soon and then he can explain to you himself exactly what happened. In the meantime, however, your mother has got hold of the wrong end of the stick and convinced herself that I attacked him!
>
> You may not want to hear from me, in view of all that has happened, but I cannot allow this to pass. Whatever you may think of me, I cannot let you think that I would wantonly attack your brother. I love Fred! In spite of all that has happened, I have always loved him – like a brother. Think of all the times we went swimming together, the nights we have sat in pubs and talked of politics. The idea that I would wish him harm is grotesque. I have no brother of my own and when I met Fred at the university – and especially in view of the way we met – I embraced him as the brother I never had.
>
> Oh Grace, you cannot understand how important you all are to me – you were my other family and, I had hoped, my own too, to be. And now this has happened and your mother is going to tell you all sorts of things about me which are completely untrue. How can I convince you? Why would I fetch a cab and carry Fred to the hospital? Why am I lying here with my knee smashed in, unable to walk?
>
> The simple truth is that I came across a gang of roughs beating Fred outside a pub and went to the rescue. Your mother refuses to believe this. Well, there's nothing I can do

about that except to hope that Fred will recover soon and
that his memory will return. In the meantime I can only
beg you not to judge me until you have heard him speak.
Matt Byrne

The police did call, and Matt made a statement about the affair,
but until Fred recovered his memory there was nothing more
they could do. They had only Matt's unsubstantiated statement
and the statement made by the surgeon who examined Fred. He
corroborated that Matt too looked very badly beaten.

After a week the enforced inactivity was too much for him, and
he got out of bed and, in the teeth of his mother's protests and
with some help from the butler, dressed and, also with his assistance and the use of a stick, managed to get himself down into
the drawing room. What a relief to be on his feet again! There
was still no chance of his going out however, and day by day he
would sit in an armchair, vaguely opening a text book. The
moment he did so, however, the night outside O'Leary's was
present again to him and he was running it over again in his
mind. Restless, he would struggle to his feet, hobble to the window
and, leaning on his stick, stare into the street and the gardens
opposite, now thick underfoot with fallen leaves, and think himself
accursed; not merely had he insulted Grace, but her mother was
now his bitterest enemy (if she hadn't been before) and Fred was
lying in hospital, his memory gone. It seemed that he was destined
to bring trouble to everyone he knew.

Even as he thought this, his eye settled on the street sweeper
who at that precise moment was looking up at him. Matt leaned
on his walking stick and looked down at the sweeper, at his
battered bowler hat and spade beard, at the strings tying up his
trousers. So they were keeping a watch on him. He hadn't thought
of the Vindicators since the night of the fight, but seeing Hanlon
brought it all back with a rush. They were wondering what had
happened to him; what's more, they didn't trust him, it was clear.
They were probably wondering what had happened to their gun,
too. A wave of irritation swept through him.

Then a thought struck him like a violent blow across the head.
Suppose the Vindicators had had Fred beaten up? Matt concentrated

trying to remember that night. It had been dark, to be sure, and he had scarcely seen any of their faces but he was sure he hadn't recognized any of them. Even so it raised a horrible suspicion in his mind and, remembering his conversation with Walsh in the doorway, it seemed only too likely.

Hanlon made no sign of recognition as he turned back to his sweeping. Matt too turned away and hobbled across to his armchair and the book he had been reading, or not reading.

He drew a breath. Were they the kind of men to have Fred beaten up? He had to admit, they were. And these were the men with whom he had sworn to live or die. He remembered all the years he had sat at Brother Ronan's feet, those passionate vows he had made to himself in the darkness of the night. Was this how he had sworn to serve the white maiden Erin – by murder, by a brawl outside a pub door?

Twenty-six

He looked up. Bríd was in the doorway, a letter in her hand. 'I am having an old friend to tea this afternoon and I'd like you to meet him.'

'Who is it?'

She smiled awkwardly. 'You'll see – but I just wanted you to know – around four. And you'll be here?'

'Where else would I be?' Matt waved his walking stick.

'Quite.' She laughed unconvincingly. She was just leaving the room when he stopped her.

'Mam?'

She turned. He was watching her closely. 'Are you all right?'

'All right? Of course, darling, fine.'

She went out, leaving Matt staring after her. She had seemed very nervous. However, since he was not going to learn any more, he turned his attention back to his book and tried to concentrate on wills and probate.

That afternoon again she was fussing about the drawing room, following the housemaid and rearranging things she had just set straight, giving little unnecessary orders about the arrangements of the cloth, and the china and the place settings.

'Mam, did you say he's coming for tea?'

'Yes – why?' She looked up nervously.

'You're carrying on as if it were dinner for sixteen. What on earth is the matter?'

'*Matter?*' She jumped.

He limped across to her and took her arm. 'Mam! Who is this visitor? You're as nervous as a mouse.'

She couldn't meet his eye, and at last muttered, 'Just wait and see.'

At the appointed hour Matt, who was again in the window, saw a stately carriage roll up, a very stately carriage indeed. It had a crest on the door, there was a servant in plush velvet livery and white stockings on the box who leaped down nimbly, opened the door, and let down a couple of tiny steps. Matt couldn't see the owner's face as he stepped out because he was holding a top hat which he placed on his head immediately as he crossed the two paces to the house steps. Matt did see the street sweeper, however, who had reappeared across the square and was watching.

There was a distant rap at the door and the voice of Dunne the butler. Bríd, who was at the looking glass doing something to her hair, turned hurriedly as Dunne appeared at the door and announced,

'Lord Elphin, madam.'

His Lordship was right behind the butler and came quickly into the room. He was in afternoon dress, a grey cutaway coat, striped trousers. He stopped as he saw Matt. Bríd, who was all nerves, came a step forward.

'Lord Elphin, I am so glad . . .' She faltered as Harry's glance had switched to Matt, who was watching them both from the window.

'This is Matt,' she said breathlessly. She saw instantly that Harry was pleased with the sight of his son. She was turning to Matt to introduce him but Harry interrupted hurriedly, 'The stick – have you been injured?'

'Harry,' she went on, 'this is my son Matt. Unfortunately he has been—'

But Matt interrupted her too.

'A friend of mine was attacked in the street a few weeks ago, Lord Elphin, and I went to the rescue. Unfortunately I was some-what damaged in the process.'

There was an awkward hiatus as Bríd crossed quickly to the bell-pull and tugged it. And for a moment all three of them stared in silence at each other. Matt was reeling at the sight of the Viceroy in his own house, and his mother calling him Harry, as if she had known him for ever.

Bríd turned to the butler who was hovering near the door.

'Dunne, you may serve tea.'

'Very good, madam.'

She turned again to the Viceroy. 'Harry, won't you sit down – not there –' she laughed nervously – 'we keep that for Matt at the moment since he hurt his knee – he finds it easiest to get out of. Won't you take that chair?'

Under this barrage of instructions the three of them sat, facing each other, and there was another hiatus. Matt had now been able to get his breath under control but his mind was racing and he still struggled to make sense of the situation. Of course, he realized, his mother had moved in all sorts of circles; it was not at all unreasonable she should be on speaking terms, on first name terms even, with the Viceroy of Ireland. Even so it was a horrible shock. He waited, his heart thudding, to hear the outcome of this. With his broken knee there was no way he could make his escape.

'You are at present studying – the law, I understand,' the Viceroy enquired politely.

Matt nodded, still uncertain of his voice and staring mesmerized at the Viceroy.

'A good choice, if I may say so,' the Viceroy went on. 'There are many aspects of the law as it pertains to Ireland in particular, that need to be looked at. Gladstone made a very good start with the Land Act, and we may look forward soon to Home Rule, it is to be hoped.'

'Harry!' Bríd was surprised. 'I never expected to find you a Home Ruler!'

He looked down modestly, then turned to Matt. 'I was for some years Governor General of New South Wales, Matt, and it taught me a lot. The people being thrown upon their own resources, with the British Government so much farther off, gave them a measure of independence, of resourcefulness, I might say, which I could not fail to admire.'

It took Matt a few moments to take this in. He had been struggling so hard to account for the Viceroy's presence in the house that he had not been listening very closely. But gradually the sense of his words began to filter into Matt's brain and he was able to make sense of them. In the meantime Bríd was handing the teacups round. The Viceroy was a very softly spoken, modest man who seemed to offer his opinions hesitantly. But the opinions he did offer were based on his own experience, not got out of books. Matt relaxed; it was clear that they were not after him and that this must be merely a conventional afternoon call to his mother. He was consequently able to take a closer look at the Viceroy. He seemed very old and rather sad, with his drooping moustache and his uncertain, diffident manner. How had a man like this ever become the representative of the British Government in Ireland?

'There are other measures which might be advanced to the great advantage of the Irish people,' Harry went on thoughtfully.

He hesitated and Matt was forced to ask, 'Such as?'

'Well, for one thing, the government is thinking of a fund from which loans might be made to farmers to buy their farms from the landlord. It would be an advance on the Land Act and I believe would relieve much ill-feeling.'

At this some distant memory chimed in Matt's mind and he remembered with a jolt that this man was the son of that earl who had insulted and humiliated Uncle Patsy all those years ago. He felt a chilling, a tightening inside him. When it came to the crunch would this man behave any differently? Yet looking at him, he thought he might.

The Viceroy was now sipping his tea. Bríd turned to the butler who had been hovering nearby.

'That will be all, Dunne. I will ring if we need anything.' She turned to Matt. 'I asked Lord Elphin to call, Matt, for a special reason. You see, I wanted him to meet you – and he wanted it too – very much.'

She glanced at Harry and Matt was suddenly conscious of the two of them in some way in league against him. Frightened again, he searched quickly in his mind; this could have nothing to do with the gun, could it? Or the Vindicators? Or the attack on Fred?

She now leaned forward and took Matt's hand. 'Matt,' she began breathlessly, 'I promised to introduce you to your father.' She hesitated as Matt glanced quickly between them. There was a moment's silence.

'You mean—?'

They both nodded, staring closely at him. Matt was flung back in his chair. 'You!' he gasped at last.

Harry nodded, smiling. 'I hope it isn't too much of a shock,' he said, and then went on rapidly, 'My dear boy, I assure you, I had no idea that you even existed until a few weeks ago when your mother told me about you. You cannot imagine the delight it gave me. I – who had no child of my own and never thought to have one, suddenly to be told that I have a son – and such a fine one too. A son to be proud of!'

Matt saw to his bewilderment that there were tears in the old man's eyes.

'You're my father?' he gasped, still reeling with the shock. 'But – *how?*'

Harry leaned back too, relieved now that the truth was out. He glanced at Bríd who took up the story.

'I am going to tell you, Matt – everything! But it would take too long now. Let's just say we were both very young. Oh goodness, how young we were, Harry!' She glanced to him. 'How absurd it all was!'

Matt looked from one to the other, both with tears in their eyes. His mother had impulsively reached for Harry's hand. Only for a moment, she gave it a squeeze.

'Mam, I don't understand any of this.' Matt was blushing with confusion and embarrassment.

Bríd, picking this up, hurried on in spite of herself, 'You see Matt, Nora was my aunt and I was brought up by her just as you were. Then, when we were seventeen Harry and I met.' She caught his eye, and smiled. 'You had a riding fall, didn't you, Harry – and were knocked unconscious and brought to our cottage, and the doctor said you must not be moved, so you lay in my bed and I tended you . . .' She glanced back to Matt. 'Matt, I'll spare you all the details. Let's say only that I ran away to London to be with Harry, and then – his father—'

'Matt,' Harry interrupted. 'You must not blame your mother in any way for what happened. The fault was all mine!'

'No, Harry!' she cried.

'Yes, yes it was! Matt –' he leaned forward – 'my dear, dear boy, whatever you may think, the fault was not your mother's! It was all mine,' he repeated. 'You see –' he looked down, gathering his thoughts – 'I was a younger son, never expected to inherit the title. But just after Bríd – your mother – had come to London, my elder brother the heir was murdered—'

'*Murdered?*' Matt jerked the word out in an unnatural voice. Harry nodded.

'Your brother was murdered?' Matt repeated anxiously. 'How?' Harry drew a breath, shrugged. 'Fenians. This was years ago, in the sixties. There was unrest – anti-British demonstrations, and, in short, my brother was MP for Roscommon and he was shot one evening on his way home from a meeting in Athlone.' He was thoughtful. 'My mother never recovered from the blow. So –' he drew a breath, and looked up again – 'suddenly I was the heir. My father sat me down and explained that our family was almost bankrupt – we had never recovered from the famine – and since I was the heir it was imperative that I marry a girl with money.' He hesitated, and the silence began to draw out. At last Harry looked up at Bríd, searching her face for a response. As she saw his difficulty, she reached for his hand. 'You must not be too hard on yourself.'

'Don't say I was too young!' he burst out, with agony written all over his face. 'I was old enough! Bríd, I was weak! My father went on and on at me about the family, how we were all about to sink and that it was imperative I marry money. He said I could not allow my personal happiness to weigh against the fortune of a noble house! A noble house!' He leaned forward, his elbow on his knee, and covered his face. 'How noble was I?' he muttered.

Matt was watching him with burning attention.

'Matt,' Harry looked up at last. 'The truth is, I abandoned your mother. Left her almost penniless in London.'

'Harry!' Again Bríd reached for him. 'Don't! It was all a long time ago. I got through! I survived! The important thing is that you and Matt have been able to meet at last.'

'I could not come to you as a father without your knowing the truth – the full truth, Matt. Don't say anything, my boy – don't judge me too hastily. Take time to think. I won't press you in any way. But you must think it through – talk to your mother – and then decide whether you will accept me as your father,' he ended almost in a whisper.

Matt was still utterly confused in his feelings, still trying to take in the import of this story – so briefly told. He looked again between the two of them, both watching him earnestly.

Harry could see that Matt was uncertain how to reply, and stood up. 'It might be better if I left now. Matt has heard what happened – I am sure there will be much for you to discuss—'

'No!' Matt gestured. 'No – don't go! Not yet. Just give me a moment. It's so much – I can't take it in all at once.'

Harry glanced at Bríd.

'You say your brother was murdered?' Matt went on. 'Returning from Athlone – to Ballyglin?'

Harry nodded.

'And you were – seventeen?'

Harry nodded again.

Thoughts of murder were going round and round in Matt's brain. Had he really been going to kill this man? His head was swimming. This harmless old man, earnest, modest – had he actually intended to shoot this man? The horror of it filled him until he shook. The past, Harry's story and his guilt, did not affect Matt so intensely as the thought of what he himself had so nearly done. After all, the story which had been told in part sounded like something out of a novel – he could not quite believe it, or imagine it. The idea of this man and his own mother as lovers was not something he could visualize. Lovers? The way he and Grace had been on Howth Head? It was impossible and Matt closed his mind against it. What he could see, however, was this old man sitting before him, humble, contrite, the trace of a tear in his eye: this old man begging his pardon. It was all too strange; it should be he, Matt, who ought to beg his pardon for intending to kill him.

But where to begin? What to say? How could he reach out to him, welcome him as a father?

Harry could see that Matt was very confused and turned again to Bríd. 'I really think I should go. We can meet again,' he added more cheerfully, 'and, I hope, in time get to know one another better. Now that I have found you,' he went on tentatively, 'I want to – and of course,' he added rapidly, 'if there is anything I can do—'

Bríd stood up. 'Of course, Harry. We shall meet again, soon, I'm sure. And Matt –' she glanced down to him in his armchair then hesitated – 'Matt and I will talk, and I'll write!' she finished quickly on a cheerful note.

As Bríd followed Lord Elphin out of the room, and Matt heard their voices on the stairs, he hauled himself from his chair and crossed to the window. The street sweeper was on the other side of the garden watching the house. A moment later Matt heard the door open and close, saw his Lordship enter his carriage and drive away. He was feeling in a very strange state, as if he had suddenly been called upon to grow up, to embrace ideas and states of feeling that he had hitherto been only vaguely aware of. Suddenly this afternoon he was face to face with the adult world; it was frightening, and exhilarating too, like standing on a high cliff and feeling the stiff breeze in his face. It was a dizzy height, but how much farther he could now see!

Bríd reappeared at the door, and Matt turned to face her.

'You don't have to say anything, Mam,' he said calmly, elevated by this new feeling and able now to treat his mother as a fellow adult. 'He seems a good man.' He paused thoughtfully, 'I'm sorry for him that his own brother was murdered.'

She was watching him carefully and after another pause, she said, 'He was never intended to be an earl. He never saw himself as Lord Elphin. He was a younger son; he had no money and all he wanted to be was a soldier.'

'A soldier?'

She nodded. 'When I first knew him he was a soldier.' She turned away to the window, looking out where the carriage had departed. 'I must say,' she went on dreamily, 'he did look very handsome in his uniform. It's difficult to understand now, perhaps, but he really did look very dashing, very handsome,' she repeated in this far away voice. She turned to Matt. 'I must tell you, Matt, that Harry, your father, has not had a happy life – he has not been lucky. There was his brother's death. Then his father, who was a horrible man, cold and unfeeling, forced him – good God, Harry was barely eighteen! – to leave me and to marry another girl.' Bríd was writhing her fingers together, as she spoke in these rapid, jerky phrases. 'And then Stella – that was the girl – Stella died in childbirth. So Harry lost me, and he lost Stella and after that he told me, he didn't trust himself ever to marry again, for fear of what fresh disaster he might bring on his wife. And now, poor man, he seems so lonely. I hope you can understand Matt, from all this, how important it has been to him to learn that he has a son after all – and such a son as you – that any father would be proud of!'

'It's all right, Mam, I understand.' Matt could not bear to see his mother upset. 'You don't have to go on. I am happy to know he's my father.'

'You are? Really?'

He nodded, and she crossed and took him quickly in her arms. 'I am so glad!' she murmured pressing herself against him. 'I can't tell you how it has preyed on my mind, worrying what you would think when you learned the truth, whether you would accept him, or blame him for abandoning me.'

Matt was thoughtful for a moment. 'It seems a shame in a way, never to have told him before.'

'I was very angry. I had nothing, Matt, I was alone in London, and I did not know a soul – scarcely a soul,' she corrected herself, 'but I had my pride! If he rejected me, so be it! I would survive on my own. But of course I could not understand the pressure he was under. Poor Harry! He is a gentle man, and only looked forward to life as a soldier. Instead of which he had these terrible decisions thrust upon him.'

'Because of the—'

'Because of the murder, yes.'

There was another pause, they were both thoughtful and at length Matt hobbled back to the armchair and sat down. 'I suppose a cup of tea would be out of the question?' he asked mildly.

Bríd jumped to the bell pull. 'I'll order a fresh pot! And look at all these sandwiches and cakes! We haven't touched them! Please, Matt, do eat something!' She clapped her hands together. 'Oh, I can't tell you how glad I am, how relieved I am!'

'It's all right, Mam. Sit down. We've got plenty of time – we've got all the time in the world. And I will have a sandwich, thank you.'

She sat opposite him, offering a plate. 'And of course, I know he would do anything for you – not that you will ever need anything that I and Garrett can't give you! But he is the soul of generosity.'

'I won't need his generosity,' Matt said quietly as he took a sandwich, 'but it's kind of him to offer.' He was thoughtful. 'In any case, it might be awkward for him to give me anything, or do anything for me – as you put it. People would only ask questions. And I suppose someone in his position must be careful.'

He caught Bríd's eye, as the import of this occurred to them both. 'Your being – your birth being – irregular –' she struggled to find an appropriate euphemism – 'makes no difference to him.

You saw yourself how glad he was to know you! And I can assure you, Matt, that the very moment that I told him about you, he was overjoyed. Really! So all that – I don't know – social disapproval, really doesn't matter. It's not important and it won't affect you, you have my word. No one will ever know.'

'It's all right, Mam. It doesn't bother me. Not any more. It did, years ago. But not now. I'm twenty-one, and it's time for me to stand on my own feet, take my own chances in life. I'm not blaming you, or him.'

But I'm having to square things with Hanlon, he thought, and he might not be happy about it.

Twenty-seven

Several days later when he still had not come up with a plan to resolve this crisis there was a knock at the door and as he looked up from his book Grace walked into the drawing room. He struggled to his feet. His mother was behind her, and was muttering something about a cup of coffee, Grace was pulling off her gloves and saying she couldn't stay long, and so forth. Matt stared at her. It was a cold November day and she was well wrapped in a long overcoat and hat. As Bríd left the room, Grace came across to where Matt was still watching her, frozen. She was not looking very pleased to see him, it was clear. After a moment she began,

'I have been with my brother—'

'How is he?' Matt interrupted quickly.

'He has begun to remember,' she continued quietly. 'Not much, but a little. He still has no memory of you in what happened that night.'

Matt waited.

'And he has no idea how he came to be in the hospital.'

'But you had my letter?'

She nodded.

'Well, you must know – I would have gone to see him myself before now but – you see . . .' He indicated his knee, and the walking stick.

'Come with me now,' she said. 'If he sees you he may remember more clearly. I want to know what happened. I cannot be quiet until I know how he came to be in this terrible state.'

'I will come,' he said immediately and as his mother came into the room soon afterwards he asked, 'Mam, can I borrow the carriage? Fred has begun to remember. I must go and see him.'

'Are you sure – your leg—'

'It'll be all right. I'm stronger now.'

'Grace –' Bríd turned to her – 'how are you? We haven't seen you since—'

'No.' Grace looked down.

'I hope – one day – we may all be friends again,' Bríd went on with difficulty. Grace did not reply. It was an awkward moment and Matt watched her with a sinking heart. Nothing had changed, it was clear. She was here solely on Fred's account.

Twenty minutes later the carriage had been harnessed up and Matt managed to hobble down to the front door and out into the street. He paused on the step with Grace beside him.

'It's so good to breath the fresh morning air; I feel like a prisoner let out at last.'

'I don't want to talk about what happened. I mean – between us,' she said when they were in the gloom of the carriage together. She wouldn't look at him. 'I only want to see whether, when Fred sees you, he can remember anything more.'

There was nothing Matt could say to this and they travelled through the morning streets in silence.

'Is he recovering – apart from his memory, I mean? His bruises. The surgeon said he had three broken ribs.'

'He is still in a lot of discomfort but he is out of danger. In a week or two we hope he will be well enough for us to take him home.'

'That's some comfort.'

After another pause, during which Matt sat in misery, Grace said grudgingly, 'The surgeon said you had been badly bruised too.'

Matt didn't want to talk about himself and there was silence until Grace went on, 'Are you recovered – apart from the knee, I mean?'

Again Matt said nothing but nodded assent. Finally, he muttered, 'You don't have to worry about me.' He could not look at her and it seemed she could not look at him. They both waited until the carriage arrived at the hospital.

'You'll have to wait a while. I don't know how long we'll be,' Matt told the coachman.

He hobbled along beside Grace along corridors and up stairs until they came into a long ward, brightly lit by high windows. Nuns hurried by and they made their way between the beds until they came to one where a man lay still, with his head bandaged up. As they stood before him, Matt was horribly upset to see Fred so bound up, so helpless, his face still black and swollen. Fred turned his head with difficulty as he recognized Grace.

'I've brought Matt,' she murmured bending over him.

Fred turned his attention to Matt who stood behind her. Matt waited as Fred scanned his features. At last he murmured, 'Matt? How are you?'

'You remember me?'

'Of course I do,' he said more clearly. 'How are you?'

Matt shrugged. 'Fine – apart from the leg.'

'Why – what happened.?'

Grace turned to hear Matt's reply. He gathered his thoughts.

'It was in Dame Street,' he began, 'outside O'Leary's bar – you remember?'

'O'Leary's? Yes.'

'It seemed you got into an argument and a fight broke out.'

'You were there? I don't remember—'

'I wasn't there. I only saw you when the fight spilled out of the pub. I was just coming up the street when I saw a gang of men all kicking and beating you.'

He paused to see whether Fred remembered. Fred was staring at him. 'There was a fight,' he began weakly, 'in O'Leary's. I don't remember how it started.' He paused, thinking hard. 'And then we were outside. I remember that.' He paused. 'And then somebody did come up. He was shouting at them to stop and trying to pull them off. I remember that. Was that you?'

Matt nodded. Fred was staring at him. 'I don't remember anything – no, wait, we were on a car – an outside car – somebody was holding me up.'

'Yes.'

Fred was still struggling to remember. He closed his eyes and shook his head slightly. 'Sorry it gives me a headache trying to think.'

'Don't strain yourself,' Grace said hurriedly. 'There's no hurry. We have plenty of time.'

A nun came up. 'Would you like a chair, madam?'

'Thank you.' She and Matt sat on either side of the bed. They waited. After a while Fred began again. 'The hospital at night, and the nurses, a surgeon over me, and there was another fellow there – he had brought me.' He paused looking up at Matt. 'Was that you?'

Matt nodded. Fred was staring at him. 'Matt – it *was* you, I remember now. Yes, it was you in the hospital – and you had brought me?'

'Yes.' Matt was conscious of Grace watching him.

A little later the nurse came back. 'It's not wise to stay too long. He's still very weak.'

Soon afterwards Matt and Grace were walking back to the entrance.

'Where are you going now?' he asked.

'Back to my aunt's.'

'I'll take you.'

And when they were in the carriage and out in the street again, 'They said he will make a full recovery – eventually,' she said. There was another pause. Then almost grudgingly, 'I suppose I ought to offer an apology. It seems it was you after all.'

He said nothing at first, then finally with difficulty, 'I didn't think about it at the time but later, afterwards, I thought, perhaps I did do it because of you – and us – and your family and all, and well, I owed you something, and this was a way of offering you – I don't know – something like that.' He shrugged helplessly. 'I know what I did was unforgivable, but I thought . . . well – you might not think quite so hardly of me after—'

Then to his horror he realized she was weeping. 'It was so unlike you! I couldn't believe you could say such a thing to me! We were all having such fun, and I was seeing all those people I hadn't seen for a long time, then suddenly you were pulling me out of my chair, hauling me across the room shouting at me in front of everybody, calling me – unspeakable things. It was all horrible.'

Without thinking he put his arm about her and her head fell on to his shoulder as she wept.

'I was stupid and jealous. Oh, Grace,' he sighed, 'you were just so beautiful, like a dream. The most beautiful girl in the room and I couldn't believe you were for me, that you were all mine, that I could be so lucky. So when I saw you with those fellows, laughing and joking, it seemed to confirm all my doubts. I am not asking anything of you, honestly. You must decide for us both. But I have thought about it every day and I swear to you that there will never be another girl like you, and whatever may happen to us, I shall think of you all my life, as the one.'

She looked up into his face and they gazed a long time into each other's eyes, until at last he bent and kissed her a glancing, grazing kiss, a healing kiss.

'Don't say anything,' he murmured. 'I am not asking anything. Perhaps later, when Fred is well again, and we are able to put all this behind us. Then – then I'll ask you again.'

She pulled herself up, and taking a handkerchief from her sleeve, blew her nose, sniffed and drew a long breath. 'Perhaps you are right. We don't want any more misunderstandings. Still –' she glanced down at his walking stick – 'I won't forget what you did. To walk into a fight like that . . .'

Neither were taking any notice of where they were or the traffic clattering about them, but in fact they were on the Carlisle Bridge, a notorious bottleneck, and at that moment both doors of the carriage opened abruptly and three men clambered in. The carriage rocked with the unexpected weight as they slammed the doors behind them and arranged themselves with difficulty in the seat opposite. There was not room enough and one of them was half standing, half crouching in the narrow space between them and Matt and Grace. One of these men was Hanlon, another Walsh. Matt did not recognize the third man.

It was clear that they had not calculated on finding a girl in the carriage. As Matt and Grace were exclaiming, the men were looking at each other.

'Who's the girl?'

'Never you mind. What do you want?' Matt said firmly, unconsciously putting his arm about Grace's shoulders.

Hanlon glanced at the others. 'No matter. Matt –' he collected himself – 'we – the lads and I – were just wondering how you were doing. We were sorry to learn about your leg. You've been withdrawn from circulation, like. And then, seeing the Viceroy himself calling on you, you see, we were concerned – for yourself, like. However –' he glanced again at the others – 'this isn't the time for a talk, I see. We'll arrange a visit for another time. Come on, lads.'

He threw open the door again. The carriage was going at barely a walking pace as it crossed the bridge in the press of traffic all about it. Walsh, however, couldn't resist saying as he was about to leap out – 'We've got our eye on ye, son. Don't forget.'

A moment later all three had leaped out and Matt reached to pull the doors shut.

For a long second there was a silence as they both absorbed what had just happened. Matt was thinking furiously until at length Grace gasped, 'Who on *earth* were they?'

Matt's mind was still a complete blank.

'Matt?' No reply. '*Matt!* They knew you. Who are they? And what did he mean – he's got his eye on you?'

Matt leaned forward, his head in his hands. 'Jesus.' A new page in his life had just been turned; there was hope that eventually he and Grace would be friends again; there was everything to work for, to look forward to. And now this . . .

He realized almost immediately, however, that if there were ever to be a future for himself and Grace, he would have to explain everything.

'*Matt?*' He had still not answered.

'You must trust me,' he whispered and reached for her hand. 'If I tell you, you must trust me.'

'Very well,' she said uncertainly, 'but what did it mean? Who were they?'

Another long silence, and at last he began in little more than a whisper. 'I've been a big fool. Even bigger than you thought. I don't know how I have the impertinence to remain in your presence. Those men, they're part of a secret gang dedicated to Irish freedom—'

'Yes?'

'I mean, dedicated to fighting – no, not even fighting – murdering for Irish freedom. Stupidly I allowed myself to get mixed up with them.'

'Tell me you're joking,' she whispered.

He shook his head, leaning forwards with his elbows on his knees, and speaking in a low mutter. 'It all started in the village when that family were evicted for not paying their rent. I was arrested and taken to Boyle Castle and thrown into a cell. I told you about it. What I didn't tell you was that while I was in the cell, I was visited by a priest and soon after – that night anyway – they let me out. The priest was waiting, and gave me to understand that it had been through his intercession. I found out later that actually it had been all arranged between my step-father and the colonel of the militia.' He paused again. 'Well, the next thing I know is, I meet this man, Gerry Hanlon – that was him with the gold-rimmed specs – while I was waiting for the train. I didn't recognize him at first but it turned out he was the priest. He had been in disguise. He's an expert at disguise, I should tell you. So, on the train, he tells me about this organization, dedicated to Irish freedom, and when we got to Dublin I went along with him and was sworn in.'

He paused, and Grace whispered, 'But you said – murdering—'

He nodded. 'Murdering it was. I don't know what I was thinking of. I actually planned a murder. It sounds insane, immoral, call it what you will. And then, the most amazing thing happened. You see, I never knew my mother and father. I had been brought up since I was ten by – well you know her – my aunt Bríd. And one day she told me she was actually my mother!'

Grace gasped.

'Yes, my very own mother! I can't tell you what this meant to me. All my life I had believed my mother was dead – and she wasn't dead at all. She had been there all the time. But that's not all. Because as soon as she told me that, I wanted to know who my father was, and then, only last week, we had a visitor. Can you guess who?' He didn't wait for a reply. 'Only the Viceroy of Ireland himself, in his carriage! And he sat down before me together with my mother – and they, Grace, they told me he was my father!'

There were tears in his eyes. 'I had found my own father! I couldn't take it in. I still can't. This old man, so sad, and – you know – modest, he was my father! Can you imagine how I felt? I had found my parents – after all this time I had my parents!'

Grace reached for his hand and squeezed it.

'But that's not all! No, because I had already agreed with the Vindicators—'

'Vindicators?'

'That's them – Hanlon and the others. I had agreed with them . . . to murder the Viceroy. Murder my own father! And they still think I am going to go through with it.'

'Oh, Matt!' She clutched his arm and there was a long silence, a silence which seemed to drag out and drag out.

'What are you going to do?' she whispered at last.

'Obviously, tell 'em I can't go through with it. I would have done already but I've been stuck at home with this leg.'

Another pause before she began tentatively, 'And the police?'

'I've been involved in a conspiracy to murder,' he said flatly. 'And if the police don't get me, they will.'

'They — the Vindicators?'

'Betrayal of the Vindicators is punishable by death. It's the first thing they told me.'

'My God,' she whispered.

At that moment the carriage drew up outside Grace's aunt's house. Matt turned to her.

'Grace — I never thought I'd hear myself saying this but the safest thing for you would be to keep as far away from me as possible.' He paused. 'I can't allow you to be involved. They have seen you. And you have seen them. You should return to Sligo. Go today.'

'I'm taking Fred back with me.'

'No! Don't wait! Go today. God knows what's going to happen now.' He paused again, thinking furiously. 'Actually, now I think of it, they don't know anything. Not yet — not till I tell them.'

'You mean—'

'They still think I'm going through with it. It was only the sight of the Viceroy's carriage outside our house that made them suspicious.'

'So there's no danger — not till you tell them. Matt, don't tell them — don't go near them. Tell the police.'

'Tell them what?'

'Say you overheard something in a pub.'

'There's nothing to tell. If I reported what I know the Vindicators would simply deny it. It's only my word.' He turned to her. 'Grace — do you realize? Either I do nothing and risk my father's life — or tell them I'm not going through with it, and risk my own.' He paused. 'Either way, I risk dragging you into it. You must leave Dublin, better go today. I mean it. They're bound to watch you, at the very least. The longer you stay the more dangerous it'll be for you.'

'Come with us.'

For a long moment he held her look.

'You mean it?'

'You'd be safe in Sligo. They'd never find you.'

'And what about my father? Even if I run away they will still go after him.' Matt was still lost in thought. Then unexpectedly, as if in a delayed reaction, he turned to her again. 'Did you mean that? What you just said?'

'Yes.'

'After everything I've just told you?'

'Yes.'

He clasped her hands. 'Oh, Grace, I do love you.'

'I know you do. I knew you did even when you shouted that word at me. I knew you loved me and were saying that – because you couldn't bear to share me with anyone.'

'You understood that?'

'Yes. I knew we were destined for each other when you first came to Sligo; I was pretty certain the moment I first saw you and after the night I told you about Val, I was certain. So even though you hurt me very much, I understood it was out of your own pain.'

He took her head in his hands, and they kissed slowly, lovingly.

'We will be together, and everything will be all right. But I must make sure my father is safe first. You take Fred back to Sligo and I will come as soon as I can.'

Twenty-eight

After Grace had left him and he returned to Fitzwilliam Square Matt sat down to think. The one person he couldn't take into his confidence was his mother. And yet the Viceroy – his father – must be warned. Matt didn't want to be seen going to him in person and he didn't want to put anything in a letter. In the end after such hard thinking that it gave him a headache, he decided to take Garrett into his confidence. He could warn his father through Garrett. Garrett was a man who understood the world, a man who had come to dominate his environment, a man not at the mercy of chance, competent, in charge. In a word, a successful man. Compared with Harry, Garrett seemed – and Matt grasped this now for the first time – Garrett seemed paradoxically to be Matt's true father, while the Viceroy appeared to him more in the role of grandfather.

Whatever he might think of Matt's judgement, Matt knew Garrett would stand by him, and in particular, could be his channel to the Viceroy. It was imperative to warn him of the danger to his life as soon as possible.

Matt knew that Garrett was often at the Kildare Street Club in the early evening before returning home. This was the premier gentleman's club in Dublin and as always Garrett made sure he was in the right place to mix with the men he could use.

Matt needed to speak to Garrett but not at home, so that evening he made an excuse to his mother about calling into the college and took a cab to Kildare Street. It was the first time he had entered the club and, preoccupied as he was, he could not help pausing to look about him at the vaulting of the entrance hall, and the fine marble staircase. Doors opened into large, elegant, brightly lit rooms, the morning room, the drawing room, the dining room, and the air was thick with talk and cigar smoke. The hall was crowded with men coming and going. To one side was a porter's cubby hole, and Matt asked him whether Mr Doyle was in. He was, and Matt sent in a message by a porter to summon him out.

'Matt? You're out and about again, I see. What brings you here?'
Garrett was smoking a cigar.

'I need to speak to you and I did not want to talk at home.'
He paused. 'Do you mind coming outside for a moment?'

Garrett glanced out into the dark street. 'It's cold. Can't we talk in here?'

'I'd rather not. Its urgent – and secret,' he muttered.

'Really? Then I'd better get my coat.'

A moment later they were strolling up towards St Stephen's Green. Garrett said nothing, and puffed meditatively on his cigar. Matt could not look at him, but hopped along, one hand in his pocket, the other leaning on his stick. 'Something terrible has happened,' he muttered at last. 'I need your help.'

Garrett stopped and turned to him. Matt caught his eye and after a moment stumbled out the story as he had told it to Grace.

Garrett did not expostulate, did not criticize, did not even express surprise. He merely said calmly, 'Who have you told?'

'No one apart from Grace. She's going back to Sligo.'

'So you want me to get a message to his Excellency?'

'It's essential. I don't know what's going to happen.'

'Do you think these men still believe you're going through with it?'

'I don't know! Ever since they saw the Viceroy visiting our house, they've got suspicious.'

'Hmm.'

'And Garrett, there's something else. Mam knows nothing of this.' He paused. 'I'd better tell you everything. I had a gun—'

'A gun!'

Matt nodded. 'It sounds incredibly stupid, I know – evil – but I had this gun.'

'Where is it now?'

'At the bottom of the river. And Garrett – I must tell you something, I mean thank you, actually. That night when I met you outside the Shelbourne, and you shouted at me about Grace—'

'Yes?'

'You made me see sense. I mean – that this was not the way – and not the way ever to win back Grace. I realized how criminal, how evil the plot was. Thank you for that.'

'Hmm. That's good anyway.' He was thoughtful. 'The man we need to speak to is not the Viceroy, it's the Chief Constable. As a matter of fact he's in the Club now. Come on.'

He turned and they made their way back to the club. 'Wait here,' said Garrett and disappeared into the crowd of men coming and going through the lofty smoke-filled rooms.

'Get your coat, Charlie,' Garrett said coolly, 'we need to take a stroll.'

The Chief Constable was a slim man of Garrett's age, somewhat lean in the face, with a small moustache. He looked like an ex-army officer.

Outside the door Garrett introduced Matt. 'My son.' And turning to Matt, 'Charlie O'Malley, Matt. He's our best man in this case. Tell him what you told me.'

Strolling up the street again in the cold and the dark, Matt ran through the story again. At the end when they stood facing St Stephen's Green, O'Malley was thoughtful, stroking his chin. 'Sam Walsh we know. He was in the States for a long time – has a lot of contacts there, I believe. But Gerry Hanlon is new to me. I'll have to look him up, see whether we have anything on him.'

Matt realized now that Hanlon's passion for disguise, which hitherto he had regarded as childish, did have a practical use. It seemed likely that the police had no knowledge of him.

'We'll go round to my office now, and see what—'

'No!' Matt stopped him. 'I can't be seen going into the police headquarters. And I must be home soon. My mother is expecting me – and I can't let her suspect anything!'

Garrett turned with a surprised look to Matt. 'Quite right,' he said after a moment. He turned to O'Malley. 'Perhaps I could see you in the club tomorrow lunchtime?'

O'Malley nodded and turned back to the club. Garrett hailed a cab and they made their way home.

'That reminds me – we have guests tonight. Better not be late. As for the other business . . .' He paused. 'It's in the hands of the police now, Matt, and we'll have to wait for instructions from them. It's as well you told me now – and we told him. I'm not sure what might have happened to you otherwise. Plotting the life of the Viceroy – they could have taken a very dim view if they had caught you earlier.'

Matt was chilled with fear. Plotting a murder: was that a hanging offence? At the very least it would have meant many years in prison; ruin and disgrace. As for Grace herself – Matt closed his eyes and prayed it was not too late to straighten things out.

As they entered the house, and encountered Bríd in the dining room doorway, Garrett announced cheerfully, 'I picked Matt up on the way back. Get changed, Matt; we have guests – remember?'

Matt was still in a state of acute trepidation. He had no idea what the police chief intended – or what he would find out in his files. Had Matt been followed, for instance, when he met Hanlon in St Aloysius? Or had there been spies in O'Leary's bar? His head was filled with unanswered questions, but all of them led back to Grace now that they appeared to be reconciled. He sat on the edge of his bed, his head in his hands. How could this nightmare have descended on him? How had he allowed himself to get into this situation?

When he descended to the drawing room he heard voices, and on entering saw Garrett in conversation with a man and a woman. Matt recognized them immediately as Mr and Mrs Haynes. He attempted to join the conversation, wrenching his mind with difficulty from his own preoccupations and answering their well-meaning questions – about his law studies, and his limp, the fight and so on. He soon found himself in conversation with Mrs Haynes as Garrett and the man diverted off into a private talk of their own, and as Matt came eye to eye with this lady, his answers became more and more awkward. Of course she recognized him, only too well, so that her questions too became strained, halting, with embarrassing pauses as they continued to look into each other's eyes.

It was worse because she was undeniably very good-looking, and had a charming and quite seductive manner. Questions were racing through Matt's mind: what was she doing here? Had she been deceiving her husband? And many other questions too. Again Matt felt very much out of his depth. What had she been doing with Garrett in the Shelbourne that night? He vividly remembered Garrett's impassioned speech to himself. It was impossible that Garrett had betrayed his mother. And a fresh question arose: What did his mother know of this woman?

At that moment Bríd herself appeared and announced that dinner was ready and they went down to the dining room.

Throughout the evening Matt watched the woman – and her husband. He could detect no sign of friction, no suspicion or awkwardness. On the contrary, Mr Haynes was in very high spirits, laughing and joking with Garrett and even flirting a little with Bríd.

'And are you back at college now, after your scrimmage?' Mrs Haynes asked innocently at one point. Matt said he now felt strong enough to return to his lectures. 'I've lost a lot of time this term and I have finals next summer.'

The following day Matt was conveyed to the college in his parents' carriage, and he limped back into the lecture theatre. He was still using a stick, but the swelling of his knee was much reduced and he felt he might soon be able to dispense with it.

However, as he was standing outside the front gate at lunchtime staring idly across at the imposing façade of the Bank of Ireland and his mind far away, still running the conversation with the Chief Constable through his mind, he was startled to find Mrs Haynes standing in front of him. She was well wrapped against the cold, a toque on her head, and her hands in a muff.

'Matt?' She peered into his face. 'Do you remember me?'

'Mrs Haynes, of course.'

She did not allow him to go on because releasing one hand from her muff she slipped it through his arm. 'We must have a little talk, Matt. I owe you an explanation.' She was about to steer him up towards Grafton Street when he stopped her.

'I was expecting my mother's carriage.'

The carriage did in fact pull up at that moment. She glanced at it and then said hurriedly, 'Well, perhaps we can ride a way together – if you don't mind?'

He shrugged and followed her into the carriage.

'Where do you want to go?' he asked.

'It doesn't matter.' She drew a breath. 'You seem to be much recovered now.' She gave his arm a little squeeze. 'As I said, I owe you an explanation,' she repeated.

He waited.

'You see, Matt, and I beg you not to tell anyone – don't on any account tell your stepfather I'm saying this – some time ago my husband got into difficulties. I don't know all the details but I believe it was to do with the exchange rate of the dollar and instead of making a profit, as he expected, he made a very big loss. He first approached Mr Doyle for a loan. Doyle unfortunately was not inclined to advance him. The money market was volatile, everything was uncertain. We had sleepless nights and I really thought for a while my husband was going to do something desperate. That was when I plucked up courage and decided to approach Doyle myself.'

All Matt's suspicions were confirmed. He listened in silence as she continued.

'Matt, you're only a young man, but I have to tell you this – because I don't want you to get the wrong idea about Mr Doyle.'

'What wrong idea?' he said brusquely.

'I think you know.'

Matt said nothing.

'So,' she resumed, 'I went to see Mr Doyle. I first spoke to him at the Horse Show where you saw us. We made an assignation – or rather,' she corrected herself awkwardly, 'I asked him to meet me – at the Shelbourne. Actually I had sent him a message in my husband's name but I went alone. Matt, I am ashamed to confess . . . I had booked a room.' She disentangled her arm and reached a tiny scented handkerchief to her nose. 'That's how desperate I was!'

Matt was feeling intensely embarrassed that this woman who was so much older, was sitting beside him in the darkness of the carriage spilling her most intimate secrets and getting so upset about it. 'Why are you telling me this?'

She looked up desperately into his face. 'I don't want you to think badly of your stepfather – because you saw us coming out of the hotel that night.'

'I don't understand any of this. You met Garrett in the Shelbourne – and then what?'

She looked away. 'I told him we were in desperate straits, and that I would do anything – I mean, anything Doyle wanted – for the money.'

'Anything?' Matt whispered after a moment as he watched her.

She nodded, looking away from him with her handkerchief over her face. 'Now you know what a woman will do for her husband!'

There was a long silence. Finally Matt stuttered, 'Well . . . what—'

'What happened? That's what you want to know, isn't it?'

Matt waited until finally she drew a long breath, dabbed at her eyes, and turned to Matt. 'Nothing,' she said simply. 'Garrett listened to me and at last he said he would see me home. He said it wouldn't look good if anyone saw us sitting there together. We were going out into the street and I caught his arm – I said I was sorry to trouble him about the money. He just said he'd sort something out. That was all. Then he called a cab, and then you appeared.'

'Well – did he sort something out?'

She nodded. 'He has a friend at the bank, and Haynes managed to get a loan. Doyle endorsed the bill. You're a lucky young man. Doyle is one in a million.'

When they met the Chief Constable again – by night and in the street as before – O'Malley was able to tell them a little more about Walsh and one or two of the others, but as he suspected, the records contained no mention of Hanlon.

'What we need is corroboration,' he explained. 'Your word is not sufficient in a court of law. You have got to take one of our men with you, when you meet them to discuss the job.'

'What man?'

'I don't know yet. I'm working on that. But we'll find someone. Don't worry, leave it to me.'

That evening around ten, Matt strolled into O'Leary's bar. He looked a lot more relaxed than he felt. He leaned on the bar, ordered a pint and as the barman placed it in front of him said casually, 'Evening, Tom. Any sign of Gerry?'

'Gerry who?' said the barman without expression as he took the money.

'You know – Gerry Hanlon.'

'I don't know any Gerry Hanlon,' he replied with a stony face.

Matt looked him in the eye for a moment as he rearranged his thoughts. 'Well, if you do happen to meet a Gerry Hanlon would you tell him to get in touch?'

'In touch with who?'

'With Matt Byrne. He'll know where to find me.'

'If I see any Gerry Hanlon I'll tell him.'

That was the end of the conversation. Matt finished his drink hurriedly and left the pub. He found himself shaking as he walked quickly home.

A couple of days later he received a note at college making the usual appointment at St Aloysius.

'I've found a new recruit,' Matt said.

'Oh?'

'A chap at college. We've been planning it between us.'

'I told you, there'll be no private arrangements. This is an operation by the Vindicators, and Sam and me'll give the say-so.'

'To hell with that! Why do we need to bring them into it? The more men that know about it, the more likely we'll be betrayed – how do you know one of them isn't a traitor? Didn't you once tell me about Kevin Meany? Look, the Viceroy is a friend of my mother's. That makes it all the easier. I can arrange to meet him in the park for a chat, my friend will have a trap ready. One shot will do it and we're away safely.'

Hanlon was thoughtful, studying him carefully. Matt was cool. At last Hanlon said, with an ironic note in his voice, 'So who is this "*chap at college*"? I have to see him before anything is decided.'

'Didn't I tell you, the fewer men know about it the better.'

Hanlon was clearly uncertain. However at length he repeated, 'This is a job for the Vindicators. There'll be no private armies. You need us more than we need you, Matt. You'll need a network to get you out of the country after. Bring your friend along to Tom's next Tuesday at nine.'

'There's another thing.' Matt remembered Fred. 'That friend of mine, the one you saw me talking to in O'Leary's once. He got beaten up outside one night. Was that your doing?'

Hanlon was awkward. 'You'll have to speak to Sam about that.'

'Sam? You mean he did organize it?'

Again, a pause. Hanlon couldn't look at him. 'Maybe.' Finally, he turned to Matt, serious. 'The Vindicators don't tolerate spies. It was a warning, that's all. He got off lightly.'

'*Spies?* He was innocent. He's never heard of the Vindicators. He has no idea about them.'

'That's as maybe.'

Twenty-nine

The following day Matt received a letter from Sligo.

Dear Matt,

As you see we are home again, and have brought Fred with us. Poor man, he is making a very slow recovery. He had the most awful beating and it's a wonder he survived at all. I now realize how brave it was of you to go to his rescue when he was so heavily outnumbered. Fred is remembering more and more each day and his memory is nearly back to normal. He told me how you came to the rescue – though he didn't recognize you in the dark. I believe you saved his life. And for that, if for nothing else, I must always remain grateful to you.

Dear Matt, I believe we can put the past behind us now and go forward together. (Though, when I say that, I have not forgotten the day on Howth Head, which is burned into my memory – the most beautiful day of my life.)

So, I beg you, come to Sligo now. I am so frightened for you thinking of those horrible men who climbed into the carriage. I have scarcely been able to sleep since that day for thinking of it. Dear Matt, do come to stay until all this has blown over. I shall not be easy until I know you are safe.

Bless you again for what you did for Fred,

Yours,

Grace

The following night Matt and Garrett met the Chief Constable again. He was accompanied this time by a thin little man, a weasel-faced man in shabby clothes, a shrimp of a fellow with a furtive sideways sort of expression, who ducked and feinted sometimes as if he had been a boxer once.

The Chief Constable introduced him as Timmy O'Farrell, 'The best man we've got,' he told Matt when he saw the expression on Matt's face, 'and clean – hundred per cent.'

Matt took the constable's arm and led him a few feet away.

'I can't take him – I told them I was bringing a chap from college. They'll take one look at him and suspect something. They're already suspicious of me.'

The Chief Constable frowned. 'I haven't got any one else.'

'Look, it's my neck going in the noose,' Matt whispered. 'Am I really supposed to introduce him as a chap from college?'

'Not all of us have had the benefit of a university education, Matt,' the Chief Constable said brusquely. 'Make something up – tell them he's a college servant or something. A gardener, anything. And you don't have to worry. He'll be armed, and we'll be outside. But this is the only way we can do it. We must have independent corroboration.'

On the Tuesday Matt met Timmy, who was a man of few words – and those uttered in a heavy Dublin accent – and they made their way to O'Leary's.

This time it appeared Tom the barman recognized Matt after all and nodded them through a door to the stairs. When they got into the upper room, Walsh was there with four or five of the gang and a few others drifted in after them.

'No sign of Gerry?' Matt looked round the room.

'He'll be here,' said Walsh in an offhand voice as he studied Timmy. 'Matt here says you're a "*chap from college*",' he said suspiciously.

'Timmy works in the college kitchens,' Matt interrupted. 'We got talking one day and I found out he's a staunch Republican. True to the cause. Isn't that right, Timmy?'

'True enough,' said Timmy with that curious sideways feint as if Matt had thrown a punch at him.

'What's the matter with you?' asked one of the others suspiciously.

'I used to be in the fight game, welterweight. Did ye never hear of Timmy O'Farrell, Dublin schools junior champion in '68?'

'And what makes you think you'd be any use to the cause?' Walsh went on, still suspicious.

'Try me,' said Timmy.

There was a moment's silence.

'We may just do that,' Walsh said ominously.

'Yes, you will do that!' Matt said aggressively. 'Timmy and I have it all thought out. None of you will have to risk your necks. You'll all be safe in your beds but it's Timmy and I will do the job! And then you'll see what he's worth!'

'Hold on Matt,' Walsh said coolly. 'No need to raise our voices. No one's accusing you or Timmy here of anything. It's just that we've never set eyes on him till this moment and naturally we want to satisfy ourselves that he's clean.'

'Clean? Why wouldn't he be?'

'You don't know much,' Walsh went on in his suspicious voice. 'This town is full of police touts. We have to be careful.'

'Tell him about your brother, Timmy,' said Matt.

'Ah well, ye see,' Timmy began with another twist of the neck as if easing it in his collar – though he was wearing no collar. ''Twas me brother Joseph was sent down for a stretch in New South Wales by this very same Lord Elphin when he was a magistrate over there. I swore I'd get even if ever I got the chance – and now it looks as if the chance has come.'

'Joseph O'Farrell,' said one of the others whom Matt did not know. 'I remember the name.'

'Ye were there?' Timmy turned on him.

'Hmm. Seventy or seventy-two, that would have been.'

'Seventy-two it was.'

'So you're his brother?'

They were all looking at O'Farrell. He said nothing, waiting.

'Ye see,' the man went on, 'I remember Joe O'Farrell, and his mother and father too, and his sisters. But I don't remember any talk of a brother.'

'That'd be because I never went out. I was fostered on me grandparents as a baby. To ease the load, like.'

'Ah,' the other man looked thoughtful. 'To ease the load.'

At this moment there was a knock at the door. The others started and looked round. It opened and the pot boy from below slipped across to Walsh and passed him a folded paper.

'Gentleman said to give ye this,' he whispered.

Walsh opened it. 'Jesus!' He looked round at the others in the utmost alarm. 'It's Gerry! He's outside and he says there's the polis in the street.'

He turned and stared at Matt with dawning recognition. 'This is a trap, isn't it?'

But before Matt could say anything, Timmy cried out in terror, 'Oh Jesus Mary and Joseph, is it the Peelers? What have ye done, ye've brought me here and now we're trapped!'

'I always thought it!' Walsh leaped up 'A bloody spy, and your friend too.'

'Oh Jesus, Matt, what'll we do?' shouted Timmy, ignoring Walsh. His tone had terrified the others who had started up in confusion.

'The back stairs,' said Walsh with authority in his voice. He turned to Matt as he pulled a pistol from his pocket. 'And you're coming too, sunshine. We need you.' He thrust his pistol in Matt's side. 'By the hokey but you'll pay for this night's work!'

In the confusion Timmy had slipped through the door and disappeared in the direction of the bar. Walsh saw this. 'I thought as much – the little rat.'

Matt saw the effect Timmy's disappearance had on the others who were in headlong panic.

'This way.' Walsh had his pistol in Matt's side as they came out of the room, and in a moment Matt was being pushed among the others down the servants' staircase to the kitchen. There were men in front of him and behind. And right behind him, with his pistol in Matt's back, was Walsh. He was incandescent. 'Ye've a heavy debt to pay, me boy. I had me doubts about ye from the start,' Matt heard him mutter.

In a moment they were hurrying through the kitchen, but as they were almost at the door it opened and a burly constable of the Dublin Metropolitan Police in a dark greatcoat and pointed helmet filled the doorway. Without hesitation Walsh raised his pistol and fired. The noise was deafening in the kitchen as the workers screamed and dived to the floor and the constable lurched to one side clutching his shoulder.

They emerged into a dark alley leading down to the river. 'Don't try anything, or you're a dead man,' Walsh shouted. Matt was forced to run, but almost immediately his knee began to hurt and he slowed.

'Keep up! Keep up or you're for it!'

Matt was limping. 'I can't go any faster.' Walsh was behind him and kept glancing back up the alley in the direction of Dame Street.

'Faster!'

'I can't, I tell you! I had an accident with my knee.'

They emerged on the quay. It was quiet but coming towards them was a cab, a four-wheeler.

'Stop him!' Walsh bellowed and two of the others seized the horses' reins. Walsh wrenched open the door, reached in and seized a man by the arm. 'Get out!' he shouted in such a tremendous voice, that the man leaped out followed by a very startled woman.

'Now get in and don't try anything!' Walsh shouted. Matt realized in this instant that it was now or never if he was to get out of this alive. His knee was already in exquisite pain but he hauled himself into the cab, across and opened the other door, almost fell out, made two hops to the parapet of the river and threw himself over. In the darkness he hit the water.

A cold shock, a rushing, floundering, gasping, and then with a whoosh he broke the surface, gasping for air. At that moment there was a gun shot. Matt was not hit, but with a sudden access of energy he twisted in the water, dived again, swimming towards the wall and came up close in its deep shadow. As he was gulping air, he heard noises and shouts above him, running feet, a clatter of horses' hooves and more shouts. He waited, treading water, listening, breathing hard. The cold of the water had quietened the throbbing in his knee. Then the voices moved away, and things seemed to go quiet. He waited until it seemed they had gone away then began cautiously swimming downstream until he came to steps. He hauled himself out and sat for a moment getting his breath back as the water ran off him.

As soon as he stood, however, the pain shot through his knee again, and he collapsed on the step. This was ridiculous. He couldn't wait here unless he wanted to freeze to death. It was a very cold winter night. With an effort he pulled himself up again, and half hopped and half crawled until he was on the quay. Pulling himself upright he looked about for a cab. The quay was quiet – since it was nearly midnight, but there were signs of move- ment and traffic further along on the Carlisle Bridge so he began to hop and stumble towards it. Then to his relief a cab did approach, mercifully free and he stopped it and dragged himself inside.

When he got home he let himself in with his own key and

worked his way up to his room. The house was in bed and he was careful to make as little noise as possible. He peeled off his wet clothes, towelled himself and fell into bed.

When the maid arrived with his hot water the following morning, he asked her to send his mother up.

'I've made a fool of myself again, Mam.'

She looked about the room at the wet clothes scattered about.

'I was bragging to the fellows how Fred and I went swimming down at the Forty Foot Rock, so a fellow bet me I wouldn't swim the Liffey . . .'

He looked up at her helplessly.

'What time was this?'

'Near to midnight.'

'Near to midnight on a November night, and you went for a swim?'

He looked up her helplessly. 'And I think I strained my knee again.'

'Oh Matt! Have you no sense?' She clasped her hands together. 'You may end up doing some permanent damage! What were you thinking of?'

'I know,' he shrugged helplessly. 'So I think I'll just stay here for the morning, if you don't mind. To rest the knee. And Mam –' she was just going out – 'could you ask Dunne to send up the papers?'

The raid on O'Leary's made the headlines that morning. Eight men had been taken into custody, including Walsh, and had been charged with conspiracy to commit murder. Matt bit his lip as he read this. Clearly the police would be round to talk – probably this morning – he would be called to give evidence and that meant that his mother would have to know. The real trouble was that Hanlon was still at large. And if Matt had to be in Dublin ready to give evidence, the chances were that Hanlon would be after him. Hanlon knew where he lived. Without Matt's evidence the men could not be tried. There seemed no way out of it.

Sure enough later that afternoon there was a visitor, and the Chief Constable was shown into his room where he still lay in bed. Behind O'Malley stood Bríd with worry all over her face.

'Mam, can you leave us please?' Matt said helplessly.

The conversation was brief. As Matt had guessed, he would be the key witness of the trial of these men. Equally importantly Hanlon was still free.

'How long until the trial?'

'A month perhaps. Can you arrange to be out of Dublin till then?'

'Yes.'

'In a safe place?'

'Yes.'

That afternoon he wrote to Grace, explaining the situation and asking whether she would still like him to come down to Sligo. The reply came the following day by telegram. 'Come.'

In the meantime Garrett had come up to talk to him, and Matt explained what he intended to do. Garrett undertook to explain the situation to Bríd after Matt had left.

That afternoon he was on the train. Though it was late November, the weather on the west coast was clear and not particularly cold. Grace was waiting for him at the station, well wrapped in a long overcoat. Matt was hobbling again on a stick.

'I seem fated to be propped up on a stick,' he said as she greeted him on the platform. 'Still, who knows, perhaps in the end I'll get used to it. I might even grow to like it. Don't you think it lends me an air of authority, of dignity? Of *gravitas*?'

'*Gravitas*? You'll be a long time waiting for *that*, me boy,' she said. 'A midnight swim in the Liffey? A wild boy indeed.'

'The Liffey saved my life and I shall be eternally grateful to her cold, dirty waters. In my old age, I may even endow a prize for swimming, a midnight race for the Matthew Byrne Cup. To be awarded to the silliest, drunkest student in Dublin.'

'Come on, it's cold standing here. Let's get you home.'

She slipped her arm through his and led him out to where the trap was waiting.

That evening Matt dined with the family. Fred was on his feet again, and seemed at first sight to be completely recovered. However, 'He does still have headaches,' Grace told Matt later. The parents were all smiles and friendship and Matt was hugely relieved that the horrible moment in the Gresham was at last put behind them and he and Grace could look forward to their life together. Ardnashiel, so remote, right on the brink of the winter ocean, with its scrubbed skies and clean, white beaches, seemed a million miles from the dirty streets of Dublin, and for the first time it seemed in ages Matt felt able to relax and to concentrate on Grace. And once the trial was over . . .

The following morning they walked along the beach together. The clouds reared up in huge banks over the western ocean, the wind blew into them, filling Matt with a wonderful zest and energy. The white sand was strewn with bladderwrack and fragments of driftwood driven ashore by the strong, clean, life-enhancing west wind and the sea swept up in huge grey-green rollers that exploded at their feet, filling the air with a fine spray. Matt couldn't help stopping, his arm round her shoulders staring out to sea at this magnificent spectacle.

'It's wonderful here. I never want to go back.'

'Then don't,' she said simply.

'What do you mean?'

'Come and work for Fred. I don't know whether he may post-pone his degree for a year – he's lost so much time. But either next summer or the one after he's coming back to work for Pa. Eventually he's taking over.'

'He told me about it once.'

'Well – you could be, like, a partner. Or agent, or family lawyer. It doesn't matter what you're called. We'll be here. What more do we want? Where else do you want your children brought up?'

In a flash Matt saw everything clearly. A simple life with Grace and their children. What more do you want, she had asked. He stared out to sea, with his arm about her shoulders, as his imagin-ation was filled with this prospect.

'I do so love you,' he murmured. 'And to think I so nearly lost you.'

'Don't talk of that,' she said crisply. 'You didn't and that's what matters.'

Thirty

It was the relief most of all. The thought that he was safe here. He still had to go to Dublin for the trial, but for the moment he was safe, and could be with Grace all day. They seemed to have so much to say to each other, and whenever he remembered the events of the last few days – which he did during the night – he would remember the moment when Walsh pulled out a gun and he thought his last hour had come. It was only the river, he thought, which had saved him. Then he would wake up breathing fast, staring up into the darkness and realize he was safe.

As for the trial – he would face that when it came. He did not think Hanlon would try anything. It would be far too dangerous. It would be a good idea too, Matt thought, when he returned to Dublin to stay at a hotel before the trial. Hanlon would be bound to watch the house and might have tried to attack him there. Just get through the next month, he told himself, and it would all be over.

In the meantime he was free to be with Grace. He had also written home to Garrett to ask him to send up some of his books. Although his degree had been nearly forgotten since the night of the fight, it seemed, now that his life appeared to be regaining some semblance of normality, it was time to resume his studies. He was still uncertain, however, whether to sit his exams in the summer or postpone them for a year. He too had lost a lot of time.

One morning, a week after writing home for his books, he and Grace arranged to go riding along the beach, and he was just coming downstairs into the hall when Grace, who was before him and was standing near the front door called, 'Your books have come.'

'Oh good.' He hurried down.

'Just got here this minute – delivered from the station.'

Matt hurried down to where she was standing with a cardboard box at her feet. But almost immediately he knew there was something odd. As he picked up the box, there were two things wrong with it. First it was far too light. And secondly he did not recognize the handwriting. In fact there were three things wrong with it, he now saw – there was no sign of a railway address sticker. Standing in front of Grace holding this box, Matt had a sudden premonition. Some unconscious thought prompted him, he did not know how.

'Open the door!'

'What?'

'*Open the door!*'

Grace, suddenly nervous at his ferocious tone, jumped to obey and Matt ran out of the door and a further fifty yards before setting the box on the grass.

'Don't touch that box. Leave it! Grace – don't go near that box and don't let anyone touch it till I get back!'

A groom had just appeared at the corner of the house with the two horses. Matt ran as fast as he was able, hopping and stumbling, seized the bridle of one, and was helped into the saddle. 'I shan't be long! Don't touch the box! Remember!'

In a second he was galloping up the drive and in a minute was at the gate, turned into the road towards Sligo town. And sure enough after a few minutes he saw a man on a trap half a mile ahead of him where the road came out on the coast above the cliffs. As he came in sight the man on the trap turned and saw him and immediately lashed his horse into a gallop. He did not have much chance of outrunning Matt, however, who quickly overtook him. As he drew level Matt glanced at the driver and beneath the beard and the bowler hat drawn down low over his brows he recognized Hanlon. At that moment Hanlon drew a pistol from an inner pocket and fired at him. Although they were almost side by side Hanlon missed his mark and there was nothing Matt could do but leap from his saddle on to him and send the two of them crashing to the ground from the trap. They hit the ground locked in an embrace, rolling over and over. The breath was knocked out of him and he had a pain in his shoulder where he had fallen but Matt managed to get over the other man, raised his fist and smashed it into his face. Hanlon, who was slim and wiry and surprisingly strong, jerked upwards, threw Matt to one side, and raising himself on to his knee, pulled a knife from his pocket. Matt wrenched to his face but only seized the beard which immediately came away in his hand as Hanlon, free now, raised his arm with the knife. Matt rolled away backwards to give himself more space and as Hanlon leaped to his feet Matt, suddenly crippled by his knee, fell back with a gasp of pain as Hanlon sprang over him. But in that moment, as if inspired, as Hanlon was leaping on him with the dagger poised to drive it into his throat, Matt contrived to seize his arm and, taking advantage of Hanlon's lack of balance, suddenly rolled backwards. Hanlon flew over his head and over the cliff.

Silence. And then, gradually, the sound of the rollers below and a curlew somewhere high above him. Struggling to regain his breath, Matt lay staring upwards as the peace and silence of day gradually permeated his consciousness.

Eventually he twisted himself, half crawled to the brink of the cliff and looked over. Far below he could see Hanlon's body. It was not moving. Then, remembering Grace and the box, he tried to struggle to his feet but fell back again. There was no sight of his horse so presumably she had made her way back to her warm stable. There was no sight of the horse and trap either but presumably she had made her way back to Sligo town. Matt remained in perplexity for some time until Fred appeared on horseback.

Matt was still sitting on the grass, feeling curiously empty, as Fred drew up.

'What's going on?'

'No one has touched the box, have they?'

'No. Why, is there a bomb in it?' Fred was almost joking.

'I think so.'

Fred dismounted. 'I imagine you're going to explain all this eventually. In the meantime, what are you doing here and where's Marigold?'

'She's on her way home, I hope. As for me – give me a moment and I'll explain everything – just so long as no one has touched the box. Let's get back. I want that thing safely disposed of.'

Fred helped him to his feet and Matt stumbled to the horse. Fred helped him up. 'I really don't know how you do it,' he murmured at last, shaking his head.

'Do what?'

'You seem to attract trouble wherever you go. I hope it isn't going to be like this after you're married to Grace.'

'So do I. Let's go.'

Fred looked at the horse. 'Do you think she'll take us both?'

'It's not far. I expect she'll manage it this once – as a special favour.'

Fred, with some difficulty, helped Matt into the saddle, hauled himself up behind and they jogged back to the house. The entire household was standing outside the door and there on the grass, fifty yards away, stood the box.

'Matt! What's happened?'

'I'll tell you later. We've got to decide what to do with *that*, first.' He pointed. 'The main thing is not to open it.'

'The man carried it in and put it down,' said Grace helpfully.

'That was Hanlon,' Matt muttered.

'Hanlon? Who's he?' Fred turned to him.

'I'll tell you one day.'

They all stood, the family surrounded by the entire household staff, looking at the box.

'The man carried it in, you said, Grace?' said her father.

'Yes. He set it down on the ground at my feet. He didn't ask for a signature, though. I thought that was odd.'

'So – presumably it won't go off until we open it. I suggest, the thing to do is to pour a bucket of water over it.'

'Don't go near it!' cried his wife, clutching his arm.

'My dear, Matt himself carried it out of the house,' Sir William said mildly.

'What about the garden hose?'

'Sound suggestion, Fred,' said Sir William. 'Liam, go and fetch the garden hose. We'll give it a good dousing.'

After some preparation a hose was unrolled, and a foot pump set up, and Liam and Mick set to work until the box was thoroughly soaked through.

'We'll just leave it where it is until the police arrive.'

'There's a body too,' said Matt, almost as an afterthought, 'at the foot of the cliffs back there.'

They all turned.

'It's the man who brought the box,' he said simply. 'Someone called Hanlon. He was trying to prevent me giving evidence at the trial. Somebody had better go for the police.'

That evening Matt began to develop symptoms of a fever and the following morning he had a temperature. His shoulder also ached abominably.

'I'm sorry to be such a nuisance,' he said as Grace stood at his bedside the following morning, her arms folded as she inspected him.

'So long as you're sure there's no one else gunning for you.'

'I don't think so.'

'You don't *think* so? You mean, you're not sure?'

He rolled his head on the pillow. 'No one that I know of.' He smiled wanly.

'So, do you think it'll be safe for you to give evidence at the trial?'

'Yes. Pretty sure.'

She sighed and turned away to the window, staring out at the sea. 'And I used to think *I* led an exciting life.' She turned sternly. 'Once the trial is over, we are coming back here and we are going to lead a *quiet life*, me wild boy.'

'Hear hear.'

Matt was a week in bed recovering from the emotional after-effects of his struggle, running a temperature, babbling in his sleep, pored over by the doctor. Gradually, however, his natural resilience bounced back, he recovered, was out of bed, resumed walks along the sands. He couldn't open a book, though. The print would just run together on the page and he would get a headache.

The day of the trial approached and, as he had told Grace, he moved to the Gresham, where he was visited by his mother.

The trial came and lasted all day. Matt gave his evidence, then Timmy O'Farrell appeared and gave a very coherent account of what he had heard. Strangely, the twists and feints, the bobbing and ducking, had all disappeared. He seemed quite sane, quite unlike the man who had accompanied Matt to O'Leary's bar. 'I told you,' the Chief Constable told Matt one day afterwards, 'he's our best man.' Matt never could decide who the real Timmy O'Farrell was – or even whether that was his real name.

Dear Harry,

I thought I should write and give you an account of the wedding. Matt was so sorry – as were we all – that you could not be with us on this special day, but of course we understand the reasons. Still, Matt wants to bring Grace to meet you soon after they get back from their honeymoon and I am sure it can be arranged quite discreetly. They are in Ballyglin for a few days at the moment, and then going to Italy. Matt wanted to take Grace to see the place where he was brought up and to visit Patsy and Nora's grave. Matt is recovered now after all his adventures though his knee may never be completely healed and he walks with a slight limp.

As for Grace, I need hardly say she looked a vision at the wedding. She is a lovely girl and on this day of all others, she looked quite radiant. Matt seemed quite besotted with her, so proud of his new wife. It was all very touching and everyone was in tears. I will send you some photographs as soon as they are ready.

Grace wants Matt to go to work for Fred on the estate in Sligo, but I think he is still intent on going into the law and involving himself in legal work on behalf of the Land League and Home Rule. I think they intend to settle eventually in Sligo to be near her parents . . .

It was a hot afternoon, the grass smelling of summer. High above, the sky seemed fathoms deep where small puffy clouds hovered at an immense distance, serene, detached. The air was filled with the humming of insects; suddenly a dragonfly would zigzag erratically across the water's surface and there was a sudden 'plop' as a fish broke the surface as another insect skimmed too low.

Across the valley the trees were thick, lush, bright with fresh growth and away at the far end of the meadow on the other side of the river a few cows lay in the shade of a broad sheltering oak, their tails flapping idly across their bony backs.

Grace slipped one foot out of its sandal and dipped it into the water.

'Bliss.'

Matt was lying on his back staring up into the afternoon sky biting meditatively on a long grass stalk he had plucked at random.

'Uncle Patsy used to bring me here as a boy. He taught me to tickle trout.' He went on dreamily, 'He taught me all sorts of things. How to break a rabbit's neck—'

'Horrid man! I don't think I like the sound of your uncle Patsy.'

Matt turned to her. 'He was the gentlest man alive,' he said seriously, 'unlike my aunt Nora. She was a tartar.'

'And how on earth do you tickle trout? I've never heard of such a thing. Do they giggle? Do you tickle them under the armpits?'

'You reach down into the water where they hover in the shelter of the bank, very, very slowly –' he sat up and reached a hand over Grace's hair, and stroked it down her back – 'and then you stroke her very gently at first so that she hardly notices—'

'Oh, it's a female, is it?' Grace murmured, reacting to the movement of his hand down her back.

'Very likely.' He continued caressing and stroking her back as she pressed herself against his hand. 'You go on like this for quite a long time, and gradually the trout goes into a dreamy, ecstatic state. She just enjoys being stroked so much.'

Grace lay back on the rug and Matt ran his hand up and over her thigh and her belly to her breast. She was looking into his eyes.

'The trout goes into an ecstatic, dreamy state,' he repeated gently, as he leaned over her to kiss her, 'and then, quite simply, you can do anything you like with her . . .'

Author's Note

Readers interested in the earlier story of Bríd, Harry and Garrett will find it set out in full in the author's *Far From Home*, available through many outlets on the Internet.